DEVILED EGGS AND DECEPTION

A SEASONED SOUTHERN SLEUTHS MYSTERY

NANCY NAIGLE

KELSEY BROWNING

KICKSASS CREATIONS

DEVILED EGGS AND DECEPTION

ISBN: 978-1-944898-21-2
Print ISBN: 978-1-944898-30-4
Large Print ISBN: 978-1-944898-31-1

Cover Art Design by Elizabeth Mackey

Digital release, April 2015
Trade Paperback release, April 2015
Second Edition release, March 2020

Kicksass Creations
P.O. Box 49662
Athens, GA 30604

BOOKS IN THE SERIES

IN FOR A PENNY

COLLARD GREENS AND CATFISHING

DEVILED EGGS AND DECEPTION

FRIED PICKLES AND A FUNERAL

WEDDING MINTS AND WITNESSES

Jenny & Teague Stories

CHRISTMAS COOKIES AND A CONFESSION

SWEET TEA AND SECOND CHANCES

This book is dedicated to Nancy's mom, Bettie, who reminds us to rest when we work too late, pours the wine when we're working from NanLand, watches the dogs when we work from the cabin, and reads every single version of these stories over and over and over again.

Thanks for your unlimited confidence in the two of us.
And for being our biggest fan.

CHAPTER 1

Summer Haven's front doorbell rang in rapid-fire succession, making Sera freeze mid-stretch into a *janu sirsasana* pose on the kitchen floor. She glanced over at Maggie and Abby Ruth sitting at the farm table with Sheriff Teague Castro. "Were we expecting anyone?"

"Not that I'm aware of." Maggie straightened her dark ponytail and tucked her appliquéd shirt into her pants.

"So help me." Abby Ruth's tone was as sharp as the creases on her trademark slim jeans. "If it's Angelina Broussard coming around to stir up more trouble, I'm gonna wring that woman's neck."

Teague's voice dry, he said, "Aunt Bibi, it's not smart to plan a murder right in front of the sheriff."

"No offense," she said. "But you're like family, and you know what a pain that woman is. Don't you think I could get off on an insanity charge?"

Teague shook his head, obviously not daring to step into that conversation, especially not with the mother of his dream girl.

Sera hopped to her feet. "I'll get it." To forestall violence against the woman who had final say over Summer Haven remaining on the historic register, Sera raced for the foyer, her bare feet slapping against the wooden floor. She flung open the door and there stood Hollis Dooley with that stinky hound dog of his.

The man was a hundred and sixteen if he was a day. Bundled up in a coat that made him look like a cross between a Ninja Turtle and the Michelin Man, Hollis leaned on his silver walker. Goodness, it wasn't *that* cold outside. Here at the end of March, the shrubs had already taken the hint that spring was around the corner, displaying buds and tender greens so welcome after the cold of winter. Still, his false teeth were chattering.

"Hi, Hollis." Sera waited for him to say something, but he just stood there staring at her. Could he be lost? "What are you doing here? They didn't miss your Meals on Wheels delivery again, did they?" She had her suspicions he was either sleeping through his doorbell or simply couldn't hear it anymore.

"No. Somethin' else altogether," he said.

She leaned out the front door and looked around. No sign of a car anywhere. "Did you walk?"

Hollis rubbed his gloved hands together. "It's cold as a witch's tit out here. You gonna invite me in or not?" He nudged her foot with his walker, jostling his old bloodhound, Ritter, in the process. Poor Ritter wasn't getting along any faster than his master. Sometimes it was hard to tell who was walking who.

"Of course." Sera stepped back and opened the door wide enough for him to navigate.

But why was Hollis Dooley paying them a visit? He hadn't been out to Summer Haven since the historic preservation committee's inspection, and even then he hadn't been much help, mainly sitting in the parlor drinking iced tea while Angelina checked the place from top to bottom, her eagle eyes missing nothing.

"You got a fire going? Thinking I could get warmed up was the only thing keeping me walking up that endless driveway." Hollis hobbled in with a *thump, thump, thump*.

Sera took Ritter's leash and patted the old boy on the head. "Why in the world are you walking?"

"My damned kids said it was too dangerous for me to be driving my car. They took the keys to my Bonneville. 1967. They don't make 'em like that no more. Now I gotta catch that damned give-a-senior-a-ride bus to get to my job. Pain in the ass is what it is." His face went slack for a moment. Then he said, "What about that fire?"

"No fire today, but we're all back in the kitchen where it's nice and toasty. I've been baking all morning. Whole wheat prune-bran muffins."

His face scrunched up. "Sounds like something my colon sure don't need. You got coffee?" He aimed his walker toward the kitchen as if he'd been there a hundred times. Maybe he had.

Sera didn't know much about who'd been a frequent visitor at Summer Haven before she landed here in Georgia and became roommates with Maggie and Abby Ruth. Unfortunately, Lillian Summer Fairview, the woman who owned this stately old money pit, wasn't in residence. Sera and the others had to keep Lil's true whereabouts on the down-low because her current address was Walter Stiles Federal Prison Camp. Not something Lil wanted the good people of Summer Shoals to know.

"Coffee? That I can do." Sera matched her steps to Hollis' and together, they slowly made their way toward the back of the house. "It's a pleasure to have you visit."

"No pleasure," he grumbled. "I need some help. There's problems. Lots of problems."

"Are you watching the news again?" she asked. "You shouldn't. It's a real downer. Focus on the positive, Hollis. That's what I always say."

"Well, that's a little hard to do when people are up to no good right in your own backyard. Don't need the news to remind me of that."

"Your own backyard?" Sera stood back to let him shuffle into the kitchen. "What's going on?"

When Hollis saw Teague sitting at the farm table with Abby Ruth and Maggie, he stopped in his tracks. The old guy pierced Sera with an accusing glare. "You didn't tell me you had company."

You didn't ask. Just kind of barged right in. "The more the merrier." She aimed a cheery smile in his direction, then headed for the coffeemaker. "Come on in. Sit and tell us about all these problems."

Hollis didn't budge, just mumbled, "I'll come back another time. I don't want to intrude."

"Then you should've called before you showed up," Abby Ruth said under her breath.

The old man let out a sigh. “Miss Sera, could I talk to you for a moment in private?” He lifted the walker and pivoted, bumping the kitchen counter and jostling one of Lil’s precious Depression era vases. Sera jumped to catch it before it toppled to the floor. The collective inhale from the other three people in the room carried enough force to nearly suck Hollis back into the kitchen. But he clomped out the way he’d come in.

“Maybe he’s going to ask you on a date,” Abby Ruth said with an exaggerated wink.

“Real funny,” Sera whispered. “Stop it.” She slapped her thigh and Ritter moseyed alongside her.

In the hallway, Hollis fidgeted with his jacket zipper. *Zip.* Halfway up. *Zup.* Halfway down. “Maybe I shouldn’t have come, but there’s something rotten up at the landfill.”

Probably banana peels and moldy bread, as Hollis would well know since he worked there a few times each week, but Sera just cocked her head and listened to Hollis.

“But if I tell the sheriff I noticed trash is missing, he’ll think I’m losing my mental faculties.”

“Maybe more people are finally recycling around here.” About time. Smalls towns in Georgia certainly lagged behind California in their eco-friendliness. "That's a good thing, Hollis. It shouldn't worry you."

"No. It's not like that. You know we have a spot for the recyclables. Didn't need it before you happened into town. But I know my trash, and someone's messing with it."

Strange that Hollis would be so possessive of garbage, but Sera couldn't argue with a man who was dedicated to his work. Then again, if someone was making an effort to reuse other people's castoffs, he should be applauded. But she couldn't brush off Hollis' concerns. "What do you think they're doing with the trash? And really, does it matter?"

He snatched the leash from Sera's hand. "I shouldn't have come. You don't understand."

She placed a hand on his arm, thin and frail even under his puffy coat. "Tell me how I can help."

"I know you and your friends have tracked down a couple of no-good criminal types lately."

"And you want *us* to find the person responsible for your missing trash?"

His chin angled up, and his dentures clacked together. "Stealing is stealing. Plus, they cut the fence, and that's destruction of public property. If someone's going to the trouble to break into the dump and steal, don't you think that means something is wrong?"

Hmm. Missing trash was one thing, but a damaged fence seemed more serious. As she considered the possibility of taking on another investigation, excitement buzzed under her skin. "I guess you have a point. But we're not true detectives, you know."

"You ever heard of citizen's arrest? It's your neighborly duty to look into this. We don't catch this yahoo, these thefts could lead to more dangerous stuff. I've seen those *Criminal Minds* shows. I think they call it escalation. Yeah, today they'll rip off Copenhagen cans and tomorrow it'll be cars. Then armed robbery!"

"I can't speak for Maggie and Abby Ruth..." But why couldn't she? They'd all agreed these cases made them feel more alive than ever. Besides, she didn't know how much longer she'd be at Summer Haven. At some point, she needed to turn around and face her real life. The life no one in this town knew a thing about.

But before then, she desperately wanted one last escapade with the two women who'd become her best friends in the world. "Why us?"

"Because y'all can be what they call *covert*. I

don't need neither the sheriff or my kids catching wind of all this."

"But—"

"But nothin'. The sheriff would think I was making a mountain outta a mold hill—" he chuckled at his own joke, "—and my kids are looking for any reason to throw my keister in the old folks' home. And I sure as hell ain't ready to play canasta and eat applesauce all damned day. Besides, they don't 'low no pets. Where would poor ol' Ritter go? I can pay cash money." His droopy eyes pleaded with her. How could she say no?

But with Hollis on Social Security and Meals on Wheels, he sure couldn't afford to pay them much. And they were always strapped for funds to keep up with Summer Haven's maintenance. Then again, investigating this for Hollis wasn't really about the money. It was about the adventure. "We'll do it."

His face softened, not at all like the old curmudgeon she'd come to know. "Thank you, Sera. I knew you'd be the one to understand." He took an envelope from his jacket pocket and placed it in her hand. A surprisingly *thick* envelope.

"What's this?"

"Payment in advance."

Sera slid her finger under the flap, but Hollis put his gnarled hand over hers.

"When you see what's inside, you'll see I'm serious as a four-alarm fire about all this." He held a finger to his lips. "Don't forget, not a peep to anyone. I don't need the sheriff or my meddling kids up in my bin'ness."

LIL PRACTICALLY SKIPPED ACROSS THE PRISON camp's courtyard toward the cottage she shared with Big Martha, one of the toughest broads at Walter Stiles Prison Camp. After what the warden had just told Lil, she wanted to dance around and hug every one of the women in this place. Even the mean ones.

"Hey there, Grammy Lil," one of Martha's protégés called out. "What're you grinnin' about? The cafeteria serving hot dogs for lunch today?"

Oh, her news was so much better than questionable franks and white buns. But she didn't want rumors to start swirling around the prison before she had a chance to talk with her roommate. Martha might be a bit rough around the edges, but over the past few months, she and Lil had become friends. A totally unlikely friendship since when Lil first arrived Martha had been a big ol' bully. "I'm just happy to see the sun shining."

"Amen to that, sister."

And it was a beautiful day—a little cool still, but with soft blue skies and clouds Lil felt she could float away on—full of beautiful news. She hummed a lilting tune, did a grapevine move up the cottage stairs, and cha-cha-chaed across the threshold.

Martha was reclining on her bed, flipping through the latest copy of *Redbook* magazine. That woman had a way of getting her hands on anything her heart desired—nail polish, makeup and magazines. Admittedly, she was a good gal to know. "Martha," Lil sang, "I have some good news."

"Hot dogs for lunch?"

Lord, if she could accomplish one more thing before she left federal prison, it would be to teach these women to appreciate something more sophisticated than a twelve-year-old's diet. "Better."

"Not when they serve them with the chili and cheese," Martha said without looking up. "That's hard to beat."

Lil flounced down on her bed, her bottom bouncing on the thin mattress. Today, even the feel of metal springs poking her in the behind couldn't get her down. "I just came from the warden's office."

Martha glanced up, her eyes sharp. "Don't tell me she's tapping you for another project."

Since Lil had voluntarily surrendered herself into the kind keeping of the federal prison system nine months ago, Warden Proctor had found several ways to utilize her refined background. Lil had taught an etiquette course and helped impress a crew of BOP suits so they'd keep Walter Stiles' doors open. "Not at the moment, but she did tell me I'd be getting my good conduct days at the end of the year. If I keep it up, I could be out of here in just a few more months."

"Oh." Martha's tone was flat and she looked back down at her magazine. "And here I thought you had something worth getting all excited about."

The helium filling Lil's chest eked out so fast, she was surprised it didn't make a tooting sound. "You don't think early release is worth a little excitement?"

Martha lifted a shoulder. "At your age, you could probably be out of here next week."

"Excuse me?"

"You really had an idiot for an attorney, didn't you?"

"I saw no need for legal help when it was obvious I was guilty. Why waste any more of the taxpayers' money?" After all, she'd already "borrowed" money from the Social Security system to pay for her husband's funeral. Why toss compound interest on top of an already substantial principal?

"I will never understand you, Miss H&M."

Over the past few months, Martha's nickname for her, Miss High & Mighty, had become endearing. But now it grated on her last nerve. Lil's mouth drew tight, her disappointment carrying the taste of lemon. "Perhaps they *are* serving hot dogs and your dining experience will be more satisfying than my news."

"Lord have mercy. If there was a snooty category in the Olympics, you'd be a gold medalist for sure." Martha huffed and tossed her magazine aside. "But someone's gotta look out for the high and mighties of the world. Guess it might as well be me. How's your arthritis treating you? I noticed you messing with your hands a lot lately."

"It's fine." Without thinking, Lil rubbed her thumb against the knuckles on her opposite hand. "Well, actually it's always worse in the winter. I suspect everyone's joints will feel better once spring blooms fully."

She and Martha shared nicer quarters than the women who lived in the pods inside the main building. But one January night when the Georgia temperatures dropped well below freezing, she'd discovered the cottage's downside. A building made from cinderblock was colder than a well digger's boots, and this darned thing was drafty.

"Nah," Martha drawled, "I want you to tell me it's real bad."

"Listen, if this is another way for you to get my goat, it won't work. I may be…mature, but I'm in good health." In fact, maybe too healthy with the bit of weight she'd put on recently. But she didn't like all the meals the cafeteria served so she always made sure to double up on those she did. The result was khaki prison-issued pants with a tightly stretched elastic waistband.

Martha pushed her dark straight hair over one shoulder and shook her head the way you did right before saying *Bless her heart* about someone. "You ever heard of compassionate release?"

"No."

"You should keep up with stuff like that. If you'd stop nosing into everyone's business, trying to teach people how to eat with a crab fork and whatnot—"

"It's a seafood fork."

Martha's head dropped forward, and she pushed her thumbs against her eyes as though Lil had served up a massive headache. "See what I mean?"

"You were saying something about compassion?"

"So there's this racket the BOP started a few years ago. And it's a way for folks who're long in the tooth to wiggle their way out of the system."

Lil sat up straight and scooted to the edge of her bed. She didn't want to miss a word of what was about to come from Martha's mouth. "Go on."

"It's because of prison overcrowding, and on account that most geezers ain't in any shape to go out and knock over a liquor store or pop a cap in someone's as—"

Lil leveled a disapproving stare at her roommate.

"—assets."

"Why haven't you told me about this before?" Part of Lil hoped it was because Martha liked her and didn't want to see her leave. Probably a barrel full of wishful thinking.

Martha waved a careless hand. "You never asked."

A nice deep breath was definitely in order here. "So how does one become eligible for this compassion program?" And why hadn't the warden ever mentioned it? She'd talked for months about the potential for Lil's early release, but never said a word about compassionate release. Maybe she'd been stringing Lil along the entire time. Maybe that was all this talk about good behavior credit was.

"It's actually not all that hard. If I had a few more decades on me, I'd try it myself. All you have to do is be real sick…or real old like you."

Lil's spine straightened. "I'll have you know *Cosmo* says seventy is the new fifty."

"Fine, you don't wanna age out? Then all you gotta do is play the sick sympathy card. And the warden already knows your arthritis acts up now and again, right?"

"But it's not debilitating."

"You know that and I know that, but does the warden have to? One thing about you *mature* folks, one day you can be right as rain, the next day, you're four legs in the air."

A chill inched over Lil's skin. She didn't want to be four legs in the air anytime soon. "If I ever meet your mother, I'm going to mention she should've enrolled you in charm school."

This time, Martha just chuckled. "Look, I know how much your precious Summer Haven means to you. After all the septic system mess a few months back, I figured you wanted to get home as soon as you could."

At the mention of her family estate, Lil's heart shrunk. This was the longest stretch of time she'd ever been from the home where she was born and had lived her whole life. "It's beautiful, you know."

"I'm sure it is." For a few seconds, Martha stared off into the distance as if longing for her own home. Her mouth was flat when she turned her attention back to Lil. "Look, if there's a good chance you'll blow this joint by the summer, what's the harm in trying to scoot out a little earlier? Sounds like your friends could use you there."

It was true. When she'd turned over Summer Haven's care to Maggie, she'd put such a burden on her best friend. Maggie had done a standup job, but it would be so much better for them all if Lillian could return home and handle the family estate herself.

Lillian swallowed, then rubbed her hand along the side of her knee and moaned.

"What was that?" Martha sat up quickly. "You okay?"

"Practice." Lil smiled. Then she inhaled to fill herself with courage and on one exhale, blew away her honesty. "Tell me how I should go about this."

CHAPTER 2

When Sera came back into the kitchen without Hollis trailing her, Teague's suspicious nature ramped up. A man didn't come all the way to Summer Haven just to turn around and leave within minutes. "What happened to Hollis? Thought he was coming in for coffee."

"He…uh…" Sera glanced away, smoothed a hand over her hip, then shot Teague a sunshine smile, "…had to get home. Forgot he left a pot pie in the oven."

"Pot pie?" He wasn't buying that smile for a second.

"Far be it for me to get between a man and his crust-wrapped chicken."

Abby Ruth snorted out a laugh. "Even to me that sounds a little wrong."

Sera pulled a chair close to Teague, batted her eyes in a way he now knew wasn't a cougar come-on but one of her tools of persuasion. "I noticed you've been stressed since the Christmas holidays."

Of course he had. He and Jenny Cady had reconciled after ten years apart, and he'd hoped she and her son would be moving to Summer Shoals in January. Because Jenny wasn't allowed to sublet her condo, she had to sell it before she could leave Boston. He was so anxious, he'd barely been eating or sleeping the past three months.

"You know what would fix you right up?" Sera said. "My morning yoga class."

"Tadpole doing Downward Dog Fixin' to Pee?" Abby Ruth's snort-laugh was now coming from her belly. "I'd give my JO.LO.AR to see that."

Teague sat for a second, considering. That old Spanish semi-automatic pistol was one helluva gun. He'd love to get his hands on it, but if it meant putting both his feet behind his head and walking around Summer Haven's lawn on his hands, the price was too steep. "On that note, I think it's time for me to get on home."

He headed for the foyer and opened the front door to find Colton Ellerbee standing there, his hand raised to knock. Apparently living in his own artist's world, Colton didn't pause his motion, nearly pummeling Teague right in the noggin. Teague stepped back to avoid the man's knuckles. "Hey, Ellerbee. How's the sculpting going?"

Calling what Colton did *art* was a stretch as far as Teague was concerned. Michelangelo and marble? Sure. But Ellerbee's so-called masterpieces were made from random junk. Using the word *sculpting* was about the best Teague could do.

Colton's bright red beret made him look like a woodpecker, and his wind-chapped cheeks matched his hat. "It's been better. I'm glad to see you here, Sheriff."

"Teague," Maggie called from down the hallway, "who's here now?"

"Colton Ellerbee."

Maggie, Sera and Abby Ruth joined Teague in the foyer. "Bring us any more of your *work*, Ellerbee?" Abby Ruth drawled.

Colton shifted his gaze to the grannies. "Not in this lifetime. I can't believe you'd separate the nativity scene. Tell me, are you selling it off piece by piece to get more money for it? Don't you know it's plain wrong to profit from someone else's hard work?"

As Colton verbally blasted them, Sera and Maggie both stepped back, but not Abby Ruth. No sirree. She stepped right up into the artist's space and lifted her chin. "Son, I don't know what your problem is, but these outbursts of yours are getting old. What on earth are you yapping about this time?"

"Oh, yeah." Colton didn't back down a centimeter. "Should've known you'd stoop to something like this. Apple doesn't fall far from the tree. First your grandson ruins my nativity scene, and now you're profiting from my work."

Teague suppressed a smile at the memory of Jenny's son playing catch during the holiday art show. The sweet baby Jesus from Colton's nativity scene had sustained some serious injuries. Jenny and the grannies joined forces to repair the sculpture, and Ellerbee's nativity scene had gone on to win the show.

"That sheep was a collector piece," Colton barreled on. "I don't think your daughter will be pleased to find you cut her out of a commission either."

With the roach-killer toes of her cowboy boots, Abby Ruth crowded Ellerbee back, forcing him out the doorway and onto the porch. Her shoulders hitched at least three inches as she rose ready for the fight. Teague knew that look. It never boded well.

"Whoa now. Let's stay cool. Ellerbee, calm down and explain." He turned to Abby Ruth and lowered his hand as though quieting an orchestra. "You, simmer down. Let's hear him out."

"He—" Abby Ruth made a gun with her thumb and forefinger. Pointed the darned thing right at Colton's forehead.

Teague pushed down her faux firearm and motioned Colton inside Summer Haven's foyer. "Start from the top."

Colton shoved his hands into his pockets, seeming to make a concerted effort at remaining calm, even though his neck was pink and splotchy with hives. Wasn't unusual. Abby Ruth had that effect on folks. Made Teague itch sometimes too, but then he'd had over twenty years to get used to her.

"When I gave the nativity set to Summer Haven, I expected it would be used as part of the annual display…forever. Kind of a legacy."

Teague leaned an elbow on the stair's newel post. "I understand."

"I mean, Summer Haven is the heart of this town so I thought by donating the sculptures to the estate, I was doing the whole town a favor. It was a gift. You don't sell a gift."

"It was a nice gesture," Teague agreed.

"I didn't realize I needed to make a no-sale provision. Never in my wildest imagination did I think these ladies would sell anything."

Teague glanced toward the grannies. Sera's head was tilted to the right. Maggie pulled at her ponytail. And Abby Ruth's scowl was edged with confusion. Proving they didn't know what the heck Ellerbee was jawing about.

"We didn't sell any of your so-called art," Abby Ruth said. "You didn't expect us to leave them in the yard year round, did ya? They're in the garage because we couldn't fit those damned things in the attic with the rest of the Christmas decorations."

Colton pulled a glossy piece of paper from his pocket and handed it to Teague. "Here. See for yourself."

Teague studied the page. It had been ripped from a magazine, and darned if it didn't show a picture of a sculpture from Colton's Annual Holiday Art Fest nativity entry. Teague would recognize that gasoline-can-headed sheep anywhere.

He turned to the grannies. "Ladies?"

One look at the paper and Abby Ruth snorted.

"Someone paid $15,000 for that sheep? Another passel of idiots born every blessed day." She grabbed it from Teague's hold and held it out so Maggie and Sera could see it.

"Worth every penny," Colton said. "This is the year of the sheep, after all. But that's not the point. The point is…"

"Yeah, yeah, the point is you think we sold it out from under you. We didn't." Abby Ruth jammed her hands onto her hips.

Teague studied the other ladies. "Sera? Maggie?"

"No. Of course not. It was a gift. You don't sell a gift." Sera fiddled with something in the back pocket of her yoga pants. With all the rubbing and fiddling she'd been doing since Hollis left, she was either hiding something or had psoriasis on her ass.

"I don't even re-gift," Maggie said.

Abby Ruth caught Colton by the shoulder and tried to swing him around toward the door. "You're obviously wrong."

He ducked and eluded her. "No. That was a one-of-a-kind piece."

Lord, most of the time, Teague loved being the sheriff in a small, sleepy Georgia county, but sometimes he'd take a murder over a bunch of backbiting. "Ellerbee, Jenny told me you've made several of those nativity scenes for folks since the art show, and for quite a price tag. This rogue sheep could be from one of those sets, right?"

"No. See this?" Colton grabbed the sheet from Abby Ruth's grip and waved it in front of Teague's face. "The gas can was a vintage retro metal galvanized from Delphos, very hard to find. I'd bet you a million dollars the one in that picture is the one I left here."

"Goodness knows I'd like to take that bet," Abby Ruth muttered. "But we can put an end to these idiotic accusations here and now." She stepped around Colton and threw open the front door. "Everyone march your butts out to the garage. Now."

Fine. If this would stop Colton's bellyaching, even Teague would give in to Abby Ruth's demand. Everyone trooped outside and around the house. Teague lifted the garage door, and Abby Ruth retrieved the keys to the sacred Tucker Torpedo from atop its front driver's side tire, where Lil's daddy had always kept them. That Lil was one for tradition.

Abby Ruth jumped behind the tank of a car's wheel and revved the engine.

"Easy there," Maggie called out.

"I've got this." Abby Ruth quickly checked the rearview mirror, then the car shot out of the bay.

"Lord have mercy," Maggie gasped. "Lil would've had a heart attack if she'd seen that."

"Our little secret," Teague reassured her.

Maggie led the way to the back of the garage, where boxes were stacked four high in the corner. A large blue painter's tarp was draped over a heaping mass to the left. "Help me with this, Teague."

They lifted the tarp and let it billow to the ground.

Maggie swept her arm in a Vanna White gesture. "See."

Colton stepped forward, and Teague made a mental inventory of the pieces. Baby Jesus, Mary, Joseph. One, two, three wise men, and the menagerie. But no sheep.

He and Colton locked gazes.

"Awww, shit." Abby Ruth whirled toward Maggie. "Did you sell it?"

"No!" Maggie swiveled her head toward Sera. "Sera, I know you wouldn't have sold it. Donated it, maybe. You didn't recycle it for cash, did you?"

"I wouldn't donate something that's not mine to give away," Sera protested.

Her hands palm up, Maggie turned to Colton. "I don't know what's going on here. I can assure you that sheep was here on January tenth when we put away all the decorations."

"Well, it's not here now." Colton waved his arms wildly. "And I want it back."

Teague watched the color drain from Abby Ruth's face, and her lips pulled into a tight line that spelled trouble. If he didn't get Colton out of here within the next sixty seconds, his murder wish would come all too true. And the last thing he needed was to have to arrest his—hopefully—future mother-in-law. Because although Jenny would believe her mom had committed the crime, she still wouldn't forgive Teague for letting it happen in the first place.

Abby Ruth took a menacing step toward Colton. "I'll find out what's going on here, and when I do, you'll be sorry you ever accused us of stealing your crap."

"Crap?" Colton squawked. "I'll have you know—"

His gut twisted into a pretzel, Teague shoved himself between Colton and Abby Ruth. He'd prefer Abby Ruth didn't play murderer *or* deputy. "I'll take care of it."

But Abby Ruth's narrow eyes and Maggie's bland expression sent a warning streak down

Teague's spine. When had these gals ever listened to a darned thing he said?

Pretty much never.

SERA WATCHED TEAGUE SMOOTHLY TAKE THE PAPER from Colton's clenched fist. He cuffed him on the shoulder in that fake buddy-buddy way guys did, then led the artist a few feet away. "I don't know what happened, but I can assure you if these ladies say they didn't sell your art, they didn't. I'll figure out what's going on." Teague leveled a warning look at them, then walked Colton back toward his car.

Clearly, the sheriff wasn't a fan of Abby Ruth's notion that she, Sera and Maggie would get to the bottom of Colton's problem. Sera chuckled to herself. Hadn't the man learned anything over the past few months? His disapproval of their extracurricular activities wouldn't stop them for a minute.

A tingle of pure happiness and excitement ran through Sera. Not one mystery, but two. Maybe this was a sign that Summer Shoals was where she was meant to be. Forever.

"I told you we should lock this place," Abby

Ruth said to Maggie. "Small town or not, you can't be too careful these days."

Maggie's shoulders sagged. "I can't believe anyone would steal from Summer Haven."

Sera wrapped an arm around Maggie. "It's not your fault if someone stole that sheep and sold it. You always take these things so personally."

"You would too if your best friend was trusting you to keep her entire home all safe until she can do it herself."

Stung, Sera said, "Lillian is my friend too. Maybe nothing like what the two of you have, but she's shared her home with me, and I take that to heart."

Sometimes it seemed as if Maggie and Abby Ruth thought she was just some float-through-life flower child. Probably her fault for perpetuating the image. Yes, she loved yoga, healthy eating and good karma, but she was more than the sum of her southern California parts.

"We need to figure this out and fast." Abby Ruth turned her back to the men, and her face was pale. "If Colton blames me, he could pull his contract with Jenny. He's her first solo client, and if she wants to make the move to Summer Shoals, she sure can't afford to lose him. If he fires her, she'll never forgive me."

The reality of Abby Ruth's claim ricocheted through Sera. "Do you think Teague's even considered that Colton might be mad enough to fire Jenny?"

"I don't know, but that's why we need to handle this. You know how lovesick Teague's been for her."

It was true. Teague's chakras had been all jacked out of shape since Jenny left at Christmas and had been forced to delay her move to Summer Shoals. They'd faded from a vibrating sunburst orange to a stagnant brackish brown.

"We don't even know where to start," Maggie said.

"I do." Abby Ruth absently tapped a toe of her boot as if in deep thought. "When I looked at the paper Colton brought, I not only got a look at that ugly sheep, but also saw the folks with crummy taste who bought it live down in Palm Beach. I say a trip to Palm Beach is in order. I could probably get a flight out of Atlanta first thing in the morning."

Teague glanced back at them.

Sera smiled and waved, trying for nonchalance and hoping Teague hadn't overheard their conversation. He'd be half crazy if he thought Abby

Ruth planned to solve this on her own. “Shh. He’ll hear us.”

“Doesn’t matter,” Maggie said. “We can’t afford to fly to Palm Beach. Do you know how much three plane tickets would cost?”

“Who said anything about the three of us?” Abby Ruth said. “I can zip down there by myself.”

Unleash Abby Ruth on the good people of Florida? “No offense, but I don’t think that’s a good idea,” Sera said. “Maybe I could drive us.”

“No!” Maggie and Abby Ruth said at the same time.

“Oh, wait.” She dug into her back pocket and held a fat wrinkled number ten envelope by the corners. “Maybe this will help.”

“What’s that?”

“Hollis Dooley gave it to me.”

Abby Ruth grinned. “A love letter.”

“Why do you always have to go *there*?” She slipped her finger under the edge and ripped open the envelope. “Holy wow!”

“What?”

She tipped the envelope their way and thumbed the edges of a pile of hundred dollar bills.

Abby Ruth raised a hand toward where Teague and Colton were still talking in the driveway and hollered, “Gotta get inside for some of Sera’s tofu stew before it goes bad. Y'all have a good night, you hear?"

"Come on." Maggie motioned Sera and Abby Ruth inside, and they hightailed it through the back door of the house and into the kitchen.

The sound of two cars cranking penetrated the walls. Sera raced to the front of the house to look out the parlor window. "They're gone."

"How much money is that and why the hell is Hollis Dooley giving it to you?" Abby Ruth demanded. "I swear that old curmudgeon is in love with you."

"Stop it! Love would give him a heart attack. Walker yoga is about to do him in as it is. He wants us to look into a situation for him."

Maggie's gaze went to the envelope Sera still held. "You mean investigate something?"

"You have to admit we're getting pretty good at hunting down people who aren't on the up and up," Sera said. "He seemed pretty impressed with us. If we could make some money at it, maybe we could pay for Summer Haven's upkeep. It would be our way of thanking Lillian for letting us live here while she's away. And maybe we could afford to send Abby Ruth down to Palm Beach."

"Lord, this place is a never-ending project." Maggie sighed.

"What the heck does Hollis want us to do?" Abby Ruth paced around the perimeter of the room. "Whatever it is, it better be fast because I don't think Colton wants to stand in line behind someone else."

Sera sucked in a breath, then rushed out, "He thinks someone is stealing trash from the dump."

Abby Ruth barked a laugh. "That's bass-ackwards."

"I know it sounds silly, but Hollis is really upset."

"We can't investigate missing trash. After taking down a couple of real scam artists? Talk about a demotion."

Sera winced. "I already promised we would, and from the heft of this envelope, I think he's willing to pay for results."

"Hollis has obviously lost it. You don't give…" Abby Ruth trailed off. "Wait a minute. Just how much money?"

Sera fanned the hundred dollar bills across the kitchen table like a Vegas blackjack dealer, then counted. She slowly lifted her head. "Thirty-two."

"Hundred? Where the heck did he get that kind of money?" Maggie stared down at the money pile as if it were a big bowl of hot fudge and caramel covered ice cream. With pecans on top.

"I have no idea," Sera said. "He gets Meals on Wheels, for heaven's sake. I thought he was living off Social Security like most of the people I deliver to."

"Something's not right here." Abby Ruth kicked one foot across the other and leaned against the wall, suspicion swarming over her face. "That's too much bank to track down missing milk cartons and juice containers."

"I know he's probably overreacting," Sera agreed. "But it's serious to him. And the money? I think it's a bribe to keep us from mentioning any of this to his kids or Teague. Hollis doesn't want them to think he's gone senile. They took the keys to his car, and now he thinks they're going to make him move into Dogwood Ridge Assisted Living."

Maggie's eyes softened. "What an awful feeling to have your children start stripping away your freedom. First the car. What next? He probably should be worried."

"Yeah, he sounds downright desperate." Abby Ruth's smile was sharp and predatory. "And far be it for us to tell a desperate man no."

CHAPTER 3

Lord, the early morning trip from her cottage to the courtyard had never taken Lillian so long. This pretending to be old and feeble was already exhausting. But it could be so worth the pain.

She gazed down at one of the recently replanted flowerbeds. All the work they'd done for the Bureau of Prisons inspection was beginning to pay off in new growth. But even though it was only the last week in March, the darned beds already had chickweed growing in them. Too bad the warden hadn't allowed them to mulch the way Martha had suggested.

Lil made a show of holding her back with one hand and bracing herself against the building to ease herself to her knees. Once kneeling, she was careful not to attack the weeds sprouting around the rose bushes that would bloom pink, yellow and white in a few weeks. Instead, she acted as if it was hard to grasp the individual plants and pull. No yanking. That would give her away.

When she'd gone to Warden Proctor this morning to mention how severe her arthritis was becoming, the warden had made a *hmming* noise and sent her to the infirmary. After a rather long consult with the staff doctor, he'd sent her back to the warden. Worried they knew she was trying to pull the wool over on them, she'd nearly died of hyperventilation sitting outside the warden's office. Wouldn't that be unfair? She sure didn't want to get out of prison that way.

But as luck would have it, the warden had promised they'd keep an eye on Lillian's health and if there was no improvement, they could talk about a compassionate release.

Compassionate release. It was a real program. Martha was right…again. And with a chance at release, Lil had walked out of the warden's office fully committed to the charade.

Which meant she had to put on a good show 24/7.

Everyone—even she—needed to believe the

pain in her joints was becoming more and more unbearable by the minute. But that also meant it had taken her three times as long to weed this tiny section of flowers than it should've. But then it wasn't like she had anywhere else to be.

Martha strode out of the main building, obviously in a chipper mood since she'd had someone stop by for visiting hours. Too bad Maggie and the others couldn't come to visit Lil every week, but it just wasn't realistic. Not with the hour and a half hour drive between here and Summer Shoals and all the upkeep Summer Haven demanded.

"You got a visitor," Martha said. She walked closer and leaned forward, lowering her voice. "Make it look like this hurts." Louder she said, "Let me help you up there, Miss H&M."

Lil held out her hand. When Martha pulled her to her feet, she let out a groan that sounded as fake as a pro wrestling grunt. How anyone was buying that she was old and feeble was beyond her. But Martha was always here to keep her in role. "Maggie came today?"

"No, dark hair and same kind of shirt she always wears with those barnyard animals stitched all over it—alpacas, maybe? But this is some other chick."

An uneasy feeling burrowed under Lil's skin. Some other woman? Lillian only had three people registered on her visitors' list—Maggie, Sera and Abby Ruth. "Could something have happened to Maggie? Is it her daughter, Pam, coming to give me the bad news?"

"I don't know, but calm down, and remember," Martha said, "don't walk too fast. Make it look like every step could be your last."

Lord, between the tiny steps she had to take and the lingering smell of the wintergreen-scented arthritis cream she was rubbing into her skin like it was some kind of French lotion, Lil was already half-sick of pretending she was sick.

Still, she replayed Martha's nagging voice in her head the entire way down the long hallway toward the visitors' room. All this time and itty-bitty steps for a visitor who wasn't even there to see her. But when she entered the room, the guard on duty waved a hand toward a table on the opposite end and said, "She's been waiting a good quarter hour."

But who was *she*?

As Lil minced her way closer to the woman, who had her head down and face averted, the whole thing became more and more odd. Her hair was dark like Maggie's but without the sprigs of gray that sometimes sprouted here and yon. She was, however, wearing an appliquéd shirt. Lil squinted. No, those weren't alpacas. They looked more like emus. And rhinestones on the collar? Those weren't exactly Maggie's speed.

And although Maggie had slimmed down lately, this woman looked like a stringy flank steak to Maggie's rump roast.

And something about the way the woman's skinny fingers drummed the table made Lil want to hurry over and slap a hand across them to stop the restless movement. She controlled herself for the sake of show. She was still a half-dozen scuffling steps from the table when the woman looked up and turned in her direction. "Hello, Lillian."

She didn't have to fake it this time when she grabbed for the wall to steady herself, because her legs had turned the consistency of the cafeteria's tapioca pudding. Shock and fear would do that to a body. How she forced herself to pull on a social smile, she wasn't quite sure.

Then again, she wasn't part of the Summer family for nothing. The Summers were known for having plenty of backbone. But it took every bit of spine Lillian had to pull out the chair and carefully settle herself before addressing the last person she ever wanted to find her here at Walter Stiles.

"Well, this is certainly a nice…surprise, Angelina."

NICE? LILLIAN STRUGGLED TO KEEP THE PLEASANT smile pasted on her lips. There was absolutely nothing *nice* about a surprise visit from Angelina Broussard. Lord, Lil's momma had taught her not to be a liar. After all, Daddy had been the most honest man in Bartell County back in his day.

And this whopper of a lie would likely send Lil straight to H-E-double-L. Inside her chest, her heart was playing those crazy X-Games she'd watched on the rec room TV. Kids on skateboards and bikes and skis, just begging for a broken neck.

Angelina's toothy smile was wide and wicked. "Isn't it? It's been so long since you and I have had a chance to visit. I thought a little girl time was in order."

So they were going to pretend all the way around, were they?

Lil circled a finger in the general vicinity of Angelina's chest, taking in the horrible sequined animal scene sewn onto her cotton shirt. "I must say, this is a new look for you. Maggie's obviously become a fashion maven in Summer Shoals."

Angelina's smile had more bite than balm.

"Desperate times. But then again, you know all about desperation, don't you?"

For the first time in her well-born life, Lil wanted to lunge across the table and wrap her hands around someone's neck. What would it feel like to take Angelina down to the ground and wring her like a stubborn chicken?

Heck of it was, if she jumped and wrung like that, the arthritis hoax would be all over.

So Lillian inclined her head toward the badge on Angelina's shirt. The badge labeled *Margaret Rawls*. "I'm sure Maggie didn't let you borrow her property, and last I checked theft was a crime." Lil leaned in a little and tilted her head. "Maybe *you're* interested in renting a room at Walter Stiles."

"Very funny."

"It probably won't be when I have the guard check your handbag for your real identity." Lil made to rise, but her required slo-mo gave Angelina enough time to clamp a manacle hand around her wrist.

"I know you don't like to make a fuss." Angelina's broad smile was as fake as Hollis Dooley's teeth. "That's just not the Summer family way, now is it?"

On second thought, Maggie had caused quite a stir at the prison when she'd lost that badge over the holidays. What if the warden wouldn't allow Maggie to visit again if she found out about this ID switcheroo? Lil didn't know how closely the guards kept track of how many times a visitor lost a badge, but if they somehow realized Maggie created another security breach it would be bad news. Lil sure wasn't about to bring it to their attention. What a teetotal mess. Lil edged back into her seat, lifted her chin, and forced a casual note into her voice. "Since I can't serve you tea and cookies, I assume you're here for some other reason."

"I expected you to explain. Or at least defend yourself," Angelina said.

Lil simply gave her a tight smile and waited. Angelina wanted something, and Lil wouldn't give her the satisfaction of asking what that something was.

"I see prison hasn't changed your high and mighty ways."

Lil's right eye gave a twitch. From Angelina's mouth, *high and mighty* sounded like some of the salty vocabulary Lil had learned here in prison. "Good manners are never out of place."

Angelina eyed Lil's prison getup, distaste clear from the way the corners of her lips pulled downward. Lil often made the same expression when she caught sight of the yellowish khaki on blueish khaki ensemble in the mirror. "How does it feel to have fallen so far from grace?"

The way Lil was grinding her teeth together to maintain her composure, she'd be making an emergency appointment with the prison camp's dentist. "I believe in being accountable."

"And what is it you have to be accountable for?" Angelina asked. "I find it terribly interesting you started all this *vacationing* right around the time another Summer Shoals resident was arrested for Social Security fraud. But surely a member of the Summer family wouldn't stoop so low as to become involved with something like that."

Any hope Lillian had that Angelina was still in the dark about why she was here caught fire and poofed like ash. The woman might be a royal pain in the patootie, but she was a smart one. Too smart.

"Can you imagine what your friends and neighbors would say if they not only knew where you've spent the past nine months but also learned you'd been stealing from them?"

"Now wait just a minute. I didn't—"

"Those Social Security checks were taken out of Bartell County mailboxes. Can you honestly sit there and tell me you had nothing to do with that?"

Lillian built a mental shell around herself to deflect Angelina's barbs because they were coming so close to making her lose her cool. And even though she'd promised herself she wouldn't, she asked, "What do you want?"

Angelina sat back, the expression on her face pure I'm-the-cat-and-you're-the-canary. "Oh, I want so many things." She looked toward the ceiling and tapped her crimson lips with a well-manicured fingertip.

Lil glanced away, trying to temper her jealousy at the perfection of Angelina's nails. Of all the things to think about when much bigger trouble was brewing. Lil couldn't fathom everyone in Summer Shoals knowing she was a jailbird. Yes, she'd come to terms with her fate, even embraced it to some extent.

But there was accountability, and then there was humiliation.

"For instance, I wanted to head up the historical preservation committee." Tap, tap, tap. "But I got that."

Yes, but she hadn't been able to strike Summer Haven from the register no matter how hard she'd tried.

"And I wanted to be the president of the Summer Shoals Junior League." Tap, stroke, tap. "Oh, but I got that too."

The way Lil was gripping her hands together under the table, her knuckles really were aching.

"But you know what I don't have? I don't have a one-of-a-kind car. I'd use it for very special occasions, and my husband would look so handsome riding next to me in town events. I'm sure you're about ready to hand off those duties anyway, aren't you?"

If Lil thought her hands were aching, they were nothing compared to the throbbing pain in her midsection. Angelina wanted Daddy's Tucker Torpedo. An extremely rare car, and one of the only convertibles in the world. "I heard that guy over off Old County Line Road often buys collectible hot rods at auction down in Florida."

"Please don't play dumb." Angelina leaned on the table, pushed her face so close to Lil's that Lil could see her Botox handiwork up close. By the time Lil got out of here, she'd need a ton of that stuff pumped under her skin to get rid of all the stress lines around her own mouth and eyes. "It only insults us both."

Angelina had to know how much losing the Tucker would tear Lillian up inside. Everyone in Summer Shoals knew how much that car meant to her. "I…I need some time to think about this."

"Really?" Angelina's brows winged up into the

bangs fluffed to look like Maggie's. "Then I suppose I need some time to think about the situation as well. And sometimes when I'm in a thinking mood, I also get into a talking mood, if you know what I mean."

"Hold your wild horses, Angelina. I need to consider a few things. A week or so," Lil said quickly, trying to keep the panic out of her voice and failing miserably. "I'll let you know something by the end of next week."

"No." Angelina stood and looked down at Lil, making her feel like a chastised child. "You'll call me by Monday. You know how small towns are. Doesn't take any time at all for gossip to spread like wildfire. Don't make me strike a match."

CHAPTER 4

When Maggie hit the kitchen for a midmorning snack of cereal and coffee, Sera, dressed in a neon pink long-sleeved T-shirt and florescent tie-dyed skirt, was beaming with joy. If Maggie didn't love her so much, sometimes Sera would be too bright to look at straight on. "You're in an awfully good mood this morning."

"It's a gorgeous day." Sera did a little ballet leap, bounding across the kitchen like a deer with a strawberry blond hide. She poured coffee, pirouetted and handed the cup to Maggie. Even though she didn't drink coffee herself, Sera was always a sweetheart about making it for Maggie and Abby Ruth. "A perfect day to get started on Hollis Dooley's case."

"*Case* may be overstating."

Sera pointed to the desk drawer where they'd locked the cash he'd given her last night. "If the man is willing to pay us that much money, then the least we can do is call it a case."

"Still say he's a nutcase," Abby Ruth grumbled as she walked in the door and made directly for the coffeemaker.

"You're entitled to your opinion, but Hollis offered cash," Sera said. "We can't take the man's money and blow him off."

Abby Ruth poured coffee up to the tiptop of her cup, raised it to her face and sniffed. "This chicory smells great, but with that sheep missing from our very own garage, I still think something stinks like Roquefort cheese. If we didn't move it, then it means someone else did. Ever think about that?"

Maggie tugged at the collar of her shirt, one of her favorites, embroidered with tulips and bluebirds. Abby Ruth was right. Here they were trying to figure out two mysteries when their safety might be at risk. "I wonder if we should install a security system."

"We don't need a security system." Abby Ruth frowned and patted her ribcage. "I got all the security we need right here. Say hello to Mr. Glock."

A thread of panic wound through Maggie. She'd be darned if she wanted Abby Ruth to play security around here. That woman would as soon shoot as ask questions, and that worried Maggie more than the bad guys.

A security system was a much better idea, although she hadn't tackled one of those in over twenty years, and now the security systems were all computerized, not mechanical. It took some technological know-how. Over her head.

But a bright thought tickled her brain. Security probably wouldn't be over Bruce Shellenberger's head. They'd seen each other around town now and again since the Halloween party last fall. That night, Maggie had worn a risqué Maid Marian costume, and the way Bruce had looked at her, his gaze warm and appreciative, she'd thought he might call and ask her out. Then again, even though his wife had passed away a couple of years ago, he might not be ready yet.

She understood. She'd gone back and forth on the topic of dating lately herself. How did a person ever know when she was ready?

"If we go check out the dump for Hollis, we'd have the money for a security system." Sera's hopeful smile reminded Maggie of her grandkids begging for triple ice cream cones.

Really, what would it hurt to spend an hour at the dump, or as Bartell County called it, the Waste Disposition Center?

Sera's cell phone rang, and she pulled it from under her shirt where she always seemed to have it tucked into her skimpy bra. "Hello."

She immediately turned away from Maggie and Abby Ruth, making tracks toward the hallway. Still, Maggie heard her say, "Baby, this isn't a good time."

"Who do you think that is?" Maggie asked Abby Ruth. Sera rarely received phone calls and Maggie had never heard her call anyone *baby* before.

"Maybe it's Hollis and they're setting up a date."

"Seriously, you need to stop the teasing."

"Fine."

When Sera returned a few minutes later, her face wasn't nearly so animated, and something about her expression told Maggie this wasn't the time to butt into her friend's business, so she just said, "Let's get moving, gals. We've got a date with the dump."

It was a little after eleven when they turned onto

Lavender Hill Road, and Sera's van jounced over the pitted gravel and dirt track. Abby Ruth pointed out the front window. "Looks like we're not gonna stroll right in."

Sure enough, the front gates were locked. Maggie wanted to pop herself on the forehead. She knew the place wasn't open on Fridays. "I guess we'll have to come back another time."

"Now what's the fun in that?" Abby Ruth asked. "You hauled us all the way out here. We might as well have a look-see."

They got out of the truck and Maggie said, "Remind me what we're looking for."

Because honestly, how would they know if a couple of cardboard boxes and soiled diapers had been taken? Hollis was a much better judge than they'd ever be. Then again, that gave some merit to his claim things were missing. He would know, wouldn't he?

Sera piped up, "The universe has a way of leading us in the direction we need to go."

"Then why the hell are ninety-nine percent of the men in this world lost and won't stop to ask for directions?"

Maggie snickered. Abby Ruth had a point. Her George had been one of those men who'd drive all the way to Timbuktu claiming the whole time he was headed for Tallahassee.

"Fine," Maggie said, even though she felt a tad uneasy snooping around when the place was closed. This probably wasn't what Hollis had had in mind. "But how will we know if we've found something important?"

"I have a feeling it's like a lot of things in the world," Abby Ruth said. "We'll know it when we find it. I say let's start by scouting the perimeter. Ol' Hollis probably sits up in that booth all day long. No way he could get all the way around this fence using his walker."

True. Gopher holes dotted the ground around the eight-foot chain link fence. Hollis would wedge one leg of his walker in a hole and topple over like a bowling pin.

They trooped single file, scanning the hole-pocked and scraggly ground. About two-thirds of the way around, Maggie spotted a pile of items outside the fence line. A rickety yellow footstool, a beat-up ancient stand mixer in an awful shade of green with one beater missing, and a bathmat that appeared to have been feasted on by moths.

Although they could see the stash of trash, it wouldn't be in the line of sight of anyone sitting in the security booth.

"Clues," Sera squealed.

"Looks like a mound of crap to me," Abby Ruth said.

"What about this?" Sera grabbed hold of the fence and pulled, revealing a section that had been cut, with a gap just big enough for a person to slip through.

A part of Maggie—the part excited to jump into a new adventure—sat down, sighed and put up its feet. Case already closed. "Well, we know Hollis was right. Someone has been taking things from the dumpsters. But this is harmless. Probably just some broke kids trying to outfit their first apartment."

"Oh." Sera's shoulders folded in and her face clouded.

Abby Ruth waved a hand in front of Sera's nose. "Don't know why you're so down in the mouth. We made over three grand in less than ten minutes."

"Not exactly," Sera said, pushing at the fence and slipping halfway inside. "We may know stuff is being stolen, but we don't know who's doing the stealing."

"And you think going in there will help us figure it out?"

Sera's hopeful smile lit up her face. "Can't hurt."

Lord, the things Maggie had gotten herself into since she met these women—breaking into a high-rise condo in Hilton Head, a beekeeping date, even wearing thong underwear. One thing was for darned sure, as long as Sera and Abby Ruth were around, she'd never be bored.

Following Sera, Abby Ruth ducked to ease her lanky body inside the fence. Maggie did the same, pretty dang happy when the exposed fence wire barely grazed her hips.

Sera rounded a large metal trash container and stood looking up at it. Unfortunately, Maggie wasn't paying enough attention to where she was going and her foot sank into something. She closed her eyes and swallowed. Anything but cabbage. She couldn't stand the rank smell of cooked cabbage.

One glance down told her it wasn't much better. She'd stepped in a heap of used coffee grounds, cigarette butts, and what was either the remnants from a guy's dip cup or prune juice.

Abby Ruth stopped and looked back at her, then down at her own boots. "Oh, sugar. That's not good. Handy you're wearing tennis shoes instead of good leather like me."

Unfortunately, Maggie's sneakers were made of canvas, and she could already feel the prune-juice-spit cocktail seeping into her sock.

Abby Ruth called to Sera, “You see any shoe protection in there?”

Sera moved closer to the dumpster and snatched out a couple of bags. “How about these?”

“I’d prefer something made of industrial grade plastic, but I guess beggars can’t be choosers.” Abby Ruth took the bread bags and with a frown, dumped out the moldy bread. Somehow, she was able to turn the bags inside out without getting a speck of green gunk on her hands. Pretty as you please, she slipped the bags over her cowboy boots and tucked the tops down between the shaft and her jeans to secure them. “All set.”

“We should look inside these bins,” Sera said.

Maggie shook her foot, trying to dislodge specs of coffee, but her white sneakers were now the color of the cesspool that had flooded Summer Haven’s yard not so long ago. The thought of climbing into that trash made her insides shrink and hide. Sure, she could muck around in the septic system without a problem, but something about other people’s trash gave her the willies.

“I’ll do it.” As easy as if she were skipping up Summer Haven’s steps, Sera boosted herself onto the bin’s exterior latch and then the rim, about the width of a paperback book. She held out her arms and placed one foot in front of the other as though she'd been walking on a balance beam her entire life. Not a wiggle. Not a wobble.

Sera continued to make her way around the bin's perimeter, all the while staring into its depths. "Aha," she said when she was halfway around.

Abby Ruth went on her tiptoes, trying to get a look at Sera's aha inspiration. "Whatcha find?"

Gracefully, Sera rotated her body and sank into what Maggie knew from watching a few of her granddaughter's ballet lessons was a second position turnout plié. At fifty-something, Sera had perfect form—back straight, hips tucked in, and knees over toes. As though she did this Swan Lake Dumpster Dive every day, she reached down and plucked something from the mound. When she stood, she held a bright red slow cooker in her arms.

She scampered back around the bin's edge, tossed the appliance to Abby Ruth and dismounted with a flourish.

"Dang," Abby Ruth said. "I thought maybe you'd come across a stash of *Playgirl* magazines."

Maggie choked. "Do they really still publish that?" She'd only ever actually seen one issue. The one with Burt Reynolds. Quite honestly, she'd kind of preferred the mystery of his clothes on.

"Saw one down at the Curl Up and Read Bookstore the other day."

Lord have mercy on them all. Word would get out that Abby Ruth was ogling naked men, and the people of Summer Shoals would decide they were a bunch of aging Jezebels out there at Summer Haven.

Abby Ruth let out a howl. "I'm just giving you a hard time, Maggie. They don't stock those at the bookstore."

"You're a regular comedian."

Sera took the slow cooker from Abby Ruth. "You do know what this means, right?"

"That someone's not having pot roast tonight?"

"If someone was really collecting all that stuff outside the fence to outfit an apartment, don't you think they would've grabbed this too?"

"Sugar, if this trash stealer is a man, he wouldn't give a hoot in hell about this thing. Only thing I've ever seen a man cook in one of these is deer-sausage cheese dip."

"Ew," Sera groaned.

"It doesn't even have a power cord. Looks like it's been chewed off by a rat."

Sera fumbled the cooker, and Maggie caught it before it fell on her foot. "That's easy enough to fix. Plus, it's a new latch model where you can cook and carry. We could use one of these at Summer Haven." She tucked it under her arm, and then had second thoughts. They'd come to find a trash thief, and now she was about to steal something herself. "Do you think Hollis would consider this stealing?"

Sera gave Maggie a smile. "I'll let him know we took it as evidence. I doubt he'll mind a bit."

And once Maggie stopped by the grocery store and Holloway's Hardware, they'd be having pot roast for dinner tonight.

EARLY SPRING STORM CLOUDS WERE GATHERING AS Sera pulled around to the back of Summer Haven and the three of them piled out of her van. "We better strip down out here before going in. I don't think I've ever smelled this bad in my life."

A mouse-like squeak escaped from the passenger seat. Her mouth agape, Maggie was pointing at the open garage door. She stammered, "H-h-how did we forget to put the car up last night?"

From the back seat, Abby Ruth poked her head between Sera and Maggie. "I don't know. You flash thousands of dollars in front of people, they get a little sidetracked, I guess. It's fine. I'll pull it back inside."

"No." Maggie reached for the door handle. "I saw the way you moved that car out of the garage last night. Looked like a NASA rocket launch. I'll put it away as soon as I get my shoes off. If I track kitty litter and grocery guts onto the floor mat, Lil would never forgive me."

"I said I can do it." Abby Ruth slid open the side door of the van and hopped to the ground, swatting at the dirt on her pants. She'd tossed the plastic bread bags back in a dumpster at the landfill.

"Why don't you go see if Jenny knows anything about the buyers down in Palm Beach? That might be time better spent," Maggie said, her tone no-nonsense. She was rarely short-tempered, but both Sera and Abby Ruth had learned not to push her.

Abby Ruth disappeared into the house without another word.

Trying to change the subject and soften Maggie's mood, Sera said, "I feel a little bad for taking Hollis' money for this case. He's paying us a lot of money for something anyone could've done. Plus, we got a crockpot out of the deal."

Maggie put her shoes on the porch and peeled off her soiled socks. "Me too, but it wasn't like we set the price. We could give some of the money back to him, but then again, maybe this is one of those good karma things. Who're we to deny that?

Besides, once we find the trash culprit, we can move on to Colton's case." She pushed herself up from the porch. "I'll move the car, then we can check the garage again for any clues as to who might've taken that sculpture. If someone had broken in, I would have noticed. It doesn't make any sense how someone took it without us knowing. Something's not right."

"You don't think one of us really sold it, do you?"

"I don't know what I think…except something going missing is real odd."

Sera noticed the deep lines in Maggie's forehead. It was like her to take accountability for the incident. It would have been so much easier for someone to have stolen one piece of the nativity scene while it was out in the yard. Breaking and entering, that was a real crime. Not like pilfering discarded kitchen appliances.

Huge raindrops began to plop against Sera's van like a warning from God. Maybe he was trying to tell them they weren't safe here. What if one of them had surprised the intruder? That could have been really bad news.

"I better get the Torpedo inside," Maggie said.

Sera watched Maggie take off into a jog across the yard. She was proud to see her new friend getting more and more fit. When they'd first met, Maggie probably would've had to stop and take a breather at the halfway point between the house and garage. But now, she made it all the way and jumped into the car, started the engine, then began to slowly edge it forward toward the garage opening.

A roll of thunder shimmied the earth, so loud it seared Sera's eardrums. Surely, the lightning was still miles—*Crack!*

Sera screamed. Oh, not good. "Maggie, we need to get inside!"

That one-two punch meant the lightning was less than three miles away. It could hit Summer Haven next.

The next crack of lightning proved her right, flashing above her. Sera dropped to her knees and covered her head with her arms. "Maaaggie!"

As if in slow motion, an old oak belched a wad of smoke. The ripping sound of a limb coming loose set off a shiver deep in Sera's muscles and jolted her heart. The branch's descent seemed almost languid, graceful as she watched it fall.

Until it hit the apex of the garage, changed trajectory, and spiraled one end over the other. The thick, ragged edge of the limb landed on the Tucker's hood with a sick *thud.*

Abby Ruth ran outside in her sock feet. "What in blue blazes was that?"

Sera clutched her chest and stumbled to her feet, trying to force some get-up-and-go back into her thighs. Her run across the yard probably looked as if she was dragging her legs rather than they were propelling her.

When Sera made it to the driver's side window, Maggie was sitting inside the car with her hands wrapped so tightly around the skinny white steering wheel, her knuckles gleamed.

"Are you okay?" Sera fumbled for the door handle, but it was locked. "Maggie, open up."

She didn't budge.

Across the car roof, Sera called to Abby Ruth, "I think she's in shock."

Abby Ruth crawled through the passenger side to Maggie. "Sugar, are you okay?" She snapped in front of Maggie's face. When Maggie blinked, but still didn't utter a sound, Abby Ruth gave her a light tap on the cheek. "Talk to me."

"Lil's car," Maggie said brokenly.

At the sound of her friend's voice, Sera lay her face against the car's cool surface and let the rain mix with her tears.

CHAPTER 5

"Oh. My. Lordy. Goodness." Maggie whispered the words, afraid if she said them louder something else would fall from the sky. "How much damage?"

Sera pushed away from the car, and if her expression was anything to go by, the situation was bad. Spelled in capital letters. "Who cares? It's only a car. Maggie, you could've been squashed like a spider."

Maggie slowly reached for the lock, then eased open the door. It didn't squeal in displeasure, but that didn't mean the car was fine. She already knew by the limb's impact, this situation was most definitely not fine. "Lil is going to kill me."

"She'll be glad you're alive!"

"No." She avoided glancing at the Tucker's front end, instead keeping her focus directly on Sera. "You don't know how much Lil loves this car. If Sera won't tell me, you do it, Abby Ruth."

It took a few seconds for Abby Ruth to respond. Finally she said, "It's gonna need some work."

"Even if it does," Sera said, "our Maggie can fix anything."

"I hate to tell you—" Maggie's voice cracked, and she took a breath to steady herself, "—but I'm more a drill gal than a torque wrench one." Still, she had to take a look at the car.

C'mon, Mags. You're a big girl, and you can handle this.

She blinked a few times, clearing the slowing rain from her eyes and allowing herself a little more cushion. Then she plodded to the front of the car and took it all in. At the sight of the gash across the nose of the fancy car, Maggie swallowed. Her already sweaty palms went clammier and her heart picked up more speed.

The branch in front of the car had some heft to it, and it had done one heckuva number on the Tucker's nose. Right above the third eye, the Cyclops, the Tucker now had a gash at least two inches deep. Maggie grabbed one of the sprawling arm-like branches and tried to tug the limb out of the way.

"Sugar, you're never going to budge that thing alone," Abby Ruth said. "It has to weigh dang near as much as the car."

"It's not that big." Maggie yanked again, desperation clawing at her, but the darned thing didn't even wiggle.

Sera ran to Maggie's side and wrapped her hands around the limb. Abby Ruth let out a sigh and joined them. With the three of them working together, they were able to inch the thing off the hood. But with every movement, the sound of smaller limbs scratching across the metal were like witch's fingernails on a tombstone.

Maggie's eyes filled with tears, but still she could see the gouges and scratches in the Tucker's paint. "This is awful. Everything is going to hell in a handbasket. I've got to get the car in the garage."

"Little late for that," Abby Ruth said.

Maggie wanted to lash out, to say it was Abby Ruth's fault the car had been left out in the first place. But that wasn't fair. Maggie had forgotten, and she was ultimately responsible for everything at Summer Haven. "Still, I need to protect the rest of it from the rain."

She climbed back behind the wheel and idled

the car forward into the garage. As she walked out, Abby Ruth yanked the garage door shut behind her.

The rain was tapering off, and Maggie said, "That limb has to be moved. Sera, go get me the chain saw."

Sera eyed her, doubt clear in her gaze. "I'm not sure this will work, Mags."

"Aren't you the one always saying we have to send positive vibes out into the universe to be rewarded with positive outcomes?"

"Yes, but—"

"No buts." Maggie puffed out a breath, sending her bangs up in the air. "This limb has to go." At least the chain saw was something she could handle. And right now, she needed control. Of something.

AN HOUR LATER, MAGGIE FINALLY CUT THE chainsaw motor. Her arm muscles were shaking and she was far from done, but she'd tackle carving these behemoth stumps into firewood later. Lord, Summer Haven's heat could go out for a month, and they'd still be snug from burning fires.

That was one positive way to spin such a horrible accident.

Cutting up the limb had burned off some of the adrenaline still coursing through her veins, but it did nothing to correct the car problem. Now only a sick emptiness filled her.

The Tucker was damaged and she had to get it fixed. Admitting the accident to Lil after the car had been restored to its pristine condition would be much better than telling her now. No reason to give her something else to fret over while she was stuck in Walter Stiles and couldn't do a thing about the problem. And what a doozy of a problem it was.

Maggie went inside to Lil's desk and flipped through the notebook Lil had left for her. The mechanic's name was on the emergency list. *Thank goodness.*

Maggie picked up the phone and dialed.

"Wally's Garage."

"Hi, this is Margaret Rawls. I need to get some work done on Lil Fairview's '48 Tucker Torpedo. I have you listed as her mechanic."

"Oh, yeah. Not me. That'd be my dad. He was the only one who ever worked on that car."

"Is he in?"

"I'm sorry," he said, his tone sad and low. "He passed away six months ago."

"Oh dear. I'm so sorry for your loss." And she

was, but this situation required immediate attention. "Well, I'm sure Lil would trust you to work on the car."

"I don't mess with those old cars. Not just anyone can handle something like that. I'd suggest you contact someone from the Tucker Club and get them to track down a mechanic."

No, no, no. She didn't have time for all that. "Well, to be perfectly honest, I just need a little body work and a new hood ornament. We had a small tree incident here."

"Even more reason to call them. It's hard to lay your hands on Tucker parts. You know only like fifty of the suckers were ever built, right?"

Maggie paced back and forth in front of the desk. "Yes, but—"

"Not a lot of cars made, and not many mechanics who can work on a car like that."

Not good news at all. "Thank you for your time." Her heart as heavy as a sledgehammer, she hung up the phone, but she wasn't about to accept defeat. She opened Sera's laptop, tapped the screen and clicked on the browser button.

She stabbed at the keyboard one letter at a time. T-U-C-K-E-R-4-8.

The first site the search engine displayed

featured pictures of several cars similar to Lil's, but no convertibles. At the bottom of the page, a few links were listed. She clicked on the Tucker Club link and it pointed her back to Facebook. At least she knew how to use Facebook. It was how her daughter kept her up-to-date with Chloe's and Clint's pictures and goings-on.

One click and she'd joined the Tucker Club official Facebook group. She carefully crafted a post asking for help within driving distance of Summer Shoals.

Now she'd have to wait for a response.

Sera poked her head in the kitchen. "You okay, Maggie?"

"Yes. I was just posting something to the Tucker Club on Facebook. Turns out Lil's mechanic died. I swear this is not my day."

A notification of a friend request showed at the top of her screen, and Maggie clicked it. Chuck Tuckerlover. It was one of the men from the Tucker Club group. She quickly accepted him as a friend. "That was fast."

Not three seconds after she approved him, a private message popped up on the screen with a *boing*.

"Oh, look!" Sera said.

Maggie clicked on the conversation box.

Tuckerlover: Hi Maggie. Welcome to the Tucker '48 Club. I hear you're looking for a mechanic.

Maggie: I am. Ours died.

Tuckerlover: Sorry for your loss. Which Tucker do you have?

Maggie: A 1948.

Tuckerlover: No, the car itself, not the year. They're all '48s.

Maggie: I don't know what you mean.

Sera leaned over her shoulder and pointed to the screen. "You can just type *IDK* for I don't know."

Maggie wasn't about to start using all those silly icons and acronyms, but this wasn't the time to get into that.

Maggie: Can I call you?

Tuckerlover PMed her his number, and Maggie didn't waste a second and dialed. "Hi, this is Maggie. Thank you for responding to my post so quickly."

"You're welcome. You can call me Chuck." His voice was deep and raspy as if he was a smoker.

"It's always great to talk to another Tucker enthusiast."

"Well, it's not actually my car. It belonged to my best friend's dad. He adored that car."

"What's going on with it?"

"We had a little…accident." It wasn't easy to choke out the words.

A pause stretched out on the other end of the line. Finally, he said, "That's…unfortunate. Hope everyone is okay. Good thing about the Tucker, it was made for safety. What's happened?"

"A limb fell across the front of it. Broke the hood ornament clean in two, and put a big old gash across its nose. Come to think of it, the car looks a bit like it's been muzzled. Do you know someone who can help me?"

He whistled low, in a way that indicated bad news. "Must've been a helluva branch. If it's not too bad, you might be able to get the damage repaired. You'll need a good—no, I'd say a great—body guy. If you need a new hood, it's gonna be pricey, if you can even find one. Parts are hard to come by because so few cars were manufactured. Which car do you have?"

This man was making her crazy with that question. Wasn't a Tucker a Tucker? "It's big and blue."

"There's a chassis number for each car, and we pretty much know where all fifty are. Ten-oh-one was the first off the line. So on and so forth for each subsequent car. Some are still on the road. A few have been wrecked and culled for parts. We can track those parts to the cars still running the roads."

Wow, these guys were serious about their car lineage. "Oh, well then maybe you can tell me which one I have. Although I seem to remember Lil once saying her dad calling it the Big 20. Something about it being the same as his birth year, so maybe it's the 1020."

Another long pause made Maggie wonder if he was looking up something for her, but then he simply said, "Maybe."

But the tone in his voice shouted *I don't think so!*

"Does it matter?" she asked. "And how much will this cost? Are we talking hundreds or thousands?"

"I'm just over in Augusta. How about I come that way and see what you've got there? Maybe I can help."

Wait a minute. She'd just met this man ten minutes ago online. What if he wasn't who he said he was? What if he made a living from scamming little old ladies? Maggie had run into enough scheming men in the past few months to think twice. "Why would you want to do that?"

Her suspicion must've bled through the line because he said, "Look, Miss Maggie, I'm not trying to horn in on your business. But you sounded mighty desperate when you called. You can feel free to talk to some of the other Tucker Club members. They'll vouch for me. We're such a small group, we have to stick together when one of us has problems."

Well, if his sincere words and tone didn't make her feel like a paranoid old gal. "I'm sorry. It's just been a stressful day."

"I can only imagine. But you gotta make the call."

"Chuck, I'd appreciate it if you'd come out to Summer Haven and take a look at the Tucker. When can you be here?"

"Monday morning."

After she hung up the phone, Maggie was wearing a grin that wouldn't quit. If this guy could help her get the Tucker back in tip-top shape, no way could Lil be angry.

Feeling better, she turned to Sera, who was chopping up onions, potatoes and carrots at the kitchen counter, and said, "Where's that crockpot? Let's get her fixed up and cook a celebration meal."

"Was the Tuckerlover guy able to help?"

"He's coming Monday to check it out. Keep your fingers crossed the repairs won't cost too much."

CHAPTER 6

Lil left her cottage and made the trek to the main prison building. She still had to move slowly, but the good news about Angelina Broussard's untimely visit on Friday was Lil had barely touched a thing on her cafeteria tray since. Surely she'd dropped a pound or two, even though she was barely burning a calorie an hour.

But now, she needed to finally pull out her change purse and pay the piper. So she joined the phone line and waited for her turn.

She'd tried to think of every possible way to keep from giving in to Angelina's demand. Only Angelina holding out her hand for the key to Summer Haven would've been worse than her asking for the Tucker. Some of Lil's fondest memories of her father were connected to that car.

As she patiently waited her turn, she stared out the window. Even with the screen and bars between her and the outside, the blue sky was bright and cheerful for this time of year. In fact, it was as blue as Daddy's Tucker Torpedo.

He used to say he'd picked that particular color because it matched Lil's eyes, which were the same blue as his.

When she was a little girl, he would take her on weekly outings to the soda shop on Main Street, and they always drove there in his prized car with the top down. On sunny days it was fun even if the seats nearly burned her butt. In less favorable weather, he tucked a lap blanket around Lillian to keep her warm, and she hadn't cared if she felt like a popsicle still in the wrapper, because those dates with Daddy were the best.

On one chilly February day when Lillian was eleven, they ordered their ice cream—strawberry in a cup for him and French vanilla in a sugar cone for her—and sat at the shop window overlooking the parked Tucker. He pointed to the car and said, "Lillian, that is one of the three loves of my life. Your mother, you, and that car are my three girls. My three treasures. I can't control God's will, and one day I'll have to leave you all. But promise me you'll take care of my other girls when I'm no longer around to do it myself."

"Yes, sir."

As it turned out, her mother had passed on first. And as with many couples in their generation, her father hadn't lasted much long after. Which had left Lillian with only the Tucker.

"Phone's all yours, Grammy Lil," a twenty-something girl said brightly, pulling Lil's attention from the blue sky. "Only two more months in this place and then I'm marrying the man of my dreams!"

Lil wished she remembered what it was like to feel that young and optimistic about the future. After Angelina's shakedown, Lil barely cared if the prison system ever released her. At least in here, she was safe from her hometown's judgment and scorn.

But Summers did not hide. They faced their problems head-on. Lil had only one idea for discouraging Angelina.

Angelina answered the phone on the second ring. "Hello, Lillian."

"How did you know it was me?"

"Well, you are the only person I know currently residing at the Walter Stiles Prison Camp."

Danged caller ID.

"I suppose you have an answer for me."

"You can't honestly expect me to hand over my daddy's car to you with no compensation."

"Silence is very valuable, don't you think?"

Lord, it was. But if Lil gave in this easily, Angelina might decide she had a career as a blackmailer, and Lil would never be out from under the woman's thumb. She took a breath and plunged in. "I've considered your…*offer*. I'm open to the Tucker changing hands on two conditions."

"Go on."

"You keep your end of the bargain we made the other day by keeping my recent whereabouts to yourself."

Angelina said nothing, and a fear so strong swept through Lil that it weakened her grip on the phone.

"Or have you already let that slip?"

"Apparently, I have more restraint than you because I haven't betrayed anyone this week."

Somehow, someway, Lil would make Angelina regret asking this of her. Maybe not the first week she returned to Summer Shoals. Maybe not even the first year, but Angelina wouldn't get away with blackmail. Not without some kind of payment. But Lil just forced a smile into her voice and lowered the boom. "Excellent. And I'll also expect you to pay a hundred thousand cash."

"Excuse me?" Angelina's voice rose by at least an octave.

"You may be many things." Lil said each word with extra care to ensure they were even, rather than emotional. "But you are not a stupid woman. You must know that car is worth a great deal of money. In fact, I read a story about one of them going for almost three at auction a few years ago. Why don't we say a million?"

Angelina would no more go for that figure than she'd take a step into town without her full makeup on, but there was no reason to make this easy for her.

"You cannot be serious." Heavy emphasis on the *not*.

A tiny smile lifted Lil's lips. "Have you done any comparative shopping?"

"You don't seem to understand I have the upper hand here."

It was true, but it wouldn't do to simply roll over. Lil wouldn't be in prison forever, and she couldn't have Angelina making her life a living hell for the rest of her years. "Since these are extenuating circumstances, I suppose I could consider an offer of seventy thousand."

“What if I don’t have that kind of money?”

“You’re married to the most successful doctor in town.”

“Twenty thousand,” Angelina came back like a bullet.

Oh, this woman could make a saint smoke and drink and cuss. “Sixty-five thousand.”

“Thirty.”

“Sixty.”

“Fifty, and not a penny more.”

Lil’s tiny smile stretched a little more. Exactly the number she’d been shooting for in the first place. “You get your money right, and I’ll be in touch.”

“You do that, Lillian, but don’t take too long. I want that car in my possession by the High on the Hog event or forget it. If I don’t have it by then, you can kiss your sweet Summer family reputation goodbye.”

MAGGIE STOOD ON SUMMER HAVEN’S PORCH, HER hand shading her eyes from the welcome spring sunshine, when a man in a car as big as the Torpedo pulled into the driveway. What was it with those old cars? They all looked as if they needed angioplasty.

She walked down the steps, taking in the way

Lil's family estate was beginning to come alive. Grass sprigs pushing through the ground had turned the lawn a vibrant green and all of the pruning and planting she and Sera had done last fall was starting to pay off in new buds, giving the place a breath of fresh air.

Lil would miss one of her favorite seasons at her home. Sad for her, but thank goodness Maggie had enough time to get the Tucker back in tip-top condition.

A gray-haired man pushed open the other car's door. "You must be Maggie."

"And you must be Chuck. Thanks so much for coming out. What kind of car are you driving?"

The man looked at the big honkin' ride like it was the sexiest woman he'd ever laid eyes on. "It's a '46 Hudson Commodore," he crooned. "They don't make 'em like this anymore."

"It's one hunk of a car," she said, not really meaning it as a compliment, but he clearly took it as one. It probably sucked down a tank of gas to get from here to the corner in that thing.

He gave her a wink and rubbed his hands together. "Where's your Tucker?"

"Follow me."

He walked alongside her, his head swiveling with each step. "Nice place here."

"Thanks." He didn't need to know Summer Haven was a money pit. From the outside, the white Georgian still had all the grandeur of a stately old mansion.

As she moved forward to lift the garage door, he cut in front of her and said with a smile, "Allow me."

Was he flirting? After the online dating case she, Sera and Abby Ruth solved a few months back, Maggie was constantly noticing when men noticed her. Or maybe it was just wishful thinking on her part. Or possibly senility. Whatever it was, it was nice.

The garage door rumbled up into the rafters.

"Waltz blue," he said. He gave a couple appreciative nods, then pulled out a magnet from his pocket. He slid it down the side of the car, catching it several times as it lost connection.

Maggie hated a cheap magnet, and she was half tempted to get him one of her good ones.

He opened the driver's side door and stooped, examining the doorjamb. He ran his hand along the door pillar as if he were reading Braille. "How about we take a look at the engine?"

"Sure." Maggie moved to the front of the car and fumbled for the hood release.

Chuck's brows were knit together so tight they

looked like one big woolly caterpillar. "What are you doing up there?"

She popped the hood and motioned to the motor. "You said you wanted to check out the engine." It looked quite impressive. If size mattered, this sucker had clout, and lots of shiny parts too. That had to be a plus.

He walked around and joined her at the front of the car, then let out a hearty laugh.

"What's so funny? Looks right impressive to me."

He braced one hand on his hip and the other on the huge front end of the car. "The good news is I don't think this will cost you much to fix."

Maggie let out a whoop. "Thank goodness!"

"Less than a few grand, I bet."

Nothing to whoop about there.

"The bad news is—" his already gravelly voice lowered further, "—this ain't no '48 Tucker."

Maggie whirled toward him. "Of course it is. Lincoln William Summer loved this car as much as he did his wife. His daughter, who's my best friend Lil, has ridden in it in more parades than you can shake a stick at."

"That may be true. But I'm here to tell you this is not a Tucker. First of all, the Tucker was a rear-engine car."

Maggie's heart shrunk. "All the models?"

"Let me show you." He whipped out his phone and pulled up a website featuring a Tucker with its trunk open. Unfortunately, the car's engine was clearly visible inside the trunk. "Look here. See the rear engine."

"That can't be right."

"Afraid so. Up there, where your motor is, should be the spare tire and trunk. Besides, I can't find a chassis or body number on this thing."

"That's not good, is it?"

"Not really. Plus this car has been fabricated. Did you see the way my magnet didn't stick to the body? A real Tucker body would be all metal. Every place you saw the magnet drop? That's where the body has been sculpted to look like a Tucker."

That couldn't be true. Not with the way Lil had carried on about this car for years. "Surely there's some mistake."

"It's a decent imitation, but this is no more than a kit car. I guess it might bring you five grand from the right car guy."

Five grand? But Abby Ruth had claimed it could be worth a million. He must think Maggie was an idiot. She folded her arms across her chest. She knew what was going on here. He was probably getting ready to offer her a pittance for it and steal it from her. Two could play this game.

She lifted her chin and studied him. "Are you interested in buying it?"

"No, ma'am." He spread his arms wide and shook his head. "Not at all."

Darn it all, he was telling the truth. "What about the 20 thing? Doesn't that prove something?"

"Only that your friend's dad nicknamed his car after the year he was born. Probably kind of an inside joke. The Tucker 1020 is somewhere in Japan, and it's not waltz blue. That one is color code 600, which is maroon."

"Oh, dear." Disappointment stung at Maggie's skin, making her feel raw and tired. She wasn't sure how this could be true. Although Lil had been surprised when she'd learned Abby Ruth thought the car was worth so much money. Great. Telling Abby Ruth she'd been wrong wouldn't be any more of a picnic than telling Lil the Tucker-that-wasn't-a-Tucker wasn't worth much more than sentimental value.

Was it possible Lil's daddy knew all along it was a kit car? Maybe he'd been the one to build it and that's what had made the car so special to him. With his mechanic dead and gone, they might never know.

"I guess you could have any decent auto body person work on this car. Just contact your local shop. I wouldn't bother going the route of trying to find parts. No one with a Tucker will part it out to a non-Tucker owner anyway, but you can probably get someone to pound the dent out or Bondo this puppy for two or three thousand bucks. The paint's what'll cost you the most. This one has…had a super nice paint job. Well taken care of, in fact."

Maggie walked Chuck back to his car. "Thank you so much for driving out here. I'm sorry it was for no good reason."

Chuck took her hand and kissed the top of it. "Meeting a lovely woman, such as yourself, is never a waste of time." He slid behind the wheel of his tank of a car and drove off.

Maggie waved goodbye, her heart still thumping from the combination of Chuck's smooth talking and relief she wouldn't have to worry about finding special parts to fix the car. That made things a lot easier. The last time she'd spoken to Lil, she'd sounded optimistic about getting released at the one year mark rather than the full fourteen months of her sentence. That still gave Maggie some time to handle the car situation before Lil came home.

Between now and then she'd have to decide how to break the news to Lil.

If she even had to tell her. Wasn't like Lil would ever sell her daddy's beloved car. Maybe she didn't need to know. Maybe no one needed to know.

AFTER CHUCK THE TUCKERLOVER LEFT, MAGGIE dragged herself back into the house. Was it better or worse that Lil's car was a big ol' fake? Sure, it would cost less to fix it, but three thousand was more than they had to spare—even with Hollis' very generous donation.

She plodded into the kitchen where Sera and Abby Ruth were sitting at the farm table. "We need money." She heard the misery in her own voice.

"Lordy be, isn't that always the way of it around this house?" Abby Ruth said.

If it wasn't one thing falling through the ceiling, it was another thing falling from the sky. And even if they found a way to pay to repair the Tucker, they were still left with a tree that might land on Summer Haven at nature's whim.

"How much money?" Sera asked.

"I don't know for sure. I'm going to have to hunt down a good body and paint guy. But Chuck the Tucker guy thought maybe two or three grand."

"We still have the envelope from Hollis," Sera said. "I know we didn't think there was much to this trash thing, but we need that cash more than ever. We have to keep all of it. Which means we need to get busy and earn it."

"Wait a minute." Abby Ruth thumped the toe of her boot against the table leg. "I thought we might use some of it for me to fly to Palm Beach."

"And we said we were going to use it for repairs around here." Feeling defeated and wishing she could turn back time, Maggie closed her eyes. "We've spent that money three ways already."

"Now, don't give up, Maggie. That's not your style." Abby Ruth paced the kitchen like a caged tiger. Her boots clicked out a tune like one of those Cocklebur Cloggers. "You know, if Hollis is willing to spend that kind of money on his trash, how much do you think Colton Ellerbee would pay for us to look into his missing sculpture?"

"Oh," Sera breathed. "She's got a point."

"Plus, it would kind of clear our names. I hate a liar and I sure don't like being accused of being one," Abby Ruth said. "Makes me cranky."

Maggie tried to turn a deaf ear to most of the Summer Shoals gossip, but the whole town had been buzzing with the news of the sculptor's success since he won the Annual Holiday Art Fest. If someone had paid fifteen grand for a wayward nativity scene sheep, Colton was obviously rolling in money like a horse in green clover.

Abby Ruth waved a hand toward the laptop sitting on the kitchen desk. “Sera, go do your magic and see if you can find out the names of those folks who bought that junk Colton is convinced we sold out from under him. I didn’t catch the whole name on the paper before he yanked it back.”

“Then how did you plan to find them once you made it to Palm Beach?” Maggie asked. Sometimes this woman had more guts than sense.

“Don’t ever underestimate a Cady.”

Couldn’t argue with that.

Sera slid into the chair and cracked her knuckles like a prizefighter. Then her fingers tripped over the keyboard. She clicked and hummed. Hummed and clicked. Not three minutes later, she said, “Got it! The people who bought the sheep are Lorna and Sidney Caliper.”

“Well,” Abby Ruth drawled, “since we know we didn’t sell that thing, we should find out who stole it.. Because if someone was willing to pay that kind of money for it, we could sell a couple wise men for the Torpedo’s repairs.”

“Lord, that’s all we need.” Maggie rubbed a spot over her eye. “Can you imagine what Colton would do if he found out we’d profited from his hard work? He'd be living on Summer Haven's front steps hooting and hollering about his art from sunup to sundown. No, thank you. I'd rather pay for the repairs with Hollis' trash cash."

Abby Ruth gave Sera a hip bump. "Can you get me a phone number for those Caliper folks?"

"561-555-6269."

With a motion like she was drawing a Wild West pistol, Abby Ruth pulled out her cell phone and dialed. "Hello, there," she said. "This is Deputy Cady from the Bartell County Sheriff's department up here in Georgia. How're you today?"

Maggie clapped a hand over her mouth. They'd sunk to new depths, impersonating a law enforcement officer. She glanced at the ceiling because it was inevitable they'd get struck by lightning again for spinning this yarn.

"That's good," Abby Ruth continued. "If you don't mind, I need to ask you a few questions about a sculpture you recently purchased."

All Maggie could hear was a garbled answer from the other end of the line.

"No, you're not in trouble. And I'll be happy to tell you everything I know once we get to the bottom of this. But for now, I can't divulge the details in an ongoing investigation. You understand.

Of course. Can you tell me who you purchased the piece from?"

Pause.

"You say it was Colton Ellerbee?" Abby Ruth raised her brows until they disappeared under her choppy gray bangs. "And you're sure of that?"

Maggie glanced at Sera. Could Colton be the dishonest one? But why would he do something like that and try to pin it on them? The man was annoying, but he wasn't malicious.

"Well, we've got some conflicting stories about the provenance of that piece."

Sera mouthed *provenance?* at Maggie. Yes, their former sports journalist was a lot more sophisticated than she sometimes pretended. Abby Ruth Cady was handy to have around on occasion, not only because she was pretty darned smart, but because she would do anything it took to get a job done.

And Maggie admired that in a gal.

"Don't worry," Abby Ruth said into the phone. "If we determine the sculpture is a big, fat phony, then we'll see to it you're compensated. Would you be willing to send me a few close-up pictures? We want to verify the artist's signature and techniques. You can send them to CowgirlUp@gmail.com. Oh, my official email address? Know what? Our IT folks up here in Georgia are having a heckuva time keeping our network up. I'd hate for your pictures to disappear into the wild."

Pause.

"Yep, we'll definitely get back with you." When Abby Ruth clicked off her phone, she wore a self-satisfied grin. "Well, girls, we've just kicked off our third officially unofficial investigation. Sera, you might want to hook us up with a professional-sounding email address for future use."

Sera's fingers clicked at the keyboard. "I'm on it. And technically, this makes four investigations if you count the crockpot crooks. Which I do."

"Damn, we're good," Abby Ruth said.

"Okay, ladies, our new business email account is up and running." Sera twisted the screen toward them to show them the new account for SHHGroup@whatchamail.com.

"SHH?" Abby Ruth asked. "Sounds like one of those backup group do-wa-diddies, and I ain't dancing. I'm telling you that right now."

Sera said, "It's an acronym. Summer Haven Hotshots."

"Hotshots? It's more like hunting Summer Haven style," Abby Ruth said.

"Well, fine. You can be a hunter, I'm being a

hotshot." Sera seemed satisfied, and Maggie pondered which H she'd rather be.

Abby Ruth's phone *boinged*. "We've got mail."

Maggie pursed her lips. "I don't like it. Not one bit. What if Teague contacts those people down in Florida and finds out *Deputy Cady* got there first?"

Abby Ruth lifted her chin. "How many times do I have to tell you? Y'all just leave Teague Castro to me."

CHAPTER 7

Teague shoved another stack of paperwork to the corner of his desk. Being a short-staffed sheriff sucked. It gave a whole new meaning to hump day, and he hadn't had one extra minute all week to look into that stuff for Colton. Not only was he on patrol more than normal, but as soon as he handled everyone's reports, they piled up again.

This was what happened when a guy was down a deputy. He'd been searching for a replacement but wasn't fully satisfied with any of the candidates. Summer Shoals might be small, but that didn't mean he should compromise when it came to the citizens' safety.

But continuous backlog of work and reports around the clock was killing him.

Then again, work was the only thing keeping him warm at night since Jenny and her son weren't able to move down to Georgia as quickly as both he and Jenny had hoped. Every time his phone rang, he grabbed it as fast as he could, his heart thumping with anticipation that someone had made an offer on her condo. Otherwise, she couldn't afford to come to Summer Shoals until her residency started in the fall, and fall was too far off as far as he was concerned. Still, she'd be here for a year.

A year he wanted to turn into a lifetime.

He opened a folder and was scanning a report on a kid who'd replaced the local Baptist church's holy water with cherry Kool-Aid when a head popped around his open doorway.

"Got time for a chat, Tadpole?" Abby Ruth asked. "Or better yet, a beer?"

He slapped the folder onto his desktop and sighed. "Not sure even a fifth of moonshine would wash away all the crap I need to get through."

"Any luck on the deputy search?" The gleam in Abby Ruth's eyes told him she'd be happy to step in at any time. Lord help him if that ever came to pass. She'd have him booted out in a patrol car and take over his job within twenty minutes. This woman was one of the shrewdest folks on earth.

One of the reasons he loved her. And her daughter.

"I've been interviewing candidates. I'm getting closer." Careful to not get her hopes up, he pushed out of his chair and motioned toward the door. "Don't have time for a drink, but how about a walk?"

He needed to stretch his legs, and a stroll would get Abby Ruth away from the temptation of the sheriff's office. Once outside, he asked, "What's up?"

"Talked with Jenny Monday afternoon. She mentioned she had a couple of people looking at her place today. One looked like a real good prospect."

Teague immediately groped in his pants pocket for his phone, snatched it out to check for texts from Jenny. Nothing. She hadn't mentioned it, but then maybe she didn't want to get his hopes up until it was a sure thing.

He plowed a hand through his hair. "I wake up every day thinking this could be the day she'll call with good news and be on her way."

She eyed him, and he figured out why when they passed by the gleaming glass front of the flower shop. His reflection even startled him a little with the way his dark hair stood on end like one of those old troll dolls. She grinned. "You could always swear me in. That would give you some breathing room. Maybe enough time to fly up to Boston for the weekend. Wouldn't that be nice?"

As much as he loved Jenny Cady, and as much as he wanted a weekend of uninterrupted time in her bed, he couldn't let her mother loose on his town. Goodness only knows what would still be standing when he made it back. "I'll take that under advisement."

"You're a stubborn one, Castro."

He looped an arm around her shoulders and pulled her in for a side hug. "Just like looking in the mirror, Cady."

"Since you're snowed under, I have a proposal for you."

Suspicion swarmed over Teague, making his scalp itch like fire ants had built a nest in his hair. But seeing as he planned to make her his mother-in-law at his first opportunity, there was no need to shut her down out of turn. "I'm listening."

"Colton was mighty perturbed about that whole sheep incident."

Perturbed? The guy was one twitch away from a grand mal seizure. "*Perturbed* doesn't begin to define what he was."

"What if I could take that little inconvenience off your hands?"

"Meaning?" Man, he hoped she wasn't getting ready to tell him she'd sold the thing. Wouldn't that be just great?

"Maggie, Sera and I could do some poking around. Figure out what's going on with that sculpture."

Whew. At least she hadn't taken it. He wouldn't have put it past her to have thrown it away. "Wait a minute," he said. "You're coming to me asking for permission instead of doing whatever the heck you want and asking for forgiveness later?" Suspicion? Now those fire ants were in full-blown attack mode. He made a show of looking over Abby Ruth's shoulder. "Tell me where you've hidden Abby Ruth Cady's body."

"I may be an old dog, but I can learn a new trick now and again."

Teague snorted to himself. Abby Ruth asking instead of just plowing forward? About like an ass suddenly deciding to leave a barn full of hay and take a sightseeing trip into the Grand Canyon. "What's in this for you?"

She gave him a glare that would've shrunk another man's balls. Teague's were made of titanium. Had to be if he planned to have both Cady women around for the rest of his life. "Maybe we just want to do a good deed," she said.

"If Sera were the one talking to me, I might buy that. But you? Naw. You always have what us police types like to call *motive*."

She started strolling again. A casual movement he didn't trust in the least. "Fine. Maggie heard the rumor that Colton was grumbling about firing Jenny."

"What?" Damned if that one word didn't come out an octave higher than it should've. But if Jenny lost Colton as a client, it meant more money troubles. And her troubles meant major love life. Love life? Hell, just plain ol' life problems for Teague. "He can't do that."

"As Summer Shoals' biggest claim to fame since the first Mrs. Summer tiled the huge fountain in front of Summer Haven, I'd say he can."

"I...I need to—"

"Tadpole, I hate to point this out, but you can't do a damned thing about this situation. Not really. Only lead we've got is down in Palm Beach, which is a few miles outside your jurisdiction. What if folks in Bartell County found out you were spending more time trying to protect Jenny than you are them? Probably wouldn't go over too well."

She had a point. Summer Shoals wasn't a

violent town by any means, but his first duty was to protect the people here. Colton was a resident, but this was art, not life or death. "I don't know..."

"Tell you what, if Maggie, Sera and I get this little snafu cleared up right quick, then none of us will have a thing to worry about."

How much trouble could Abby Ruth and the others get into tracking down a sheep made out of old junk? Yeah, he probably shouldn't think that over too hard. "If...*if* I say okay, it'll be on one condition."

"Name it."

"None of you make a move without telling me about it first."

"Tadpole—" she gave him an exaggerated wink that made his head start itching again, "—you have my solemn word."

"HE ACTUALLY WENT FOR IT?" SERA COULDN'T believe her ears when Abby Ruth told her and Maggie that Teague had agreed to her scheme. Talk about lovesick. The man was obviously terminal. When Sera had first arrived in Summer Shoals, he'd nearly arrested her for boondocking. He'd been one tough cookie.

Abby Ruth plunged her hands into her back

pockets. "Told y'all not to worry about him. Besides, it makes perfect sense. He's shorthanded, and we've got time on our hands. It's a win-win."

Sera wasn't sure Teague would translate it quite that way, but what the heck. If her own days might be limited here at Summer Haven, then she was all for the chance at solving another big case. "Let's go negotiate with Colton. I'll drive."

Maggie's face squinched up like a puff of wind had hit her. "Maybe I should drive."

"Or me."

Sera quickly pointed out how being around all Colton's sandblasting and blowtorch activity would ruin their paint, and the other ladies, who adored their trucks, quickly gave in.

"Here we go," Sera said. She cranked up the old van and gave the dash a pat as the vehicle sputtered before catching and moving with a little zest.

In the passenger seat Maggie held Sera's computer on her lap, and in the back Abby Ruth was cussing up a storm every time Sera hit a pothole.

Just for the fun of it, Sera swerved hard to the right to bounce through another one.

"Hell and damnation," Abby Ruth muttered, rubbing the top of her head. "You have a sixth sense about those things?"

"Sorry," Sera said sweetly, "I was trying to miss a...a...possum."

Maggie leaned over and whispered, "Nice try, but possums are nocturnal."

Would Sera ever get used to the Georgia wildlife? Sure, she'd had a run-in or two with coyotes near her California home, and the Santa Monicas were famous for mountain lions and rattlesnakes. But here in the South? Little critters ran out in the road like they were looking to commit animal-cide.

When she'd dodged another few almost road kill victims, they made it to Colton's workshop. Even from outside, the whoosh of a blowtorch was loud. They waited until the sound stopped to make their way inside. The cavernous space was filled to the brim with bicycle carcasses, bent aluminum armchairs and other castoffs.

Colton might be a bit temperamental, but the man should get an award for his recycling efforts. If only more people would use what they already had instead of buying new. Like Maggie with that slow cooker. She'd wired it right up and the pot roast—or at least the carrots and potatoes Sera had eaten—had been delicious.

Spying them, Colton paused and shoved his welding helmet to the top of his head, making his sweaty blond hair stick out from his forehead like a shelf. His face was its normal shade of ripe tomato, and sweaty to boot. He was wearing heavy-duty gloves and a thick apron. Sera had never seen the man in anything but tweed clothes and a beret, but it was clear when it came to his art, he worked hard.

A recycler and a hard worker. She could be friends with someone like that.

"Ladies." His tone was polite yet was several thousand degrees cooler than his blowtorch had been. "Come to make a full confession?"

Abby Ruth elbowed her way through a stack of random lengths of pipe, parts and license plates. "Ellerbee, is your momma still around?"

"Yes, ma'am. She lives up in Ellijay."

"Good, because I'm gonna call her and tell her to jerk a knot in your uppity little tail."

For the first time ever, Sera witnessed his florid face dull to turnip purple.

"That won't be necessary." He folded his arms, his eyes careful. Wary, even.

"You promise to mind your manners?"

"Yes, ma'am." He clapped his hands and his tone lilted cheerfully. "What can I do for you fine ladies this afternoon?"

Abby Ruth gave a sharp decisive nod. "That'll

do. Not about how you can help us. It's about how we can help you." She motioned Sera forward.

Sera propped her computer on a worktable littered with cut glass doorknobs, a stack of folding rulers, and an old metal watering can. She pulled up the sheep pictures Abby Ruth had saved to the desktop. "Is this the piece you saw online?"

Colton leaned closer for a better look. "That's the one. I still can't believe y'all would—"

Abby Ruth held up one finger, and he shut up.

"We want you to look at some close-ups." Sera enlarged a shot featuring the sheep's poor little gas-can face. "This look familiar?"

She scrolled through the handful of pictures Mrs. Caliper had forwarded to them. Then she zoomed in as far as she could. "Here's a better angle."

"Well, I'll be damned," he said softly.

"If only," Abby Ruth muttered.

Maggie waved a shooing hand at Abby Ruth. If part of their purpose was to keep Jenny's job as his agent safe, then Abby Ruth needed to twist a lid on it.

Colton pressed his face close to the screen. "Yes, those look like my materials, similar. Someone went to some trouble. But that's not my work."

"What is it?" Sera asked Colton.

"I can promise you that is not my sheep." Colton sounded almost as apologetic as he did surprised. He strode over to what looked like a band of hungry hyenas with beer-keg bodies, measuring-cup ears, and teeth made of saw blades. "Look at the weld joint on this one's front hock."

"Nice," Sera said.

"No, not nice. I don't do fillet welded tee-joints, and that's how the sheep is put together." He upended one of the hyenas. "And take a look here."

They all crowded around the hyena's hindquarters. "See? I sign all my pieces."

"Those poor suckers bought a fake!" Abby Ruth clapped Colton on the shoulder. "Well, they say imitation is the sincerest form of flattery. Guess this case is solved."

"No, it's not. We still don't know where the original is, and someone is forging my work." Colton's color was back with a vengeance. "That kind of flattery is illegal. I want this…this…forger brought to justice."

"And we just got you one step closer to that."

"Forward those photos to Sheriff Castro and me. He'll need that to—"

"I've already had a chat with the good sheriff," Abby Ruth interrupted, shaking her head. "And that poor man. He's so darned busy, I'm pretty sure I saw him meeting himself coming and going the other day."

"But this is serious business."

"Which is why we've gotten his approval to help you get this straightened out."

"You?" Colton said the word as though he'd found himself mucking through the landfill in bare feet.

"We have solved several cases in the past few months. We find the forgery, that'll lead us right to the original."

"That does make sense." Then his left eyebrow lifted. "But in one of those cases, you were the perpetrator."

It was true. She'd tried to cover for her grandson's bad throwing arm when he gave Colton's sculpture a concussion, and repairing that junkyard Jesus had been no easy task. "But two other times, we caught people who were actually breaking the law. We do have a track record."

"Fine," he grumbled.

Abby Ruth slapped a hand on her waist and settled into a hipshot pose. "And we'll only charge you twelve thousand."

"Wha…what?" Colton choked out.

"If that sheep is worth fifteen, you're still coming out ahead."

"Local law enforcement would look into it for free."

"Are you really willing to wait? Teague's got a backlog. And if someone's forging your work, he might not stop at one. At this rate, you'll be out fifty grand before the week's done." Abby Ruth cocked her head, angling her chin the way she did when she was playing cat-and-mouse. "Especially when they made that chunk of change off the first one."

Colton hugged his midsection as though he'd been struck by a sudden case of gastrointestinal distress. "Five," he said.

"Ten," Abby Ruth countered.

"Seventy-five hundred."

"Done." Abby Ruth's lip curved, her satisfaction clear. Then she patted Colton on the cheek. "We'll take cash or check."

Colton matched her grin with one of his own. "Not until you fork up the forger, you won't."

CHAPTER 8

Lillian stared at the prison cottage's ceiling. From here on her cot, the popcorn tile on the far left looked a little like Harlan's face. If she was suddenly imagining her deceased husband was smiling down at her, maybe she was just lonely. Since she'd called and made a deal with Angelina, Lil hadn't had to *pretend* she was moping around the prison camp. She felt worse than she could have ever pretended. She'd let Daddy down three ways to Sunday and that was enough to kill her.

Somehow, early release didn't hold the appeal it had a week ago. And she felt as though she'd aged a decade in those seven days.

"Miss H&M," Martha said, "you're not looking so good. You starting to believe your own press?"

For whatever reason, Lil hadn't shared her latest problem with her roommate. Why, when Martha had been so keen to help her get out of here? "Pretending to be old is hard work."

"Maybe you should go to the infirmary for real this time."

Probably not a bad idea. It had been gray and bleak here the past few days, and not just inside Lil's heart. Maybe the nurse could put one of those blue mood light contraptions on her. That might perk her right up.

Lord, it was bad enough she was bamboozling all the people in Summer Shoals about where she'd been for months. Now she was trying to fool herself too.

"If nothing else, the walk'll do you good," Martha cajoled.

Why not? At minimum, she could ask for a little vitamin C. After all, the only cafeteria food holding any appeal for her these days was a cinnamon roll, and she was pretty sure there wasn't one good vitamin or nutrient in those half-cooked balls of dough and white sugar.

Martha kept her company on the stroll to the main building. As Lil peeled off to head to the infirmary, Martha laid her hand on Lil's shoulder. "You're going to be okay, ol' gal."

Lil wasn't quite as certain that was the case.

She scribbled her inmate code on the form at the front window of the infirmary and sat on one of the cold metal chairs. Even though she sat there alone, voices in her head taunted that she'd failed the Summer family.

"Inmate Fairview," the nurse said, "I didn't expect you back so quickly. Didn't the cream help with your arthritis pain?"

"Oh, yes. I'm doing much bet…" For goodness sake, what was she supposed to say? Continue with the lies or admit she'd been faking everything? She was just so darned tired and confused. "I'm a little achy since weeding flowerbeds."

"You don't look well today. Maybe we need to switch you to work that's not so manual in nature for the time being."

Lillian loved working out in the courtyard, but if she had to give it up to get back to Summer Haven faster, so be it.

"Hop up here." The nurse patted an exam table. "Let me take a look."

It seemed to take all of Lil's energy to lift herself up onto the paper-covered table. The nurse finally gave her a little boost and then kept a hand on her back as if steadying her.

The crinkling of the paper under Lil's butt reminded her of how thin and crepe-y her skin felt lately. Heck, she wasn't playing at being old. She *was* old.

The nurse checked Lil's mouth, nose, pulse and breathing. Then she asked, "Are you having difficulty with finding words?"

"No. Well, maybe."

"Trouble with motor functions or getting lost?"

"How would I get lost? You don't let me get thirty feet out of a guard's sight. What kind of question is that?"

"So you've been a bit agitated, I see."

"I am not agitated. I'm…I…I don't know what I am. It doesn't matter. Nothing does."

"Why don't you lie down, and I'll be back in a minute."

Probably going to fix a shot of vitamin C, D, K and any other letters of the alphabet.

But a few short minutes later, in strode Warden Proctor, her mouth drawn down. "Inmate Fairview," she said, "the nurse tells me you're exhibiting symptoms of severe depression."

What in the world? Lil had been blue a few days since coming to prison, but severe depression?

Well, that was serious. "I'm not—" She tried to sit up, but the warden placed a restraining hand on her shoulder.

"Don't tax yourself. Your physical health is already fragile, and your state of mind surely isn't helping anything. You'll be staying here in the infirmary until we make other arrangements for you."

Lil's heart rate climbed, yet her stomach felt as though she'd gorged on too much kettle corn, achy and tight. "What do you mean, other arrangements?"

"It means—" the warden smiled, a strangely sad smile, "—I'm calling the Bureau of Prisons to push for your compassionate release immediately."

In order to earn the money Maggie desperately needed to fix the Tucker and then give their full attention to finding whoever was behind forging Colton's sculpture, Sera had decided they needed to put Hollis' case of the missing trash to bed once and for all. She was driving to the landfill while Maggie and Abby Ruth rode along, only this time they were well aware it would be closed. After all, even she didn't drop off her recycling at midnight.

Sera pulled the VW Van to the backside of the landfill and hid it behind a couple of dumpsters so it wouldn't be visible from the road. She cut the engine, then grabbed her hemp tote bag from the back and hoisted it over her shoulder.

Abby Ruth pointed to a rise overlooking the fenced-in area. "We should be able to keep an eye on everything from up there."

They found a spot partially sheltered by tall pines, and Sera pulled a brown wool blanket from her bag. One flip of her wrists and it lifted into the air, billowing to the ground. Then she pulled out a huge pair of binoculars. "Look what I got at the thrift store. I knew they'd come in handy one day."

Abby Ruth chuckled. "Good Lord. Those must be circa 1960."

"Hey, they work. That's all that matters. And adjusting those massive lenses is like a bonus workout."

"And I was just thinking we should've brought lawn chairs," Maggie said. "You're getting good at this sneaking around thing, Sera."

"You ain't seen nothing yet." From inside her bag, she withdrew a cold pasta salad, crudités, and a bottle of Chardonnay.

Abby Ruth eyed the booty. "This a stakeout or a party?"

"No reason it can't be both."

Maggie's stomach roared. "Sera, I love midnight snacks and I love you."

Felt good to be appreciated. Crazy how driving over two thousand miles from California to Georgia had been what it took to make Sera really feel as if she was part of a family. And as happy as she was to be here in Summer Shoals, that thought—and the thought of what she'd left behind—made her sad.

To cover her mood, she poured wine into three glasses. Real glass glasses. No plastic stuff for her.

They made themselves comfy and settled into munching and drinking. Every so often, a noise would echo up the hill. Each time, they froze, only to be disappointed by a half-tailed cat scampering away with a frozen-dinner tray. Another time the sound was just the *swoosh* of a landslide of cardboard boxes from a recycling bin into the trash receptacle. That wouldn't make Hollis very happy.

Maggie leaned back and patted her tummy. "We should have more picnics."

"Next time, do you think we could go somewhere with a better view?" Abby Ruth said as a whiff of eau de road kill wafted their way.

"And maybe with potty facilities," Maggie added.

For such tough girls, these two sure were

weenies at times. "You can't tell me you've never peed in the woods, either one of you."

Abby Ruth turned Sera's way. "You know how they say never to squat on your spurs? Well, I try never to tinkle on my leather."

Dang it. Now that Maggie had mentioned it, Sera's bladder was complaining too. She pointed to a stand of trees farther up the hill. "Let's just run up there."

"Did you happen to pack toilet paper?" Maggie asked.

Abby Ruth rummaged around in Sera's bag and pulled out a wad of brown paper. "Looks like these were once cardboard boxes. Sure glad I can hold it."

"Well," Maggie said, "you might not have to go, but Sera and I need a lookout."

"What—you afraid a feral cat's gonna get a gander at your behind?"

Maggie shot Abby Ruth a half-snarl, half-pleading look.

Abby Ruth pushed to her feet. "Fine."

They trudged up the hill, and Abby Ruth turned her back on them to keep watch over the landfill with the binoculars. Maggie veered to the right while Sera went left.

Sera situated herself, careful to pull her gauzy

skirt over her shoulders and spread her feet wide. "You okay over there, Maggie?"

"That yoga really is something," Maggie called back. "You wouldn't believe how well I can squat and balance."

"Of all the things I didn't need to hear," Abby Ruth said.

Everything was quiet except for the sound of frogs and a little splatter now and then. Then lights cut across the hillside, and Sera felt as if someone had turned a spotlight onto her butt.

"Oh, crap," Abby Ruth said.

"What? What?" Maggie screeched.

"We got company," Abby Ruth said. "Guy wearing jeans, a baseball cap and a dark hoody. And he's skinny enough to slide right through that cut in the fence. He made straight for the third dumpster."

For Sera, it was a matter of a quick stand, tug and flip.

"Dammit, he jumped down and is headed back for the fence," Abby Ruth said. "Spooked him. We need to pursue."

From across the way, Maggie called out, "You can't leave without me. Give me a second." Her words echoed along the hillside.

Sera raced to catch up with Abby Ruth as she

barreled down the hill. No way could they let Abby Ruth be the first to arrive. She'd have the guy at gunpoint, and that thought made Sera sweat bullets. She glanced over her shoulder to check on Maggie. She was still quite a ways back, tugging on her pants as she hop-ran down the hill.

But by the time they made it back to their blanket, an engine turned over and gravel spit against the chain link fence.

"He's on the move."

Sera scooped up the remnants of their picnic, and the three of them hotfooted it toward the van. Abby Ruth swung into the driver's seat as she tended to do when situations became intense. She gunned the engine, and the tires spun. "You should replace these with tires that actually have tread."

And then they shot out onto the road in hot pursuit. Unfortunately, Sera's van wasn't exactly a turbo model. They chug-chugged along even though she'd bet Abby Ruth had the pedal pushed to the floorboard.

When they scaled the last rise before Lavender Hill Road intersected with Old County Line Road, the only thing they caught was the flicker of taillights in the distance.

CHAPTER 9

A quick cruise through town turned up a big fat nothing.

"We lost them," Sera said.

"What now, girls?" Abby Ruth turned at the next street and idled at the stop sign.

Maggie said, "We should go back to the landfill and patch up the fence to keep them from breaking in again. I've got my duct tape with me."

"Of course you do," Abby Ruth said.

It was true. Maggie was the only person in the whole world Sera had ever met who never left home without duct tape. Came in handy pretty often, though.

While Maggie wove duct tape between the

mesh, Sera and Abby Ruth discovered the thief had dropped a hibachi grill right outside the fence.

Even Sera was convinced Hollis' trash problems were the work of someone who didn't have the money to buy new furnishings. And if the "thief" was recycling to that extent, she couldn't find fault with it.

"We can't take Hollis' money if this so-called case of theft is just some kids trying to outfit their apartment, can we?"

"We need the money," Maggie said. "But no, I don't suppose we can."

All told, they didn't get back to Summer Haven until after three a.m. And the next morning, Sera learned Abby Ruth Cady was not tolerable without her beauty sleep.

Sera drove out to see Hollis on her own. The dump was closed on Friday, so she pulled up in front of his house.

She banged the knocker on his door, and waited. The sound of his walker clomping across the hardwood floor toward the door seemed take a long time for such a tiny house.

Hollis slowly pulled the door open and walker-hobbled to steady himself. "Hey there, Miss Sera. I sure am hoping you have some news for me today."

She swallowed because she had all of Hollis'

money tucked into her pocket. "I sure do. Why don't you sit back down and I'll tell you what we discovered."

"It's some pervert, ain't it?" The excited growl in the old man's voice made it clear he was hoping for something dramatic.

Too bad she had to dash his hope. She helped him settle back into a recliner in front of the television. "I don't think so. We've discovered someone has, in fact, been taking trash from the dumpsters."

"I knew it. Some hoodlum."

"We almost caught him in the act last night, but he got spooked and ran. He dropped a little grill on his way out. Hollis, it's just some young guy who probably can't afford to outfit his apartment. He's taking things no one else wants anyway."

"Damned kids," he muttered. "That stuff is still the county's property."

"Don't you remember what it was like to be young and broke?"

His tired eyes went wide and filmy. "Lordy be, the first little ol' place me and the missus rented wasn't no bigger than a minute. A minute? Make that no bigger than a second. It was actually old lady Matthew's attic. In winter, it was cold as a penguin's tail feathers and in summer, hotter'n the devil's pitchfork."

The smile on Hollis' lined face warmed Sera's insides. She'd brought back a wonderful memory of his wife, who had been gone more than ten years. She reached out and covered Hollis' thick-knuckled hand. "Sounds like those were good times."

"Uh-huh. The time when I chased the missus down those stairs and we christened the porch swing, now that was something else." His eyes snapped bright again, and color spotted each of his cheeks. "I mean…uh…well…"

"Like I said, good times."

"The best."

"Then are you okay if we put this case to rest? I have a feeling the thief probably won't be back after last night." Sera took a breath, using one of her best *pranayama* techniques. "I hate to ask this, but would you be willing to let us keep some of the cash from the envelope? I can't go into details, it would be a big help to Lillian Fairview."

This time, Hollis covered her hand, gave it a pat. "Sure thing. You brought back some memories I haven't taken out and remembered in a long time. Made my day."

Making a man's day should be worth at least fifteen hundred.

"Why don't you keep two hundred?"

The hope in Sera's heart dropped all the way to her toes. "But…but we spent several hours staking out the landfill and…"

"…and now that I'm not worried about being shoved into Dogwood Ridge Assisted Living, I need my money back to hit the bingo hall over in Wheeler County. How about five hundred and we call it even?"

MAGGIE PULLED HER LITTLE TRUCK UP IN FRONT OF the Shipper Shack on Main Street since Colton wasn't willing to pay them until they tracked down the forger, and Hollis hadn't been as generous as they'd hoped. A flight to Palm Beach just wouldn't be possible unless they dug into their own pockets, but she was determined not to let that happen unless they'd exhausted every single possible alternative. So it was time to find out who'd shipped that darned sculpture to Florida.

With Sera at her side, they entered the new storefront and walked up to the counter. Most people still shipped packages through the post office round these parts, so Maggie wondered if the business had any hope of making it here in Summer Shoals. But the owner, a retired lieutenant colonel from the Air Force, had rolled into town with all the bravado of a former fighter pilot. He'd already been appointed to the Chamber of Commerce board.

"What can I do for you two lovely ladies?" the owner asked. His glasses twitched on his nose when he greeted them, drawing more attention to his expansive forehead, shiny all the way to the bald spot in the back.

Maggie smiled, trying to project honesty. "We need to check on a package shipped out of here on February 20th."

"If you shipped it, you should be able to go online and trace it with the tracking number."

Maggie sent Sera a what-now look. Asking for this information was probably illegal or at least an invasion of privacy, but they had to get to the bottom of who had shipped the forgery.

"We're actually working for the Calipers from Palm Beach, Florida," Sera said. "They were supposed to receive that shipment. But it never arrived."

"What do you mean *working* for them?"

"Perhaps you haven't heard that Maggie, Abby Ruth and I are what you would call...private investigators." Sera whipped out a SHHgroup business card and placed it in front of him.

Maggie almost choked. That girl worked fast.

Sera leaned on the counter, which allowed her flowy sweater to part and reveal her low-cut yoga tank underneath. The girl might not be stacked, but she knew how to use what she had to its best advantage. The owner's gaze immediately went to her chest. Goodness, who would've thought that trick would still work at their age?

Then again, hadn't Maggie done the same thing with her Maid Marian costume at the Halloween party? She smiled to herself. They might be older, but they still had it.

"Do you have some kind of identification?" he asked.

Sera ran a finger from the hollow of her throat to the neckline of her tank. "I have an email from our clients with the details of the sale."

She flashed him a quick look at her phone, then strategically tucked it into the side of her tank, making a show of enhancing her cleavage as she did so.

He could barely pull his gaze away, but he finally turned to his computer. Pecked at the keys in between sneaking glances at Sera. "Hmm, yeah. It went out on February 20th. It was a Friday shipment. Looks like it was shipped by Colton Ellerbee to the Calipers in Palm Beach, Florida."

"Do you remember anything about the person

shipping the package?" Maggie asked. "It was a large box."

"Can't say I do, but that would've been when Tassy Harrison was working for me. I've only seen Ellerbee around town a few times, but he's usually wearing one of those berets made from the same stuff as a sports coat."

"Tweed."

"That's it."

"Even though the package had Colton's return address on it, we don't think he's the one who actually brought the box in. Do you think Tassy might remember who shipped it?"

"Doubtful. After a while, all the boxes seem the same."

"Do you have a copy of the slip the customer filled out?"

His brow furrowed, as if Sera had finally pushed too far, but when she twirled a lock of hair around one finger and looked up at him from lowered lashes, he blurted out, "I can print one. We scan in all the handwritten forms."

Sera gave him a come-hither smile. Dang, this girl wasn't just good. She was a master. "That would be *so* helpful."

He hit a couple of keys, then handed a sheet of paper to Sera. "Here you go."

The handwriting was crisp and neat. Like a first grader practicing perfect letters and penmanship. But the signature was such a scrawling mess, Maggie couldn't say for sure it *wasn't* Colton's.

When she and Sera strolled out of the Shipper Shack, Maggie said, "Well, we didn't get what we wanted, but we could still chat with Tassy, right?" Maggie's stomach rumbled. Not only was it nearing lunchtime, but her tummy remembered that delicious banana nut bread Tassy had brought out to Summer Haven a couple of months ago when she asked Sera to take on the High on the Hog kids' events committee.

"Sure, we have a committee meeting tomorrow and I can feel her out then."

"I bet you find out something." Maggie raised her hand and high-fived her friend. "Because, girl, you should've been an actress."

A sudden cloud passed over Sera's normally bright eyes. "I guess I missed my calling."

MAGGIE AND SERA MET ABBY RUTH AT THE Atlanta Highway Diner for a quick bite before heading over to Colton's studio. The short drive across town to his workshop was quiet. Maggie wasn't sure if everyone was feeling the effects of today's blue plate special or they were all feeling the same pressure to get this case solved, clear their names, and get the money to fix the car.

As they walked up to the metal-sided building, Abby Ruth said, "Y'all let me take the lead with Colton, y'hear?"

That was fine by Maggie. From one day to the next, it was hard to tell which Colton Ellerbee you'd get—the suave, tweed-wearing one or the red-faced, nutty one. She'd just as soon Abby Ruth deal with him.

Today, even more flotsam lay strewn about the cool concrete floor—random ceiling-fan blades, grungy computer keyboards, and what looked like the guts of an old jukebox. Rather than welding, Colton was bent over a tall worktable. He was twisting wire around the ends of two metal funnels that appeared to be in the process of becoming a pair of gigantic breasts on a CD-scaled mermaid.

When he spotted them, Colton picked up a white shop towel and wiped off his hands. "You ladies find out anything yet?"

Ah, so it was calm Colton today.

Abby Ruth thrust the copy of the packing slip toward him. "You've been holding out on us, boy. Maggie and Sera just chatted up the guy down at the Shipper Shack. Sure as heck looks like *you* were the one to ship that sheep to Palm Beach."

"I did not ship it." Colton tapped the date on the paper. "I was up in North Carolina teaching at a folk art school on that day. Besides, if you look closely, you'll see I didn't sign the form."

He picked up an ink pen and scrawled his name across the top of a cardboard box full of wire connectors. "See?"

Maggie and Sera both leaned in, nearly bumping foreheads. He was right. The signature on the packing sheet wasn't his. There, the *C* in Colton was open and slightly tilted forward. And the *L*'s in Ellerbee were fat like Mickey Mouse ears rather than the skinny feathers in Colton's real autograph.

"He's right," Sera said. "His have tall skinny loopy *L*'s which means the writer is idealistic, as opposed to these big fat loops which generally mean the writer is a good talker."

"I guess you're back to square one." Colton frowned and absentmindedly fondled the funnel. "Are you sure you gals know what you're doing?"

"Yes! We're not back to square one," Sera protested. "We know the package was shipped from Summer Shoals. That's something."

"Then figure it out who it is, and don't bother me again until you do."

Maggie steadied her voice, trying to sound as confident as possible. Channeling her Detective Kate Beckett impersonation, she rattled off, “Someone stole the original from our garage between January 10th, when we packed up the Christmas decorations, and February 20th, when they shipped a forgery from Summer Shoals. One of our neighbors is up to no good.”

CHAPTER 10

Sera and Maggie had determined the next step was to chat up Tassy Harrison, and today's High on the Hog committee meeting was the perfect opportunity. Sera walked into Gypsy Cotton Gallery, owned by Tassy and her husband, for the meeting. Only bad thing about volunteering for Summer Shoals' annual pork festival was the chairperson, one Angelina Broussard. Oh, and the barbecued piggies.

One sweeping look at the space, a renovated cotton gin and warehouse, and it was clear Angelina hadn't arrived. Perfect. Sera would have time to ask Tassy some questions. She spotted Sherman Harrison, seated near the side door, dressed in pressed slacks and a button-down shirt.

Odd clothes for a farmer. Then again, Sherman was a hobby farmer, and Maggie said that meant he just played at being a man of the land.

Tassy sat right beside him, as always. That guy seemed to be on a short leash, although he probably didn't mind, since Tassy was at least thirty years younger and beautiful.

Before Sera could make her way across the room to Tassy and her husband, Bruce Shellenberger walked up. Bruce was a sweetheart and the computer genius who'd helped them solve an online dating scam last fall. "Hi, Sera. Haven't seen you in a while."

That was an odd comment since they'd seen one another recently at another committee meeting. "Strange how people can live in a small town and still not run into one another nearly often enough, isn't it?"

The tips of his ears turned pink. Bruce was a smart one. Wasn't often a man caught a woman's subtext. Sera wanted to give him a round of applause. "How's…uh…how's Maggie been?" he asked.

"Busy," Sera replied, beating back a smile. "Seems like she has a new beau every other week." Nothing wrong with stretching the truth when it was a means to a positive end.

But poor Bruce. His ears seemed to be blinking neon now. "Oh, that's…um…good?"

"Is it?" She tapped the side of her face. "I really thought there was a spark between you two. Or is someone else defragging your hard drive these days?" She should be ashamed at herself for stirring the pot, but she wasn't. Maggie deserved companionship and happiness, and Bruce might be the man for both jobs.

"No. I mean…oh, heck. I don't know what I'm saying." He blew out a breath. "Maybe I'll stop in and see Maggie soon?"

"Excellent idea."

Bruce made a beeline for the punch bowl, and Sera wove between the rows of chairs and slid into an empty seat right in front of Tassy and Sherman. She pasted on a smile and twisted to face them. "How have you been, Tassy? I've missed you at yoga." She placed a hand on the woman's forearm. Tassy always looked so friendly and cool, dressing in blues and greens, but her aura was never in sync with her appearance, running reddish orange and blinding yellow. "Quite a few new folks are joining us in the mornings now."

"You're so sweet. I can't wait to get back to yoga, but I've been busy with some family stuff. "

She edged closer to her husband and wrapped a hand around his forearm. Probably in fear that Sera was out to steal her meal ticket. With his close-cropped salt-and-pepper hair and still toned body, he wasn't bad-looking for his age, and he was way closer to Sera's age than Tassy's. But Sera had no intention of stealing away some other woman's man. Not when she couldn't even deal with the one she'd had.

Sherman's jaw pulsed. "Her dad was in town for a few weeks."

"How nice," Sera said, but clearly Sherman didn't agree.

Tassy's lashes fluttered like pale butterfly wings. "Oh, it was. Daddy is such an inspiration, and my brother came for a few days too. I miss them already."

"Where's your family from?"

"Oh, up near Chicago."

Interesting that a northern girl would call her father "daddy," but Sera knew better than anyone how the Southern culture could creep into your language and thinking.

"The gallery looks amazing." She looked around with wide eyes, as though impressed with all Tassy had accomplished. "And it's so generous of you to let the committee meet here. So much better than down at the 4H barn or the school gymnasium."

"Happy to do it."

"I don't know how do you do it all. The gallery. The farm. Hosting these meetings. I was just talking to the guy down at the Shipper Shack and he was telling me that you filled in for him while he was out of town back in mid-February. I wouldn't think you'd need a part-time job on top of everything else you do."

"I was only there a few days. I don't mind helping out once in a while."

Sera snapped her fingers as if just realizing something. "I bet you know Colton Ellerbee, the local artist who won the holiday art show with that amazing nativity scene."

"Of course. As a gallery owner, it's my job to know the local artists. I'm always looking for new talent."

"Isn't he innovative? I mean who would have ever thought of making a nativity scene out of upcycled stuff? And I thought I was the best upcycler around. I bet when he ships out his sculptures those are some huge packages."

Tassy simply smiled. Good grief, couldn't she give Sera a break and say something useful?

"I'm surprised none his sculptures are in your

gallery since his work is in such high demand now."

Tassy waved a hand. "I can't acquire art from everyone who wants to be displayed here at Gypsy Cotton."

Sera shifted into fact-finding mode. Maybe the direct approach would work better. "You know, I was trying to find out who packaged up some artwork and shipped it for Colton."

"Why? Couldn't you just ask Colton?"

Yeah, why, Sera? "Because…uh…apparently Colton uses different people to pack up his sculptures, and you know artists. Can't be bothered to remember to put on clean underwear in the morning. I figured you were a better bet. When I asked down at The Shipper Shack, the owner mentioned you were working the day Colton's package went out, so I thought you'd know who dropped it off."

"He must've made a mistake. What date did you say it was?"

"February 20th. A Friday."

Tassy turned to Sherman, who was scanning the room and beginning to fidget impatiently.

"Honey, weren't we in Tennessee then? Remember, right before we saw Trace Adkins at the

Grand Ole Opry?" She turned to Sera and whispered, "For Valentine's Day. Isn't he great?"

He nodded absentmindedly. "Right. Yes. We probably were."

Tassy dug in her bag, pulled out lip gloss and began applying it. "The owner of The Shipper Shack must have gotten his dates mixed up."

"Oh, that's too bad." Sera infused her voice with disappointment. "I was hoping to ask the person to help me pack shipments I'm putting together for the troops." She was trying to spin a story quick. She hoped Tassy would buy it. "You can't be too careful with those overseas shipments. If someone can wrap up expensive art, I figure he can pack anything."

Sherman popped to his feet and made to edge out of the row. "If you ladies will excuse me, I need to—"

Tassy put a hand on her husband's arm. "Honey, we should make a donation to Sera's charity efforts."

Panic pulsed in Sera's chest as Sherman reached for his pocket.

"Oh, no," Sera said, gripping his hand. "You don't have to write me a check right now."

"Of course he does. Make it out for a hundred, honey." Tassy glanced at Sera. "Is that enough?"

"Just $100?" Sherman asked Sera.

She swallowed hard. "More than enough."

He closed his checkbook and pulled a crisp one hundred dollar bill from his wallet. "Here you go."

Sera accepted the money with a warm thank-you, then slipped into a chair on the front row feeling guiltier than a kid who'd broken a window with a baseball. How would she explain this to Abby Ruth and Maggie? The lie had slipped right out of her lips. She hadn't considered the Harrisons might want to actually donate money. And cash, at that. If Sherman had written a check, she simply wouldn't have cashed it.

Before she could dash to the back of the room and shove the money into the hobby farmer's hand, Darrell Holloway strode up to a small podium and announced, "Angelina is running late, so she asked me to kick off the meeting."

Resigned to keeping Sherman's money, Sera sat back in her seat. At least Angelina's absence this evening was good news.

WHILE SERA WAS DOING RECON AT THE HIGH ON the Hog committee meeting, Maggie burned off her nervous energy by dusting Summer Haven's parlor. Why couldn't Lil have sold off some of the knickknacks rather than furniture when she'd been hurting for money? "Do you think Sera will find out something useful at the meeting?" she asked Abby Ruth.

"I think we'll know once she gets home." Abby Ruth kicked back on the parlor sofa and clicked at the remote. She'd recently hauled a wide-screen TV out of the horse trailer of belongings—mostly guns—she'd brought with her from Texas, complaining she couldn't live another minute without her daily dose of ESPN. What in the world would Lil say if she discovered sixty-five inches of LED hung over her ornately carved sideboard?

All Maggie knew was the sound of high-priced sneakers squealing against hardwood floors was about to make her hate pro basketball. "Can't we watch HGTV?"

Abby Ruth shot her an amused look. "When they start giving the Larry O'Brien Trophy for slapping up sheetrock, I'll change the channel."

Lord, Maggie loved this woman, but sometimes she could be hard to live with. Before Maggie could try to make her case for one of the home shows, the doorbell rang.

Saved by the bell.

Angelina stood at the front door. "Hi, Maggie." She waltzed right past Maggie into the foyer.

"Do come in," Maggie said after the fact.

"I was in the neighborhood and wanted to stop by quickly to give you something. And I needed to give Sera her High on the Hog committee shirt since I missed her at the last meeting."

"Isn't there a committee meeting right now?"

Angelina waved a dismissive hand and reached into her sparkling rhinestone and leopard-skin purse. She pulled out a thin paper bag and tossed it in Maggie's direction. "I've been meaning to get this back to you since before the holidays."

Maggie had a bad feeling. Since the holidays? What could she possibly have from the holidays that would last until now and fit into the small paper bag? The thinnest piece of fruitcake ever?

Angelina nodded, encouraging Maggie to open the bag.

Maggie unfurled the top and shoved her hand inside. The tiny Kraft paper bag reminded her of the little bags she and George had used at the hardware store they'd owned in Virginia when they sold a few screws or bolts to customers. When her fingers skimmed smooth plastic, realization bolted through Maggie's chest.

No, it can't be.

Slowly, she eased the item from the bag, and her stomach rocked with panic.

Why yes, apparently it can be.

It was a prison visitor's badge. The one with Maggie's name on it that had gone missing late last year.

Maggie swallowed to keep her jaw from hanging slack. One look at Angelina's face, full of smug satisfaction, and Maggie took a step forward, her palm already feeling the sting of a good smack.

No. She couldn't give Angelina the satisfaction. And what if she didn't know about Lil but was just dangling a line to see if she caught a big ol' blubberfish?

Words stuck in Maggie's tight throat.

"That's all I needed." With a smile, Angelina shoved a T-shirt into Maggie's hands. "Oh, and of course, this for Sera."

"Thank…thank you for stopping by," Maggie choked out and swung the front door wide. Surely, Angelina would get the hint and leave.

But she simply leaned a shoulder against the doorjamb. "By the way, how's the Tucker Torpedo?"

Someone should buy Angelina a pair of boxing gloves because it sure as heck felt like she was throwing bare-knuckled one-two punches at Maggie's head. "Fine?" The word came out like a question. Well of course it did, because it was a dad-burned lie.

"Excellent," Angelina said. "You might want to get it cleaned up. I'll need it for the High on the Hog event."

"I'll have to ask Lil."

"Oh, I'll take care of that." Angelina gave her a wink. Not a friendly one either. "I'll just let myself out." Angelina whisked around and darned if it didn't sound like she was laughing under her breath.

Maggie shut the door, then zombie-walked back into the parlor.

"Who was that?" Abby Ruth asked. "Not Hollis again?"

"It was Angelina." Maggie dangled the prison badge from her forefinger and thumb. "To bring this by."

Abby Ruth glanced up and for once even she was speechless, her mouth opening and closing like that blubberfish struggling for breath.

"I didn't lose it. She must have taken it when the Historical Preservation committee was here for the inspection." Maggie's knees finally gave out, and Abby Ruth moved her legs just in time for Maggie to sink down on the sofa beside her. "She knows."

"Did she come out and say that?"

"Not everyone is as direct as you."

"We could tell her one of your kids is in prison."

Maggie's spine went rigid. "I will *not* do that."

"Maybe let sleeping dogs lie?"

"You can't be serious. When have you ever let a dog—sleeping or otherwise—just lie? And if you think Angelina is done tormenting us, then you may not be quite as smart as I thought you were."

Abby Ruth's mouth slowly stretched into a grin and she walloped Maggie in the arm. "There's my girl."

Lord, would Maggie ever outsmart this woman?

CHAPTER 11

Sera was relieved Angelina wouldn't be at the committee meeting. She'd never had another person look at her with so much malice. If looks could kill, Angelina's eyes would be registered weapons.

But Sera felt most sorry for Angelina's son. Poor Booger. The kid had to tiptoe on eggshells—or broken glass—around his mom.

Darrell called on each committee lead, who stood and reported their progress. Apparently, Angelina had handpicked everyone but Sera to make this year's High on the Hog event better than in previous years. Which, in translation, simply meant Angelina was trying to outdo Lil. As usual.

Sherman brought everyone up-to-date on the

cooking team. "After a close inspection, we'll need some welding done on three of the hog cookers. I can weld some, but these smokers are over my skill level."

Sera's ears pricked at the word *welder*. Colton had mentioned fillet-something-or-other joints on the sheep living down in Palm Beach. Not that she had any clue what that was, but she'd Google it later.

Tassy piped in, "I talked to Colton Ellerbee. He's a skilled welder, but when I asked him about welding hog smokers he snarled at me and ran me out of his studio. That man has some personality challenges."

A titter of nervous laughter skittered across the room.

Sherman gave Tassy a pointed look, and she sat down. He said, "I only found one person in town with the welding skills to fix the smokers and who's willing to help. Joe down at the muffler shop will do it in exchange for advertising in the brochure and signage in the cook-off tents."

"Perfect," Darrell said. "I know Angelina has some money budgeted for stuff like that, but I don't think it's much. Great job, Sherman."

Sherman nodded. "Joe said he'd come into some unexpected money so he wanted to do this for the town. Welding is his thing, and I say we let him do it."

Sera fidgeted in her seat, excitement making her muscles dance. If the shipping angle was a dead end, then this was just the lead they needed to move forward with investigating the forged Ellerbee sculpture. The box had been shipped from Summer Shoals, and Joe was apparently the best welder in town. That couldn't be a coincidence.

When she made it home and told Abby Ruth and Maggie, they would be so happy.

Sera stood to give her report. "Thank you, committee members, for the opportunity to serve as children's liaison for this event. In years past you've had face painting, a greased pig catch contest and piggy races. I'd like us to consider something different this year."

Angelina's voice rang out over the space. "The greased pig catch is the highlight of the day for the kids. They love it."

Apparently, Sera's luck had run out.

Darrell chuckled. "Especially your Booger. Last year when he did a flying leap across the ring and brought that piglet down with a pile driver, I thought it would come out from under him as flat as a sausage patty."

Angelina started to say something, but Sera

pitched her voice louder. "That's exactly the *on the hog* I want to avoid this year. I suggest we give our piggies a little break. I've done some research and in fairness to the treatment of our fine swine friends, we'll take a more gentle approach. I'm proposing each registered contestant dress their piglet up for a costume contest. We can provide a theme, perhaps fairytales or—"

"I like the costume contest idea," Darrell Holloway said. "Never hurts to mix things up for the kids, right, Angelina? Otherwise, they get bored. I'll put up some prize money for the winners. How about $25 for the grand prize, $20 for second and $5 for third?"

Angelina's smile was tight, but she didn't say a word.

Tassy said, "I love that plan, Sera, and I'd be happy to be one of your judges."

"That would be great!"

Darrell nodded toward Tassy. "All right, committee members, this is the moment we've all been waiting for. It's time to reveal this year's event poster. Tassy, come on up here."

Tassy walked to the front of the room. Her long blond hair shone as if there were stage lights following her. The tailored skirt suit she wore clung to her willowy body. In front of a row of past years' posters, she pivoted to face her peers and grabbed the edge of a white drape hanging over a large easel. She tugged on the drape, letting it fall to the floor.

The poster was beautiful. In the past, they'd been playful caricatures of a silly pig in overalls or riding a tractor. Not this time. Tassy had designed a pig portrait with a stained glass effect. Pretty enough to frame. Now that was Sera's kind of pig.

Once the meeting was over, Sera was so excited about the leads she'd discovered that she stopped by the Piggly Wiggly and treated herself to a package of Mike & Ikes. Because nothing said "we're onto something!" like the taste of faux fruit-flavored candy.

When she made it back to Summer Haven, the entire box of candy now in her stomach, Abby Ruth and Maggie sat in the parlor watching reruns of House Squatters. Sera walked in and stood in front of them, blocking their view. "You won't believe what I found out at the High on the Hog meeting."

"That everyone except for you will be eating pork that day?" Leaning almost horizontal to try to see the TV, Abby Ruth shooed Sera to move out of the way.

"Real funny. It wouldn't hurt you to cut back on the meat, but no. I have a lead for the Ellerbee case." Then she took something out of her small purse and held it between two fingers. "And this."

"A hundred bucks?"

"Yeah. I accidentally got a donation. Long story." She wadded it into a ball and tossed it to Maggie. "Add it to the car fund."

Maggie snagged it out of the air and flattened it on the table in front of her.

"But I did get a lead," Sera continued. "A good one."

Abby Ruth's head swiveled back to Sera, and she popped up to a sitting position. "Oh, yeah?"

"That's great," Maggie said, but her tone didn't support her words.

"Turns out there's only one really good welder in town." Sera grinned, enjoying being the one with the insider information. "Joe at the muffler shop!"

"But he's a nice guy," Maggie said. "He can't be involved with something shady."

"He can be a nice guy on the outside and nefarious on the inside," Sera said. "Not only is he the only one in town with the skills, but he's offering to do the welding for the High on the Hog event for free, because—get this...he's come into some unexpected money."

Abby Ruth's eyebrows shot up. "We should definitely go check him out."

"I wonder if he's open now," Sera said. "We could do a quick ride by. Maybe scope out the place for any suspicious-looking work. I'll drive."

Abby Ruth stood, but Maggie didn't budge.

"Aren't you coming with us?" Sera asked.

"Angelina dropped by while you were gone."

"That's why she was late to the meeting?"

Maggie held out her hand, and in the flat of her palm lay her prison badge.

"What in the world—" Realization struck Sera like that tree limb had crashed into the Tucker. "She didn't."

"Of course, she never confessed to taking it," Maggie said.

"She knows about Lil?"

"Another thing she didn't come out and say."

"If she knew for sure, wouldn't she have gloated?"

"Who in hell understands the way that woman's mind works," Abby Ruth grumbled.

"All I know is she was snickering as she left." Maggie sighed. "Which means I have to talk to Lil. How about we check out Joe the Muffler Man after?"

Sera wrapped her arms around her friend and squeezed. "It's all going to be fine."

"Right now," Maggie said into her shoulder, "that's just a little hard to believe."

The next morning, when Maggie handed the prison guard her visitor badge, the uniformed woman looked her up and down. Tilted her head left and right. "When you were here just last week, you sure did look a might skinnier."

If Maggie didn't already want to…to…to do something really bad to Angelina for swiping her badge, she sure as heck did now. All these months of being a little more careful about what she ate and a lot more active, and now Maggie felt like a fat girl again.

The guard nodded and said, "Ask me, a woman looks better with a layer of meat on her bones."

So there, Angelina. Skinny girls aren't all that.

Maggie smiled at the guard, then headed inside the visitors' room and took the table where she and Lil normally sat. When the inmates filed in, Maggie's heart dropped to her toes. Lord, Lil looked even more haggard than she had the last time Maggie had visited. The skin on her face was pale and looked as thin as tracing paper. And why was she moving so slowly?

But with as much backbone as ever, Lil gave

her a smile when she sat down. "This is a surprise visit."

"Is it really, Lil?"

She seemed to shrink lower into her chair and avoided Maggie's gaze. "She told everyone, didn't she?"

Maggie sighed to cover the fear jumping up her throat. It had been too much to hope Angelina hadn't made use of the visitor's badge. "I don't think so. The skinny little witch, no offense to Abby Ruth's Halloween costume, brought my badge back to Summer Haven yesterday. I came as soon as I could. I have Sera and Abby Ruth out scouting for any gossip."

"Should've known better than to trust her."

"Honestly, Lil, she was cagey when she came by the house. Never admitted straight out she'd been here. What's going on?"

Lil slumped a little farther. "It's a mess all around."

"Is she blackmailing you?"

"She definitely wants something I've got."

"Nothing new about that," Maggie said. "Tell me what it is, and the gals and I will take care of it for you."

"Not this time, Mags."

Maggie reached across and gripped Lil's hands.

To heck with what the guards thought. They could chastise her if they wanted, but right now, her best friend needed her. "We've done a good job of keeping all this under our hats for over nine months now. We can't give up the fight just because Miss Stick Her Nose in Everything is trying to bring you down."

"No, I meant I'll take care of it myself when I come home."

"But Angelina's an impatient sort. Who knows if she'll keep your secret for another few months?"

Lil's hands shook beneath Maggie's. "She won't have to keep it for months."

"Why not?"

Lil lowered her voice. "I can't explain everything to you here, but suffice it to say I'll be coming home even earlier than I thought."

Maggie's fingers contracted around Lil's before she could control them. In delight or fear. It was a toss-up. "Oh, that's…wonderful. How much earlier?"

"The warden told me it could be any day now."

The words *any* and *day* pinballed around in Maggie's brain. God had a very interesting sense of humor. But why did it have to be now, when the Tucker wasn't exactly at its prime? "Surely you have to go through review and—"

"It's something called compassionate release. The prison system sometimes grants early release to older inmates when they have terminal illnesses."

Her hand still around Lil's, Maggie jumped to her feet, almost dragging Lil clear across the table. "Oh, Lil, what do you have? How long do you have?"

"Hush and sit down," Lil commanded, some of her normal spine in full evidence. "We can't talk about this here, but I am not dying."

Thank the Lord. "But…but…"

"But that's why I'll take care of Angelina once I get out."

CHAPTER 12

Even after the hour and a half drive back to Summer Shoals, Maggie's nerves hadn't stopped jumping from Lil's news. All she could picture was the devastation on Lil's face if she ever laid eyes on the damaged front end of that so-called Tucker Torpedo.

She wasn't in any shape to talk with Abby Ruth or Sera about the news of Lil's imminent release, so she went straight to bed and prayed tomorrow she'd have enough courage to move forward and come up with a solution that would actually work.

The next morning, Maggie's feet hit the ground and she strapped on her will of iron. She didn't have a moment to waste because she was not about to let her best friend down.

Maggie made a beeline for the kitchen to grab the phone book.

"What are you in such a stinkin' hurry about?" Abby Ruth asked.

She flipped to body shops. Then thought better of it. Everyone in this town knew Lil and that car.

She couldn't have it fixed in Summer Shoals. Panic raced down her spine, and sweat pooled under her breasts.

She went to the computer and Googled body shops, but the list included places in Iowa and New Jersey. She needed help. She buried her head in her hands. This helplessness was like a black, sooty taste on the back of her tongue.

Life in Virginia had never been this stressful. If she could only turn back the clock. If George were still alive, she'd even agree to open the second store he'd wanted so much.

But the past was yesterday. A memory to hang onto, not a crutch to face tomorrow.

"What's wrong, Mags?" Sera asked softly.

Maggie raised her head, brushed away a tear of frustration. "Lil's getting out of jail."

"Oh my gosh, that's such great news! When?" Sera whirled around, her skirt poofing out in her joyous dance. But she soon stopped and stared at Maggie. "Those are happy tears, right?"

Maggie shook her head. "I've got to get the car fixed…and fast. She's coming home soon."

"How soon?"

"She doesn't know, but apparently there's some compassionate release loophole, and the warden has requested it happen as soon as possible. I should be the happiest girl on Earth, but if Lil comes home before the car is fixed, I don't know what I'll do. I can't put it in a shop here in town, and I don't know how to Google body shops and—"

"Take a breath, Maggie."

Maggie sucked in a giant-sized breath and let it out. "It's a mess."

"It's wonderful news. Now scoot over." Sera bumped her hip and slid into the chair with her. "I can find a place to fix the car, but I thought you were going to find someone who specialized in Tuckers. Didn't Chuck give you some advice?"

"Oh, he gave me advice all right."

Abby Ruth propped herself in the doorjamb. "So what's the problem?"

Maggie couldn't hide the truth any longer. These girls were her friends, and their friendship was more important than the disreputable details about that car. "The car you thought was so darned valuable? It's a big fat fake."

Abby Ruth drew up to her full height. "What do you mean?"

"The thing isn't a Tucker. It's a kit car. A Bondo-filled heap of heavy metal pretending to be a Tucker. The engine isn't even in the right place."

Abby Ruth's face went slack, not a great look on her. "I'll be damned."

"The only good news is it'll be way cheaper to fix."

Meanwhile, Sera's fingers flew across the keys. "I found a list of five body shops about thirty minutes out of town. Is that far enough?"

"I sure hope so," Maggie said.

Her lips and jaw tight, Abby Ruth said, "Just point-blank ask them if they know the Summers or Fairviews when you call." She picked up the phone and shoved it into Maggie's hand.

Maggie swept away her tears and dialed the first one on the list. They were backed up and couldn't even assess the damage for three weeks. The second was out of business and the third knew Lil. On the fourth try, she struck platinum. Forehand's Body Shop had never heard of the Summers or the Fairviews and could see her today.

"We're in business," Maggie said. "He's out doing an estimate for someone. He's going to stop by and take a look at the car. Keep your fingers crossed."

Sera jotted down three more phone numbers on a piece of paper and handed them to Maggie. "Insurance. Just in case it doesn't work out, we can call these next."

Maggie tucked the backup numbers into her back pocket and went out on the front porch to wait for Mr. Forehand. *Please be able to fix it. And fast.*

She paced the porch for what seemed like an hour, but only fifteen minutes had passed. She forced herself to go inside and make one of her special batches of tea. At least that would pass the time.

With her tea chilling in a pitcher chock full of tiny square ice cubes, Maggie set a tray with the tea and glasses on the front porch. She poured herself a glass and tried to calm her nerves. Maybe she should have kicked up the recipe this time.

An hour later, when a white pickup truck with "Forehand's Body Shop" and colorful flames painted down the sides pulled in front of the house, she forced herself not to race down the stairs and hug the stranger who got out.

"I'm Dennis Forehand," he said, shoving his hand out toward her.

"Maggie." She shook his hand, sorry she hadn't

wiped them on her pants because hers was sweaty. "The car is this way."

He followed her to the garage. When she leaned over to lift the garage door, he got there first and said with a smile, "Let me get that for you, pretty lady."

What was it with all these nice men lately?

The garage door rumbled into the rafters, and Maggie flipped the light switch, the florescent lights casting an operating-room white glow on the space.

"Nice paint. Waltz blue." Dennis let out a long whistle at the sight of the car. "I've never seen one of these in person."

And you still haven't. She let him admire the impostor a little longer.

"Looks like you took a big old whack to the hood panel there. At least the Cyclops lamp is okay. That would've been impossible to fix." He fingered the hood ornament. "This has already been replaced once, I'm guessing."

"It's not what you think."

He looked up at her. "What's not?"

"The car. It's not a Tucker. It's a replica. There's a motor under that hood."

"Get outta here."

"No kidding. But I need it restored to its previous perfection."

He surveyed the damage, then popped the hood and looked underneath. He ran his hands along the metal and raised and lowered the hood a couple times. "I can take care of the dent, and I'm the best paint guy for miles. But the hood ornament…well, that's outta my league. You'll have to find someone to make you one of those."

"How much will it cost to fix the car?"

He scribbled some figures on a piece of paper and handed it to Maggie.

Oh. Ow. The number bounced around in her head, making her a little dizzy. All her prayers for a fix they could afford weren't going to be answered. She had no idea how she'd pay for it, but she wasn't about to tell him that. "How quickly can you do it?"

"It'll take me two weeks."

"If I bring the hood ornament, will you install it?"

"I can do that."

"Make it a week and a half and you have a deal."

"Done," he said. "Bring me the car tomorrow and we'll get started immediately. I'll let you know when she's ready to be picked up."

. . .

In her van, Sera and Abby Ruth followed Maggie to deliver the Tucker to the body shop. Sera was starting to enjoy serving as the SHHgroup chauffeur, even leaving one of their company cards with the shop's receptionist.

Once the Tucker was all settled, it was time to tackle the next big task of the day. They headed back into Summer Shoals and slowly rolled past the muffler shop.

Bright sparks lit up one bay like Fourth of July fireworks so someone was obviously inside. As Sera parked her van, it did a shimmy-shake dance before finally settling into park.

"Is that Joe?" Abby Ruth pointed to the man wearing coveralls and a welder's mask.

"Hard to tell since we can't see his face," Maggie said, her tone dry.

Abby Ruth grabbed the door handle. "Then let's find out. Sooner we take this guy down, the sooner Colton pays us."

"We can't just go in there accusing him. We need a plan," Maggie said.

"I could pretend I need something for High on the Hog," Sera said, "but I don't know what that would be. Maybe some holding pens for the piglets?"

"I have a better idea." Abby Ruth grabbed a tie-dyed T-shirt from the van's back floorboard. Then she scooted out the side door.

Sera and Maggie rushed to follow her to the back of the van. Something about Abby Ruth having a better idea made Sera's chakras vibrate with nervousness. "What are you doing?"

Abby Ruth twisted the shirt into a long, thick tube, wrapped it around the van's tailpipe and tugged. Pretty as you please, a whole chunk of metal clanged to the pavement.

"Hey," Sera protested. "What'd you do that for?"

"You need a new muffler."

"Well, I do now."

"Consider it a gift from Hollis Dooley, and a gift to the environment." Abby Ruth elbowed Sera in the side, then marched toward the open bay door, tailpipe in hand as if she planned to joust Joe. Just short of the entry to the garage, she paused. "Okay. Y'all need to take this hunk o' junk in there and chat him up about Sera needing a new muffler. Sera, you keep our friend Joe engaged while Maggie takes a snoop around. I'm going out back to see if I can find anything suspicious."

"What are we looking for exactly?" Maggie asked. "I highly doubt he'll have sculptures displayed on his workbenches."

"You're right," Abby Ruth agreed. "But we've

seen Colton's studio. We know what kind of stuff he has sitting around. Those wire connector thingies wouldn't normally be in a muffler shop. Antique anythings, those wooden rulers Colton loves. You get the idea."

Abby Ruth winked and dropped to a crouch. Seconds later, she was gone.

"Do you ever worry she's too good at that?" Maggie's attention was focused on where Abby Ruth had disappeared around the side of the building.

"All the time." Sera led the way into the shop, swinging the rusty tail pipe as she walked.

The welder was hunched over his project, apparently oblivious to his visitors, so Sera took the opportunity to scan the space. Big oxyacetylene tanks lined one wall. Each chained there like a prisoner, probably to keep them from toppling over and causing a real disaster.

Sera meandered through the shop, checking out the bins of materials. Nothing looked like anything Colton would be interested in except possibly the Jack Daniels bottles and beer cans in the corner trash.

The sound of the welding machine throttled back. The man raised his visor and said, "Hello there, ladies. Can I help you with something?"

"I'm having a little problem with my exhaust system." Sera held up the sad-looking tailpipe. "I was told to bring it to Joe. Is that you?"

"In the flesh." He chuckled. "And I'd say your problem is big if you're carrying around your muffler."

"Can you fix it?"

He shrugged and wiped his face with the sleeve of his coveralls. "Not a matter of if I can, but if I have time. I've got jobs from here to Atlanta piling up."

"Really?" Maggie said. "I wouldn't think there's much call for muffler work in a town the size of Summer Shoals."

"Oh, I do some other welding jobs. You know, to make a little hustle on the side."

Hmm. *Hustle* sounded dicey. Sera tried to be nonchalant when she asked, "What kind of side jobs?"

"Oh, some fence work. And the High on the Hog committee wants me to fix up the cookers before this year's event."

Sera wandered around the space, lightly running her fingers over tools and tanks. "Welding is really a dying art. Some people think it's just manual labor, but that's shortsighted." She drew a spiral on a bump connecting two pieces of pipe. "Some welders would make a big mess of something like this, but your joints are perfect. Tiny works of art."

Joe's chest puffed out under his coveralls. "Mighty nice to hear a lady who appreciates a man's work."

While Joe was facing her, Sera watched Maggie poke around on his workbench and peek into some cabinets.

He drew Sera over to what looked like the hull of a small fishing boat. "Let me show you my butt joint."

A cough came from Maggie's direction.

Sera tried to keep lookout for a sheep or any other sculpture, but found nothing. Maybe Maggie would be more successful. "Joe," Sera said, "you're so talented. Not that muffler work isn't amazing, but do you ever make anything original?"

"Whatcha mean?"

"Oh, maybe something just for fun. Not really functional, but more like a sculpture."

"You mean like that Ellerbee kook?"

Yes, Joe, exactly *like that Ellerbee kook.*

"You have to admit he's done quite well for himself," she commented. "And there's money to be made at it."

Joe's snort echoed inside the garage. "Pansyassed welding, you ask me. But to each his own, I guess."

Sera's surge of excitement frittered away. This lead was now officially a dead end as well. When would they get the break they so desperately needed?

"But old Blackwood, the shop teacher over at the high school, must've thought there was something to all that junk because he has his kids making projects kinda like Ellerbee's. Thinks they'll do real good when it comes to raising money for scholarships at this year's auction."

"You don't say," Sera said, flashing him a smile and winking at Maggie. "Well, we've taken enough of your time. Guess we'll be on our way." She turned for the bay door.

"Wait a minute," he said. "Don't you want me to reattach your muffler?"

Maggie sighed and slowly pulled out her wallet, which meant she was about to fork over Hollis' money to fix Sera's muffler.

CHAPTER 13

The aroma of fresh coffee filled the air when Maggie strolled into the kitchen. She took down the mug Lil had given her when she first moved into Summer Haven. The saying on the mug, *You'll always be my friend, you know too much*, had been funny at the time. It had taken on a whole new meaning when Lil went to prison.

Maggie poured her cup three quarters to the top, then cooled it with enough milk to make it tan. She liked to think of it as a dairy portion, good eating habits and all.

The sun danced off the sun catcher Sera had hung in the kitchen window, casting a thousand spherical dots of color across the room.

Maggie forced herself to get her butt in gear.

There was a lot less of her butt since she'd joined Sera in her yoga class, and that was a good thing. No sense screwing up her progress now. She race-walked out to where the other yoga students had already gathered on the lawn near the white gazebo, and slipped into the back row in time to take the first inhale with the group.

"Deep breath in." Sera's voice was like a melody. "And out."

By the third deep breath, Maggie was back in the zone. She still didn't have the grace of many of the people who attended Sera's class, but then again most of them were less than half Maggie's age. From the back row, it looked like a well-choreographed dance troupe as everyone moved slowly from downward facing dog to a standing position, then folding forward and to the right in the sun salutation. The group stretched right, then left, then right again in a reed-like wave. A couple of women were bundled up in so many clothes Maggie wasn't sure how they were able to stretch at all. Not Sera. Nope, she was in yoga pants and a sleek turtleneck. In that getup, she looked as if she could transition to the role of cat burglar at a moment's notice.

Maggie's body moved from pose to pose. Then Sera took them through the final few poses for the cool down, and Maggie felt the now familiar mental high-five that amped up her confidence every time she participated.

Rather than chatting with the others today, Maggie headed for the house. As she reached the porch, a blue sedan she didn't recognize pulled up. Bruce Shellenberger, the IT guy from Dogwood Ridge Assisted Living, stepped out of the car with a hello.

A smile spread across her face, and her heart did a little do-si-do.

She threw her hand in the air and waved like a cheerleader shaking her pom-poms. She hadn't seen him in…well…way too long. She'd had high hopes she might after last fall's Halloween party, but not when she was looking a mess. A flood of anxiety rushing through her, she pushed a hand through her hair. A complete bird's nest. But ducking inside to brush her hair seemed impolite. Just her luck.

"How have you been?" Bruce walked toward her, stopping about three feet away.

"Good. You?"

"Great."

You look pretty great. Even more handsome than I remembered.

"Work's been really busy." A silence hung between them. "They asked me to work full-time for a special project, but I'm back to my part-time hours now."

"That's good." Great. Good. Surely Maggie could think of more interesting conversation. But what was he doing here? He didn't seem to know what to say, and she wasn't sure either.

"I was wondering if you'd been out to the new bookstore for any of those project weekends they've started doing?" He shifted his weight from one foot to another and stuffed his hands into his pants pockets.

"No. I've been meaning to get out there. I've always been more a library kind of a girl, but I do want to support them. New in the community and all that."

"Well, these Saturday events are really for the kids. They've partnered with Holloway's Hardware for a children's hour. One of the librarians reads to the kids first, then they host a parent/child craft project."

"That sounds nice." But why would she go if she didn't have small children?

"This weekend they're building birdhouses. My son was supposed to take my grandson, but he has to work so I'm taking Austin. Only problem is I'm not exactly handy. Give me a computer? No problem. Hammer and nails? Not my thing."

"Oh, you'll be fine with a hammer and nails. Piece of cake." She patted him on the arm and discovered that under his long-sleeved plaid shirt, Bruce had more muscle than she'd expect on a tech guy. She snatched her hand back because the other option—the one she wanted to choose—was to let it linger. "Besides, if it's a kids' project, they're probably using glue and dowels."

"Says you." He frowned down at the hand she'd dropped as if trying to figure out why it wasn't still on his arm. When he glanced back up, a small hopeful smile played around his lips. "Maybe you could give me a lesson. Everyone in Summer Shoals talks about how handy you are."

Really? She had no idea people thought so highly of her or that Bruce had been asking around about her. Either way, her confidence buoyed, and wasn't feeling good about yourself inside way more important than a good hair day?

"Or I thought…if you're free…if you wanted to…you'd like to meet me at the bookstore on Saturday. Kind of help Austin and me out during the project. Then maybe you and I could do lunch afterwards?"

He swallowed as though he wanted to gulp back his words. Was he nervous? Well, she sure knew how that felt.

Sera had kept pushing Maggie to call him, but she was old school. It didn't seem right to chase him down, but now that he was asking her, a flurry of questions popped into her head.

What would she wear?

What if he tried to kiss her?

What if his grandson was a brat?

What if she outdid him in the manly carpentry stuff…probably easy to do?

Bruce ducked his head. "Or if you're busy I understand—"

"No!" Her pause had made him think she wasn't interested, but she was. Very. "I'd love to."

Bruce's face brightened. "You would?"

"What time?"

"It starts at noon, so I'll plan to stop by and pick you up about a half-hour before. My son will pick Austin up from the bookstore afterward, so then you and I can walk down to the Atlanta Highway Diner and grab a little lunch."

"That sounds perfect." Just lunch. No pressure there, and no fuss over what to wear. "I'm looking forward to it."

He stared at his feet for a few seconds. Finally, he cleared his throat, then looked her in the eye. "I'm sorry I didn't come by after the Halloween party. I meant to. But I…well…"

Maggie felt a flush of warmth flow from her heart to her cheeks, and she reached out to touch his arm. He *had* felt a little something. She'd begun to think it had just been her all along. "It's okay, you don't have to explain."

Voices flowed in a burst of chatter as Sera called goodbyes to the last of the yoga stragglers. Bruce looked over his shoulder nervously. "I guess I'd better go. I'm looking forward to Saturday."

"I am too."

Bruce took a couple steps back, then turned and waved again. "I'll see you then."

"Yep," Maggie said.

When Sera spotted Bruce in the driveway, she ran right up to him and for a moment, Maggie felt an unfamiliar pang. Jealousy. But that was just plain silly. Sera was her friend, and Bruce had asked Maggie on a date. Not Sera.

Maggie's insides felt as though she'd sipped a marshmallow-covered cup of hot chocolate. She actually had a date. A real one.

SERA WAITED UNTIL BRUCE TURNED AROUND IN THE driveway and headed out before she broke into a jog toward Maggie. The smile on her lips made

Sera's heart joyful. "Good morning, Miss Popularity."

Maggie's lashes fluttered, and the flush on her cheeks wasn't from the yoga.

"So? What did Bruce want?"

Maggie pulled her lips together in a tight line, then burst into a Cheshire-cat-sized grin. "He asked me out. We have a date on Saturday."

"Awesome! A date! That's great."

Maggie's laugh was light. "He was pretty nervous. But he's sweet."

"Who's sweet?" Abby Ruth stepped out on the porch with a super-sized travel mug of coffee.

"Bruce Shellenberger is sweet on Maggie. He just left. Asked her on a date." Sera noticed the way Abby Ruth's spine shifted as if someone had poked her with a stick. She was jealous of Maggie and Bruce!

But Abby Ruth nodded and gave Maggie a wink, then walked over and sat on the edge of the porch railing. "About time. What's on the agenda today?"

Sera sat on the porch next to Maggie, suddenly feeling protective of her because of Abby Ruth's jealousy. "How about we scope out the Summer Shoals High School shop teacher?"

Maggie said, "How will we get in? Go after hours?"

"Nope," Sera said. "I think we'd be taking less of risk going during school hours. Then we can see him in action. Take a look around. Plus we really don't have the time to waste. We need someone to show us where the classroom is."

"You think you can get us in?" Abby Ruth's mouth pulled down on one side.

"I do." It drove Sera crazy the way Abby Ruth thought she was the only one with great ideas some days. "You in?"

"I'm in," Maggie said.

"Let's do this," Abby Ruth said. "But I'm driving."

Sera, Maggie and Abby Ruth piled into Abby Ruth's big truck and headed over to the high school. They had to park on the far side because the lot was crammed with fancy cars—a couple of Mercedes, a classic Corvette, and one shiny jacked-up truck that could've given Abby Ruth's dually a run for its money. Goodness, these kids were driving cars almost as nice as the ones that ran up and down the Pacific Coast Highway in Malibu.

Sera led the way into the school's lobby.

Maggie slowed to a stop. "Place sure looks

naked now compared to when it was all decorated up for the Annual Holiday Art Fest."

"They could use some feng shui and color to bring out the positivity." Sera inhaled, pulling in the chemical scent of industrial floor cleaner and burning her nose in the process. Yuck.

She would definitely talk with the principal about switching to green cleaning products. All those chemicals they were using now couldn't be good for young minds.

"Any idea which way to the shop class?" Abby Ruth asked.

"In my day," Maggie said, "most of those classrooms were at the back of the school."

Back was a relative term here since once you passed through the columned front entrance, the building branched off right and left.

Sera forged ahead. "It seems to work when we split up," she said, motioning for Maggie and Abby Ruth to catch up with her. "Maggie and I will go right, and Abby Ruth, you can go left."

Maggie leaned in close to Sera. "Are you sure letting her wander off by herself is a good idea?"

"If she goes alone, we can't be accused of warping young minds."

"Good point."

Abby Ruth was already striding off down the

hallway, her cowboy boots thunking hollowly against the speckled linoleum.

Before they could peek into the first classroom in their hallway, an eardrum-exploding electronic bell blasted from the hallway speakers. *Maaaa.*

"Sounds like an electrocuted goat," Maggie commented.

"They should consider something more soothing, like tongue drums or the sitar." Teenagers swarmed into the hall, bringing with them the scent of overheated bodies, drugstore cologne and pheromones. Sera grabbed Maggie's arm and pulled her against the cool tile wall.

"That was close," Maggie said.

Sera could all but see their developing sacral chakras vibrating. The kids jostled one another, shouting to be heard over lockers slamming.

The wave undulated and intersected like a massive insect colony. A boy in a blue letter jacket braced an arm against one of the lockers and leaned in close to a pretty blonde girl. Sera had seen that flirting hair twirl a few times in her life.

Seen it? Heck, she'd been a master at it once upon a time. But other than trying to charm the Shipper Shack owner, she hadn't twirled her hair for a man in over a year. Truth be told, longer than that.

And she was lonely. Not for friendship. She had so much of that, her heart was full to bursting. But male companionship…she'd been putting off a decision about that part of her life for far too long.

The sound of that hoof-in-a-socket goat bleated again, chasing away her melancholy thoughts. Once the high schoolers filed back into the classrooms, she and Maggie stood for a few more seconds, recuperating from the onslaught.

"Hope Abby Ruth made it through that okay," Maggie said, pushing her hair back.

"Are you kidding? I hope she didn't pull her gun on anyone!"

"Lord, do you remember what it was like to have that much energy?" Maggie asked, nodding toward the kids.

"Lot of angst and insecurity goes along with all that energy. Not sure I'd ever want to revisit that."

"Amen."

They strolled into another hallway, and Maggie paused to peek into the window set in a classroom door. "This doesn't look like—"

The door jerked open from the inside, and a forty-something woman with a hairdo that looked as if it had been shaped with a bowl and then lacquered with a gallon of hairspray stared at them with narrow eyes. "What are you doing? If you're the evaluation committee, you're not supposed to be here until next week."

"We're not evaluators."

"Then who are you?"

Sera motioned toward Maggie and then herself. "This is Maggie Rawls and I'm Sera Johnson."

"And…"

"And we're looking for the shop class," Maggie blurted out.

"Shop? You must mean Mr. Blackwood's Engineering and Industrial Technology class."

"Yes. That's exactly what I meant," Maggie said.

The teacher's eyes became even squintier. "Why are you really here?"

Darn it. Sera hadn't totally prepared for that question, and Maggie's slip-up had set off this over-shellacked woman's warning signals. "Because I've commissioned some art from Mr…" Sera scrambled for the name the teacher had just mentioned.

"Blackwood," the woman finished for her.

"Yes. As I was saying, Mr. Blackwood said I could pick them up today."

The teacher rocked back and propped a fist on one hip. "We don't commission our students' artwork. You must be mistaken. The Gypsy Cotton

Gallery *is* holding an auction, that's something entirely different. They're working on welded farm animal sculptures."

"That's what I said. We're here to see a man about a sheep."

"Who did you say you were again?" The teacher pushed a button near the door, and the crackle of an intercom came from the classroom's ceiling.

"Main office," a disembodied voice droned. "How can we assist you, Ms. Coffman?"

"I have two strange women standing outside my classroom. Can you please send security?"

Sera drew herself up, which in hindsight probably wasn't the best idea, because the teacher jabbed at the button again. "And hurry. They seem to be threatening me."

Good grief. Certainly, people had a reason to be wary of strangers with all the bad things that had happened in schools over the past few years, but this was Summer Shoals, not Los Angeles.

But apparently the school-employed guards were as on the ball as any Hollywood star security she'd ever seen because a blue-uniformed man strode up, his face grim and handcuffs jangling from his belt. "Thank you, Ms. Coffman. I'll take this from here."

The teacher slipped back inside her classroom, and the guard took Sera and Maggie each by the upper arms. "If you ladies would be so kind as to come with me." His grip didn't hurt, but it was certainly firm. He wasn't taking any chances. Sera's chest swelled with pride that he saw them as a threat.

He led them back the way they'd come and across the lobby to an office fronted with glass. Once inside, he told the receptionist, "I assume the principal will want to talk with these two."

"Yes, take them back to her office."

He urged them around the chest-high reception desk, and Sera felt about like she had the time she'd been caught rolling and selling clove cigarettes when she was fifteen. Although her parents had been impressed with her enterprising entrepreneurship, the school administration hadn't been nearly so forgiving.

The Summer Shoals High School principal was a very put-together woman who, if Sera had to guess, was around her same age. But while Sera lived in comfy yoga clothes and breezy skirts, this woman was dressed in a navy tailored pantsuit that brooked no nonsense.

"Please sit." The principal's voice floated on a soft, Southern drawl but carried the edge of a razor.

Sera and Maggie sat as if someone had dropped their puppet strings.

"Would you ladies care to tell me why you were loitering in our hallways?"

Loitering had such a negative connotation. And somehow, Sera didn't think this woman would buy into the story she'd told the teacher. Time to improvise. "We were just taking a quick tour. You see, I'm new to the area and very interested in the education system. I've heard Summer Shoals is a gold district."

The principal's hawk-like gaze softened slightly. "Yes, we have an excellent reputation around the state. We hire only the best staff and teachers."

Sera clasped her hands against her chest. "I'm so glad to hear that. You see, I have educational experience in California and I was hoping to substitute teach here."

"What type of experience? What subject area is your certification in?"

Maggie slid Sera a look that asked if she'd kept details to herself or was pulling another minister-of-record schtick. Sera avoided her scrutiny and concentrated on convincing the woman across the desk.

"I've…uh…mainly been involved in the

dramatic arts, but I'd be interested in subbing in any academic area."

The principal tapped her pen on the desktop. "We could use more substitute teachers. In fact, I've got two teachers going out on maternity leave soon." The woman's face softened. "Where did you say you taught?"

"Los Angeles."

"Well, if you can teach there, I'd say you can teach anywhere." The woman's eyes widened. Clearly she was thinking the rougher parts of L.A., not Beverly Hills. "But you have to pass a background check."

"No problem at all." Sera's chest expanded with hope, but she resisted glancing at Maggie. "How long does it normally take? I'm so eager to get back into the classroom. There's nothing more rewarding than helping unleash the potential of young minds."

The woman nodded. "We need someone like you around here. Talk to the receptionist on your way out. She has a gift for expediting this kind of thing."

When she and Maggie filed out of the principal's office, Sera tingled with excitement.

Outside, Abby Ruth already had her big dually idling as they approached. "I've been waiting out here for nearly twenty minutes. Where'd y'all disappear to? You left me high and dry sneaking through the band hall. Lord, give me a field house any day, but not a room that smells of smoldering wool, nerd sweat and burnt marshmallows."

Sera couldn't help but laugh, but Abby Ruth just scowled, apparently not seeing the humor in any of it.

Abby Ruth shook a finger at her. "Have you ever heard Sousa's 'Stars and Stripes Forever' from five feet away? It ain't pleasant. Cymbals pounding me senseless and off-key squawks. Lord, I thought a darned pterodactyl was about to land. My ears were ringing so hard by the time I escaped, I had to come out here to recuperate. On top of that, I thought y'all were in trouble somewhere!"

"Sorry it took so long," Maggie said. "Not only did we *not* get in trouble, somehow Sera just landed a job."

Hearing those words made Sera's insides swirl with pleasure. Not just for making another stride in their investigation, but also for the opportunity to make a difference. Even if for a little while.

CHAPTER 14

When she, Sera and Abby Ruth returned to Summer Haven, Maggie was still dumbfounded by Sera's improv with the principal. Where on earth would Sera conjure up teaching credentials? Maybe it was better if Maggie didn't ask.

But for now, their investigation was stalled until Sera could get inside the high school again.

The phone rang, and Maggie snatched it from the cradle as she walked by. Okay, fine, she was skipping through the kitchen after Bruce had asked her out and she and Sera made it through the interrogation at the high school. Investigating stuff was just so…so…darned energizing. Clearly, she'd missed her true calling. "Hello," she sang into the receiver.

"Hi, Mags."

"Lil? How are things going there? Are you okay?"

"Depends on who you ask."

Maggie's mood dipped. Why was she calling? Was there any way she knew about the Tucker? Had Angelina somehow snooped inside the garage and seen something? First the prison badge. Now this. That woman was a menace. Or maybe it wasn't Angelina this time. Maybe, Lord forbid, the body shop guy made mention of the car to someone and word had leaked out.

Lil said, "I'm going to need you to pick me up."

"When? Oh my goodness. This is great. When are you getting out?" *Please, please, please, don't let it be before we get the car back.*

"Right now."

"Today now?"

"Yes. They've already started processing the paperwork. I should be ready to go by the time you get here."

The room seemed to spin, and the sinking feeling in Maggie's gut made her wish she'd prioritized getting the car fixed over all of this sleuthing she and the girls had been doing. Her goose was cooked now. Not just cooked but charred.

"Of course I'll be there." It was amazing news, but boy if she didn't feel like she'd eaten a bad pot of crawfish all of the sudden. "How did this happen so quickly?"

"Honey, we can talk about all that after you pick me up," Lil said, her voice not nearly as chipper as it should've been. "We have a lifetime to catch up. Just get your fanny in gear and come get me."

Maggie hung up the phone with a swirl of excitement, anticipation and flat-out fear. One glance around the kitchen reminded her that they didn't keep things quite as pristine as Lil had. Maggie had always planned to put money aside to bring someone in to professionally clean Summer Haven before Lil came home, but there was no time for that now.

"Sera! Abby Ruth!" Maggie called out.

Sera came walking through the kitchen door. Then from upstairs, Abby Ruth bellowed, "What's the hurry?"

"Quick," Maggie hollered back. "Come down here."

A moment later, they were in the kitchen and

Maggie didn't mince words. "Lil's coming home. Today."

"No way," Sera said. "This is much earlier than a normal release. She hasn't served eighty-seven percent of her sentence yet."

"Doesn't matter. It's happening, and this place is a wreck. I need y'all to get the house shipshape while I go to pick her up."

"What will you drive?" Abby Ruth asked.

Sera's eyes went wide. "The Tucker is still in the shop."

"I know. Lil will just have to settle for being picked up in my truck. Sera, I need you to call Dennis Forehand and sweet-talk him. We need that car back in a hurry. He wanted two weeks, agreed to ten days, but I need it now. He has to pull some all-nighters for us. Something." She swung toward Abby Ruth. "I figure with the ninety-minute drive to the prison and another hour and a half back, we'll be home at four o'clock at the earliest. Can you get this place looking like Lil left it?"

Abby Ruth shrugged. "I wasn't here when she left, but yeah, we'll take care of it."

"Got it," Sera said. "We still have to figure out how to get the hood ornament made too. Maybe I can get Tassy to give me some names of local artisans who might be able to whip something up."

Maggie's heart expanded with her love for these two women. Wasn't always easy living together, but they came through for one another when it counted. "Y'all are angels. What would I have done without you since Lil's been away? Heck, what would I do without you, period?"

Sera put an arm around Maggie. "Don't be silly. That's what friends are for. Plus, I have an idea about how we might be able to fix the hood ornament."

Maggie picked up the phone and dialed the local market. "Hi. I need Lil's standard order sent over early this week. Can you make that happen today?"

"A cake!" Sera said. "I can make a cake too."

"Add a cake mix and vanilla ice cream to the list," Maggie said before hanging up. "I guess we do need to celebrate in some way." Thank goodness someone in this house was thinking straight.

"Not sure that's such a great idea," Abby Ruth said. "I mean, she didn't want anyone to know where she's been, right?"

Sera waved away Abby Ruth's words. "We'll just make it a small welcome home party between the four of us."

"We'll have to steer the conversation away from the Tucker and our cases," Maggie said.

"Easier said than done," Abby Ruth said. "If I've gotta keep my mouth shut about everything, I might be better off moving out."

"Don't be silly. You're family and Lil will love having a full house."

"I'm not so sure about that. Lil and I have what you might call different life philosophies." Abby Ruth kicked one boot over the other and stared up at the ceiling, clearly worried. Quite frankly, Maggie wondered how long Abby Ruth and Lil Summer Fairview could last in the same house.

HER CHEST TIGHT, LILLIAN GRIPPED THE PAPER BAG containing all her personal belongings. They'd taken them from her the day she'd checked in to Walter Stiles Prison Camp. It seemed so long ago.

She ripped open the staples and checked through everything.

"Everything there?" The guard looked down her glasses at Lil.

Lil stopped rummaging through the bag and straightened. "Yes. I was just looking."

The guard waved a hand toward the restroom at the end of the hall. "You can change into your civvies down there. Leave your uniforms in the hamper. Unless you want to buy a set." She pushed a price sheet Lil's way.

"Fifty dollars for used clothes?" Lil wondered how many inmates actually wanted to wear this stuff home. They weren't built for comfort, that was for sure. And the style was nothing to brag about. "No, thank you. I'll be fine."

"Suit yourself," the guard said.

Lil hugged the bag to her chest and scurried into the bathroom. She clicked the lock and breathed in the moment of privacy. Home. She was actually going home.

The peach suit she'd worn when she arrived at the prison camp was summer weight and the wrong color for this early in the year, but it was all she had. This outfit had always been one of her favorites. Her fingers lingered over the fabric. As fine and clean as she remembered. She lifted it to her face and inhaled the familiar powdery scent of her perfume. The perfume Harlan bought for her every Valentine's Day. No lingering smell of too much chlorinated cleaner from the prison laundry.

She couldn't strip out of the ugly prison-issued khaki fast enough, dropping the whole kit and caboodle in the plastic hamper. Good riddance.

The light silk pintuck blouse felt so good

against her skin. She unbuttoned and unzipped the suit skirt and stepped gingerly into it. But it quickly became obvious that no amount of wiggling her hind parts would make her skirt fit today. She tugged the zipper up as far as it would go, but there was still a good three-inch gap between the pull and her waistband.

And the warden thought Lil had been depressed before? That was nothing compared to realizing she'd become a frumpy fat chick after seventy years of watching her waistline. It was enough to plummet anyone into the depths of darkness.

There was no way she was dragging those ugly khakis back out of the hamper though. No, ma'am.

She slipped her arms into the blazer. Thank goodness it still fit. She unrolled the slim peach-colored leather belt. But rather than wrapping it around the outside of the jacket like normal, she pulled the belt tight around the top of the skirt to keep it up. She tippy-toed and twisted but was too short to see her handiwork in the mirror, but the blazer should cover the gap. It would have to do. Even too tight, it was so much better than the three shades of khaki that had clashed with her skin every dad-burned day for the past few months.

She slipped her feet into her shoes and found it challenging to walk in the modest-height heels after tromping around in those manly steel-toed shoes for nearly a year. She stepped gingerly across the tile floor.

When she came out of the restroom, a different guard was there waiting for her with a clipboard and a box. "Okay. This is it. I need your John Hancock in three places, then you'll be on your way."

Lil initialed and signed the forms.

"Here you go." The guard shoved the box of the few things—a comb, a couple of paperbacks and an inferior hand lotion—she'd accumulated while she'd been an inmate. "You're free to go."

A zing of excitement coursed through Lil. It was really happening.

She walked to the door and waited for the guard to hit the buzzer. Then she pushed through the heavy metal and stepped outside. The buzzer still tingling her senses like a wave of electricity, she stood there for a moment, almost afraid if she moved too quickly she'd wake up and it would all be a dream. But the door clicked behind her, and everything was still the same. She walked down the sidewalk toward the parking lot.

Freedom.

She inhaled a deep breath of slightly humid Georgia air. It did smell so much sweeter out here.

A bright clump of forsythia waved like a cheerful greeting committee as she made her way to a wooden bench at the end of the walk. Trees were blooming, starting a new year of growth.

Tears danced in her eyes, and her chin trembled. The swirl of emotion inside was strong enough to pick her up and toss her as if she were a paper cup on a wave.

One quick glance up to where she'd sat and watched her former cellmate leave on her last day here reminded her that everything on the other side of that wall was now forever forbidden to her. Why did that feel so strange? She should be kicking up her heels, but suddenly the absence of a process felt risky. Martha had made herself scarce, claiming she had something to do, but Lil had seen the softer side of Martha and she had a feeling that woman just didn't like goodbyes.

Lil placed her box of belongings on the bench and settled in next to it. She crossed and then uncrossed her legs, then simply folded her hands into her lap.

She'd prayed for this day, and now that it was here, why was she feeling so apprehensive? Must be the whole Angelina thing. Lord, if the folks back home knew where Lil had spent the past few months they'd be disappointed in her. She raised her chin to the sky.

Daddy, I sure have made a mess of things. I can't wait to get back home.

One thing she knew for sure, there would be no more Miss High & Mighty when she returned to Summer Shoals. What was wrong with her? Why had she felt the need to carry on the charade and bury Harlan in a way that exceeded her means? In the grander scheme of things, keeping up appearances didn't even matter. Heck, no one had even noticed. She probably could've cremated him and stuck him in the garden for a quarter of the price and never broken the law. Tarnished her family name. Never landed her fanny here in prison. Wouldn't have her fanny fanning out twice its size right now either.

There'd been a time when her first desire upon getting the heck out of this place would've been to get to the salon. Get her hair done and have a proper mani-pedi. Now, she'd just be happy to sleep in her own bed, in her own sheets, on her own body clock.

Prison changed a gal. Inside and out.

She thought of the goodbyes she'd shared the day her first roomie here in prison camp got out. Lil now understood her case of nerves so much better.

Maggie's little truck passed right by the bench Lil was sitting on, and her heart lurched. She leapt up, trying to get Maggie's attention. The truck slammed to an exaggerated stop, then whined as Maggie threw it into reverse and stopped right in front of Lil.

Maggie tumbled out of the driver's seat and raced to embrace her. "Lil!"

Lil pushed her face into Maggie's shoulder and cried. Tears of relief. Maggie had been her rock, as always. She would never be able to repay her.

"Have you been waiting long? I'm so sorry. I came as soon as you called, and it took everything I had not to break the speed limit."

"You're here now."

"And we can go home!"

"Home. My sweet Summer Haven. I can't wait."

Maggie picked up the box and placed it in the back of her truck, then unlocked the passenger door for Lil. "I can't believe you're coming home. It feels so good to be able to touch you again." She grabbed for Lil's hand and squeezed.

Lil climbed into the passenger seat while Maggie jogged to the driver's side. She'd never seen Maggie move with such zest. Not even back in college, and in comparison, Lil had never felt so numb.

They pulled away from the curb and Maggie slowed down at the gate. The guard marked her license plate off the list and waved her on.

Maggie said to Lil, “It’s over.”

“It’s been like a weird dream.”

“I can’t begin to imagine. I’ve missed you so much,” Maggie said. “I’m thrilled, but the timing was a little surprising.”

Lil stared out the window. Things looked so vast, alive.

“I can’t believe they let you out this early. It’s amazing. Sera said it’s very unusual for someone to get out before serving eighty-seven percent of their sentence. We’re so lucky.” Maggie’s voice was bright, but her words tumbled over each other, which usually meant she was talking fast to keep from revealing something she didn’t want to let out of the bag. “Wonderful.”

The best part was Lil wouldn’t have to fake being an old decrepit woman any longer. That had been downright demeaning and, to be honest, her acting skills had been so good she really had started to feel sickly. That had been the scariest part.

Lil cleared her throat. “Is there any talk on the street? Did Angelina spread the word?”

"No," Maggie said. "Haven't heard a thing."

Lil prayed Angelina remained true to her word, but like any blackmailer, she wasn't to be trusted. If Lil had learned anything being in prison, it was that honesty and the truth were very gray areas for people like Angelina Broussard.

CHAPTER 15

As they exited the interstate and made their way closer to Summer Shoals, Lil's hands trembled. She twitched in the seat, causing the belt securing her half-zipped skirt to roll up her tummy to darned near under her bra. A swoosh of cool air tickled at the exposed skin of her lower back. She tugged on the jacket to hide the gap, feeling self-conscious about her weight gain in front of Maggie. She folded her arms across her chest to camouflage the gaping buttons and half listened to Maggie as she continued to rattle on about Abby Ruth and Sera. Lil had about enough of those stories, and she wasn't even home yet.

The carved wooden sign that read WELCOME TO SUMMER SHOALS, GEORGIA brought tears to her eyes. She was home. Just moments away from Summer Haven.

With each revolution of the tires, Lil's body seemed to twist another rotation, like a rubber band on one of those little balsa wood propeller airplanes kids used to play with. She felt as if when the truck door opened she might zoom out like one, crashing and breaking into a million pieces.

As her beloved Summer Haven came into view, she had the unexpected urge to crouch in the floorboard. Her heart was pounding so hard it felt swollen to the point of choking off her breath.

A long horse trailer was parked alongside the carriage house. Lil cringed at the thought of how the grass must have yellowed and died under that eyesore, and what was with the tree on the left side of the house in front of the garage? From here it looked like someone had run a guillotine down one whole side of it. Teague had warned her a few of the huge oaks around Summer Haven needed attention.

"We're home!" Maggie leapt out of the truck.

Lil pushed her door open and slid out. She tugged the belt back down over the waist of her skirt and pulled on the zipper again. One sharp pull and her jacket hid the rigging. She opened the truck's tailgate and picked up the box containing her belongings. It almost felt silly to be bringing those things home now, but when she'd packed them it had been heart wrenching to think of leaving them behind.

She started toward the porch, but each step felt like an uphill climb, and she was having trouble catching her breath. She prayed it was just the excitement of being home. Lord, wouldn't that be a kicker, if after all her playacting in prison she keeled over and died from a heart attack today?

When she noticed the rockers on the porch, her mouth twisted. Normally, the chairs were placed symmetrically, three on one side of the door and three on the other. Someone had rearranged four of them in a half circle on the left. The other two lay scattered on the right at odd angles.

She grabbed the handrail to steady herself. There was no flag in the flagpole. She'd always made sure the seasonal flags were changed, and everyone around town knew it. Hadn't Maggie seen that on the list she left for her? How hard was it to put a flag up?

Lil raised her hand to the railing. She slid her nail against the yellowing and flaking paint, sending it to the deck boards below. "Summer Haven is looking more tired than I remember."

"I did the best I could." Maggie shoved her

hands into her pockets. "The bathroom upstairs is renovated. New toilet and everything. I—"

"I didn't mean that quite the way it sounded. I'm sorry. I know you did your best. I'm just a little overwhelmed. I appreciate everything you've done. More than you'll ever know." But it hurt to see things this way. Had they looked this tired when she left and she was too close to it to notice, or had things deteriorated in the short time she was gone? Well, she was back now.

Maggie lowered her head and Lil felt like a real toad for hurting her best friend.

But before Lil could say another word, the front door opened and Serendipity and Abby Ruth stepped onto the porch cheering, "Welcome home!"

Sera did something of a cheerleader leap in the air, then wrapped her arms around Lil's neck. "We're so glad you're home."

Abby Ruth reached for the box in Lil's arms. "Can I take that for you?"

"I've got it." Something about Abby Ruth's question made Lil feel like a guest in her own home. Either that or a feeble old woman. She wasn't incapable. That ruse may have gotten her out of jail, but that tale had ended when she stepped foot out of prison.

"Come in." Sera ushered her inside the foyer.

"Maggie said you love shrimp and grits so I'm making it for dinner. I bet you're starving."

Lillian was touched by the thoughtfulness of it, but she'd rather just be alone with Maggie.

Maggie leaned in. "Don't expect too much. Sera is one of those health food nuts. Not even a smidgen of butter in her recipe." Maggie gave Lil a wink, and her smile had replaced the sullen look that had hung there a moment ago. "Seriously. I have no idea how she makes things taste good. It's different, but you'll get used to it."

Used to it? You've never eaten prison food. Anything fresh is a treat. I can't wait to get back in the kitchen and whip up my special family recipes.

Inside, things looked just as she'd left them. Well, pretty much. She glanced over at Maggie, but held her tongue at the long scrape outside the parlor. Clearly the floor had been damaged somehow. She poked her head inside the parlor to find a TV the size of Atlanta hanging over her beautiful sideboard. "Wha…what in the world is that?"

Maggie grabbed her elbow and hustled her down the hallway toward the kitchen. "Why don't we all sit down for some tea?"

But Lil veered left into her bedroom and placed her box on the edge of her bed. The closet door was slightly askew, and Maggie's hair ribbons hung from the lampshade on the dresser. She was tempted to take them down and tuck them away, but Maggie walked in behind her. It had been her idea for Maggie to stay in her room rather than upstairs, so why did it eat at her to see her things disturbed?

"I'm so happy I could bust." Maggie's voice nearly danced.

"Me too, Mags." Lil recognized the lackluster in her own tone.

"You seem tired. Do you want to rest?"

"No. No. I'm good." But she wasn't good. She felt out of place while the other three women moved about as if Summer Haven belonged to them. She didn't have anything to unpack. Nothing to do. And her favorite suit didn't fit. It wasn't turning out to be as wonderful a day as she'd dreamed. Settling back in seemed unsettling at best. "I'll be out in just a moment."

Maggie backed up, then stopped in the doorway. "I feel like someone should pinch me. Welcome home."

Lillian slipped out of her outfit and found a pair of her old fat pants with elastic-waist and a flowing top that hopefully hid her expanded midsection. Looked like she'd be rotating between three pairs of stretch knit pants because she sure wouldn't be wearing any of her fitted clothes for a while. But then she spotted something she'd missed so much while she was gone. Her Passion Fruit Pink #46 lip color. For a moment, those extra pounds she was carrying fell away. She uncapped the lipstick and leaned close to the mirror, letting the color glide on. She plucked a tissue from the box and blotted, held the high-quality soft paper to her face. How she'd missed the little things. She pushed her feet into her favorite old house slippers and walked back out to the kitchen feeling somewhat more herself, confident and in control.

"Can I pour you some coffee?" Sera asked.

"I can get it." Lil strolled to the counter, but the coffeepot wasn't in its normal spot. A weird sense of disorientation struck her. Heck, maybe she did deserve compassionate release. Was her memory that bad? Her gaze darted around the room. Why in Pete's sake had they moved the coffeemaker over by the fridge? She'd always kept the mugs in this cabinet. She opened the door to find those had disappeared as well. Instead, the cupboard held a bevy of assorted seeds and funky-smelling oddities. Sera's doings, no doubt.

Lil's hands trembled so she held them close to her body and went to the opposite side of the room. She retrieved a mug from the cabinet above the coffeemaker and filled it to the brim. One sip of the brew and she made a desperate run for the sink, barely making it there before spitting out the woody-tasting mouthful. "What…what was that stuff?"

"Sera switched us over to a chicory coffee," Maggie said. "Says it helps digestion and reduces inflammation."

Only thing it had done for Lil was inflame her sense of disorientation. She poured the rest of her so-called coffee down the drain and rinsed out the cup.

Lillian forced herself to sit down at the table with Abby Ruth and Sera. "Thank you, girls, for being here for Maggie while I've been away. You can't know how much I appreciate you."

"To tell the truth," Abby Ruth said, "it's been awfully nice for me to be so close to Teague again. You know he and my daughter have been best friends since grade school. Should've been more than that, but you know how stupid college kids can be when it comes to love. But those two were meant to be, and a little Summer Haven Christmas magic seems to have done the trick."

"Sure did," Maggie agreed. "Lil, the house looked beautiful over the holidays. I wish you could've seen it."

Abby Ruth snickered. "Well, the junk Colton gave us was a bit of an eyesore, but other than that it did look quite nice."

"What junk?" Lil asked.

"Colton Ellerbee won the first Holiday Art Fest with this nativity scene sculpture."

"Made out of junk," Abby Ruth sneered. "I'm talking bobbers for eyes and license plates for bodies. Even on the sweet baby Jesus. Eccentricity? Nah. That man's flat-out weird, if you ask me."

"Well, it was an honor to accept the donation for the town and to house it here at Summer Haven. I mean this is the heart of Summer Shoals. Right, Lil?"

"Certainly." Lil nodded, but at the moment, she wasn't sure what they were talking about, wasn't sure if she even cared.

"I knew you'd be thrilled." Maggie smiled proudly.

"That's wonderful," Lil offered. "About the sculpture, and Teague." She was glad to hear Teague had found someone. Or reunited as the case may be. It would be nice for Summer Shoals to gain some younger residents. "Is everyone all settled in rooms upstairs? Have you been comfortable?"

"Not me," Sera said. "I've got camp set up down by the creek."

"Still? Dear, why won't you stay inside?" Even as she asked the question, Lil wasn't sure she wanted another person in her space.

"I have everything I need out there," Sera said. "I'd never impose on you like that."

"Yeah, and ever since she came careening through the second floor on the potty flume she's been a little house-shy." Abby Ruth chuckled, and Maggie started laughing so hard, tears were dripping from her eyes.

Sera stuck her hands on her hips. "Hey, you'd have been freaked out too."

Lillian glanced from face to face. Obviously, this was some kind of inside joke, one she was squarely outside. "Is that what happened to the parlor floor?"

Maggie put a hand on Lil's arm. "Oh, Lil, I've had my hands full. I have to tell you. So, remember I mentioned I had to replace the toilet upstairs?"

"Yes."

"Well, I didn't really give you the whole story. Didn't want to worry you, but not only did I have to replace the potty, but the flooring and the whole works. That porcelain toilet fell right through the ceiling one day…with Sera still sitting on it!"

Sera smirked. "They've teased me that it was all

the natural foods I eat making too much poop. I can assure you that was *not* the case."

"You say that," Abby Ruth said, "but I'm not sure you've used an inside bathroom since then."

"There's not one thing wrong with healthy eating," Sera said.

"She won't fix anything with sugar or real butter for us, but she'd do anything to keep Mike & Ike to herself," Abby Ruth teased.

What in heaven's name was going on in this place? Was it one big wild party? Strange men at Summer Haven might be worse than people knowing where Lil had been all this time. Surely they'd be talking.

Maggie and Abby Ruth were still laughing and by now Sera had joined in.

"Well, everyone needs a guilty pleasure," Sera said.

Lil held a hand to her thundering heart. "Two men. At one time?"

The laughter stopped, and the others shared a look of confusion. Then, Abby Ruth snorted, Sera rolled in her lips, and Maggie snickered.

Not only was Lil out of the loop, she wasn't anywhere on this darned roller coaster.

Sera shoved her hand into her pocket and pulled out a miniature box of Mike & Ike's candy. She shook it like a maraca and danced around the table. "Oh goodness no, Lil. My guilty pleasure is this."

Lil smiled politely, suddenly feeling so tired. "Oh, I see."

"Okay, whew, that was fun," Sera said. "We've had our little laugh, our auras are in a good place, but no more potty talk this close to dinner." She flounced across the room and plopped into the empty chair. "Lil, I rummaged through your recipes for the shrimp and grits and will take my best stab at making you proud. I'll even use real butter."

"Never did that for us," Abby Ruth muttered.

"Tonight is special." Sera placed a hand on top of Lil's. "We're so happy you're back home."

The doorbell rang and Sera's chair made a loud groan as it scraped the original plank flooring, sending a chill up Lil's spine.

Where were the furniture pads she'd always used?

Sera came flying back into the kitchen wide-eyed. "It's Angelina. I left her waiting at the door. What should we do?"

Lillian straightened in her chair. "You left her standing on the front porch?"

"Yes!" Sera nodded. "I didn't know what to do. I mean we have so much to catch you up on. We've been making up stories for months. That woman's aura is unnaturally distributed. Her sexual chakras aren't just bound up. Those suckers are totally blown out. She's scary!"

Lil got up and breezed past Sera. "I'll handle this." She took a deep breath before opening the door. She said to Angelina, "How on earth did you know I was home?"

Angelina smiled so sweetly that for a moment Lil almost forgot all the hell and fury the woman caused on a regular basis. "I signed up to be alerted when you were released. It's a citizen's right to get an alert when a criminal is being put back out on the streets."

ALONG WITH ABBY RUTH AND SERA, MAGGIE pressed against the front window, trying to overhear Lil's conversation with Angelina.

"I am not a criminal," Lil huffed.

"The federal government says you are."

"I don't think you subscribed to an alert because you were afraid I'd come straight to your house for a little B&E."

"Oh, B&E? You've even got the lingo down, Lil. Next thing you know, you'll be running a halfway house around here."

"Maybe I will, but it won't be any business of

yours, thank you very much. Why are you here, Angelina?" Lil rubbed her forehead as though Angelina was giving her a migraine.

Maggie rubbed her rear end in empathy.

Sera collapsed to the floor and propped her chin on the windowsill. "This is not good karma."

Angelina's voice rose. "Have you forgotten we have a deal?"

Deal? Lil was making deals with Angelina?

"Unless you have a purse full of hundred dollar bills," Lil shot back, "then we don't have a deal."

"Before I pay good money, I want another look at the Tucker."

Abby Ruth elbowed Maggie. "Did you hear that? Angelina just said something about the Torpedo."

Sera squeezed Maggie's arm.

Her breath becoming shallow and rapid, Maggie said, "Sera, quick, try to get dinner on the table. Abby Ruth, stand watch at the back door. If Lil and Angelina head toward the garage, stall them. Somehow."

"How am I supposed to do that?"

"I don't know. Shoot your gun in the air and swear there's a rabid skunk in our midst. Be creative."

Abby Ruth's grin went wide and somewhat evil.

She leaned over and pulled a small pistol from her boot. Was she always packing heat?

Maggie didn't have time for that conversation. She dashed to the front door, then slowed and strolled out to join Lil on the porch.

"Angelina. You're becoming a regular around here lately." Maggie hoped the words didn't have too much of an edge, but it probably wouldn't bother Angelina if they did. She had a the-sun-rises-and-sets-on-me attitude that couldn't be penetrated.

"Just had to ask Lil a few questions about the High on the Hog event. Being a past chairperson, we share information about these things, don't we, Lil?"

The memory of Angelina pitching the idea of using the Tucker at the High On The Hog event made Maggie's stomach flip. Having to tell Lil about the damage to the car was bad, but having Angelina witness it? Now that would be the worst thing ever.

"Maybe you can set up some time later in the week." Maggie nudged Lil toward the door. "We were just putting dinner on the table."

Angelina looked as if she would argue, but then she smiled sweetly and patted Lil's arm. "I'll be in touch. Soon." She spun on her boot heels and swished her bedazzled hips back to her pearly white SUV.

"Good riddance to her." Maggie stood shoulder-to-shoulder with Lil. "If she isn't the most conniving creature I've ever met."

Lil pursed her pink lips. "Oh, honey, she's not even an evil stepsister compared to some of the women I just spent nearly a year with."

Was Lil on Angelina's side?

When she and Lil walked back into the house, Sera and Abby Ruth had somehow transformed the dining room into dinner party mode, and by the look on Lil's face, she was impressed.

The table was set with Lil's fine china and the goldware. A pitcher of sweet tea sat at the edge of the table, but Abby Ruth was already pouring wine in glasses at each place setting.

A broad smile spread across Lil's face. "You've gone all out. Thank you."

"We have to celebrate your homecoming," Maggie said as Sera entered the room with a glass cake plate. It held a beautiful layer cake decorated in soft creamy frosting outlined in the shape of Summer Haven.

"It's lovely, Sera." They all took their seats and Lil raised her glass. "To the three women who, in my absence, have taken care of Summer Haven and my reputation. May you never have to skirt the truth again."

"Hear, hear!"

"We're starting with cake," Abby Ruth stated. "Because this is just that special of a day."

Maggie knew it was really because dinner was nowhere near ready, but what the heck? Lil seemed happy with the plan and that was all that mattered.

Dinner was filled with light conversation as they tried to bring Lil up to date on all the Summer Shoals happenings while she was away. She needed to be in the loop on the cover-up stories they'd concocted to keep her absence on the down-low.

"When Maggie left this morning to pick you up, I made a quick stop in at the diner and the post office, mentioning I was preparing for your homecoming from your trip. You know how quickly things get around in this town. Everyone should know by tomorrow." Sera leaned her forearms on the table. "I photoshopped a slew of pictures for you so you could share them with people. I mean who goes on a cruise like that and doesn't come home with pictures? I even put you in a few of them." Sera pulled the phone from inside her tank top and with one sweep of her finger, flipped through photos for Lil.

Lil's eyes were soft and wistful. "Isn't that beautiful? Wish I had been on that trip."

"Me too," Sera said. "Maybe we could really go sometime. I'd give anything to see the northern lights."

"What's that one?" Lil pointed at the phone's screen. "Looks like a hunk of junk. Is that supposed to be in Alaska?"

Sera pulled the phone back in front of her. "Oh, whoops, that was in the wrong folder. It's one of Colton Ellerbee's art pieces. We're working on a —" She cut her gaze toward Maggie.

Darn it. They'd agreed to avoid that topic in front of Lil. Maggie gave a tiny head shake.

"A what, dear?" Lil asked, forking up a bite of cake. But Maggie knew that look on her best friend's face, and it meant Lil would find a way to get the truth.

So she admitted, "We're looking into something for him."

Lil flashed Maggie a look that was far from approving. "By looking into, you mean investigating?"

"I guess you could call it that," Maggie said, "but it's more like a favor."

Lil took a long swig of her wine. "Isn't that a

little dishonest, Maggie? Representing yourselves as people with skills in this kind of thing?"

Lil's words knocked Maggie back on her heels. "We've actually done a pretty good job. Naturals I'd say, and we've done a few favors for you, or did you already forget about that?"

"That was different."

Meaning it was okay to do Lil a good turn, but no one else? Didn't she realize other people had benefitted from Maggie, Sera and Abby Ruth catching two bad guys? "That Social Security fraud and an online dating scam could've hurt lots of people, Lil."

"You also could have been in danger. And besides, it just wouldn't do for me to be associated with anything related to criminal activity." Lil looked around the table at each of them in turn. "As guests at Summer Haven, I'm sure you'd want to abide by your hostess' wishes."

Hostess? Lil had been home for all of a few hours and she'd already decided she was running some kind of house party.

"But we've already made a commitment," Sera said.

Lil swirled her fork in the air. "Let Teague handle it. It's his job."

Abby Ruth sat so straight her spine could've

been made from a power pole. "But this is personal. My daughter's reputation and business are at stake."

"All the more reason for a professional look into whatever this is."

"You can't just come in here and tell us—"

"Summer Haven is *my* home."

Abby Ruth hopped to her feet and tossed her napkin onto the table. "You know what? It's been a long time since I lived with my momma."

Sera sat across the table with her mouth agape and her gaze darting from one person to the next.

"Goodness knows I'd never want to be mistaken for your mother."

Maggie had a feeling Lil's comment had nothing to do with someone thinking she was that much older than Abby Ruth and everything to do with someone thinking she would be associated with such an outspoken rabble rouser.

Oh, Lord. Just what she'd feared. Lil and Abby Ruth together were like an oil slick in the Gulf of Mexico.

CHAPTER 16

After Abby Ruth had stormed out of the dining room the evening before, Sera and Maggie had talked her down, but with the rising tension since Lil came home, Sera thought she'd be willing to fight a Southern California brush fire rather than stay in that house any longer. Thank goodness the high school had called saying she'd passed her background check. Which meant the fake ID she'd bought on the south side of Los Angeles had been worth every penny.

She headed into town for her first teaching assignment. The only thing that had come close to creating this kind of bubbling excitement inside her was when she, Maggie and Abby Ruth were chasing down a crook together. And today, Sera was doing double duty.

Score.

Today, she'd be monitoring a chemistry class. Of course she didn't think the principal would appreciate Sera teaching the kids about a few of the chemical compounds she was most familiar with. What was business as usual in her old neighborhood in California was the devil's work here in small-town Georgia.

By lunchtime, she'd consoled a girl who'd discovered her boyfriend was two-timing her with her best friend, advised a boy watching the heartbroken girl with hound dog eyes, and fixed another girl's wardrobe malfunction. Goodness, when had fifteen-year-olds become so busty? Sera herself still wasn't much more than an anemic B-cup.

She found her way to the teachers' lounge for lunch. If she'd thought the hallways were a hotbed of activity and chatter, this room, packed with people ranging from their mid-twenties to three years past dirt, was just as lively.

For a minute, Sera was paralyzed, remembering the time her parents had moved her from Crested Butte to Santa Barbara and she'd been the new girl. Again. But acting like a scared schoolgirl wouldn't get her the information she needed. She had a lot of work to do before the last bell rang at three-thirty sharp.

So she put on her smile and strolled up to a table with an empty chair. “Is anyone sitting here?”

A man—blond, muscular and probably a few years younger than her—looked up from his massive ham and cheese sandwich. With his build, he had to be a gym teacher. He checked out her granny-square crocheted poncho and black leggings, then said, “Depends on what you brought in that paper sack.” But by his charming grin she knew that, as people in Georgia said, he was just joshing her.

“How does tofu stir fry and kale chips sound?”

“Like total hell on earth.” Still, he pushed the chair away from the table so Sera could sit. “You’re new here.”

“I’m subbing for the chemistry teacher.”

“Gotcha.”

“I’m Serendipity Johnson,” she said. The other four people at the table introduced themselves—an algebra teacher, the track coach, a European history instructor and a senior English teacher who happened to be wearing a pair of clogs.

When she caught Sera staring at her feet, the English teacher said, “We’re talking about poetry. I find my students understand iambic pentameter better when I dance it for them."

Sera beamed at her. Now this was her kind of teacher.

However, making friends had to come after picking brains. Sera forked up a bite of perfectly browned tofu. "I heard something about an upcoming auction. Sculptures or something?"

"Oh, yeah, Murphy Blackwood does this every year," the track coach said. "Last year he auctioned off a bunch of metal dustpans his students made. Between you and me, some of those wouldn't have held boulders, much less dust. But the money raised goes for a vo-tech school scholarship. Can't argue with that."

"I'd love to see this year's sculptures," Sera commented. "My friends and I out at Summer Haven are always interested in supporting the community."

"You're staying with Lillian Fairview?" The clog-wearing teacher sounded doubtful.

"Yes. Have been for quite a while now. She's such a sweetheart," Sera said, although quite honestly she knew very little about Lil. "So where's Mr. Blackwood's classroom?"

The cute gym teacher next to her said, "Last year, they moved the whole shebang into a portable classroom after one of the kids had a little accident with an oxyacetylene torch."

"Accident?"

"Caught three classrooms on fire, including part of the band hall. You shoulda seen those thirty-year-old wool uniforms go up in flames. Lord, it smelled like a sweaty pig roast in the hallways for the rest of the school year."

Sera put down her fork at that thought. Good thing too because the electronic bell sounded and the teachers all hopped up as if metal barbs had poked them from their chair seats. But the cute gym teacher took time to hold his hand out to Sera, "It was great to meet you, Serendipity."

Her hand touched his and her face warmed in response. "Same here."

When she was away from the teachers' lounge, Sera surreptitiously fanned her face. Yes, she'd been longing for companionship lately, but she was skirting a little too close to the line in flirting with that man. And since she'd recently encouraged Maggie to open herself to the chance at love again, Sera needed to keep her attention on finding out who was behind these forgeries. Maggie had her hands full trying to juggle Bruce, Lil and the still damaged Torpedo. Keeping the truth about the car from Lil wouldn't be easy.

Sera stopped once to ask a student for directions, but it didn't take her long to find the row of tan-colored metal trailers behind the main school building. She snuck around to the back and strolled past the windows. The first building held stacks of wood, table saws and other tools. Maggie would be in heaven inside there. The next was full of sewing machines. Probably some kind of fashion design class. As it so often was, the third was the charm. Sera pressed close to the open window and caught sight of teenagers working with sheets of metal and blowtorches.

Bingo.

And over in the corner was a pile of castoffs—metal pipes, industrial lampshades, and napkin holders. Sera homed in on something. Was that a beater from a mixer? Among the pile of misfit parts there were some familiar bits—bobbers, those old wooden folding rulers Colton loved so much, and all kinds of pipes.

Yes, yes, yes!

She'd finally found something good. She pulled out her phone and quickly snapped pictures of the pile and the students' partially welded sculptures. Some were quite good—a large cat, a sassy rooster and a bobber-eyed dog. But the one to the far right looked like the love child of a mule and Cerberus.

Someone around here had to be the forger. Too much welding going on to be otherwise. But was the culprit the teacher or one of the kids? She couldn't tip anyone off before she, Maggie, and Abby Ruth knew for sure, and she needed more information. She could probably walk right in and pretend she was lost, do a little flirting and get some details, but where was the fun in that?

Lucky for her, a couple of the windows were tilted open. She picked up a slim stick and fitted it against the windowsill. Then she lowered the window until it looked closed.

If no one noticed it, the gap would be her entry key later this evening.

She pulled her cell phone out and texted Abby Ruth and Maggie.

I've secured entry for later. Be ready at sundown.

When Sera came skipping into the kitchen, Maggie was slowly rearranging all the small appliances and cabinets back to the way they'd been when Lil left Summer Haven. Lord, the way she'd reacted to the changes, a body would think Maggie had swapped the furnishings of two rooms. Truth be told, the kitchen was more efficient the way she had arranged it.

Abby Ruth was with her but had threatened to leave if Lil so much as stuck her head in the room. "Well," Abby Ruth said to Sera, "if you don't look like a cat that's been at a canary buffet, I don't know what does."

"That's just wrong." Still, Sera's smile didn't dim a watt. She did a few intricate dance steps that would probably make the pros on *Dancing With The Stars* jealous. "Did you get my text?"

"We did." Abby Ruth twirled a chair around and straddled it. "Spill it, sister."

"The shop teacher was a solid lead."

"He's our guy?"

"I'm not a hundred percent sure. But when we go back tonight we can do some more digging. I'll bet you it's either him or one of his students."

"Don't you think we should at least consider calling in Teague?" Maggie asked. Lord, anything to relieve some of the pressure swirling all around her these days. She was exhausted for more than one reason. Lil had looked a little wounded that Maggie had taken over her bedroom. So, of course, Maggie had packed up her things, washed all the linens on Lil's bed, then moved up to the Azalea room. "Abby Ruth did promise him we'd keep him up to date on anything we found."

Abby Ruth snorted. "I had my toes crossed inside my boots."

Maggie shook her head at her friend.

"It's totally possible," Sera said. "Have you seen how long her toes are?"

Abby Ruth reached over and squeezed Maggie's shoulder, her way of showing concern. "Sugar, we haven't given up on one of these mysteries yet, and we're not gonna stop now. Besides, I think it might do you some good to get away from Summer Haven for a while."

Guilt shrouded Maggie. Running out the front door, down those steps, and far, far away sounded like heaven right now. She could leave the Tucker Torpedo doppelganger and the newly paranoid and grumpy Lil without looking back. She'd expected Lil's homecoming to be filled with smiles and joy. Not this…this…petulant wrestle for control of something Maggie had never wanted control of in the first place.

But Lil couldn't just waltz back in here and behave as though she should have final say about everything. That wasn't fair. And in all truth, it hurt Maggie's heart.

"Sera," Maggie said, "what do you think we should do?"

"We've all paid property taxes at one point or another, right?" Sera said.

Well, who knew about Sera? Since the time she showed up in Summer Shoals, she'd seemed to be rootless. But Maggie just nodded.

"And schools are funded by those taxes. So if you ask me, we own a portion of the public school system."

"Love it," Abby Ruth crowed. "I guess you figure our portion is inside that shop classroom."

Sera sat back in her chair, her smile broad and uncomfortably close to an Abby Ruth-style expression. "Uh-huh."

Lord, Maggie had heard some rationalizations in her time, but this was, as her daughter Pam would say, ballsy.

A scrape and clang came from the direction of Lil's bedroom. Apparently, she hadn't been happy with their cleaning efforts and was doing it all over again herself. For some reason, that made pressure build behind Maggie's eyes. And if Lil couldn't recognize the sacrifices they'd made on her account, how could she expect Maggie to drop Colton's case?

Abby Ruth crossed one leg over the other, swinging her foot casually. "If you're too chicken, then you can stay here while Sera and I check out the shop teacher's classroom."

"No!" The thought of her friends leaving her behind felt like the times Maggie had been the last one picked for the dodgeball team years ago. She was part of something now—something productive and good and fun—and she'd be darned if she was giving that up just because Lil was finally home. "In fact, I just ordered a perfect B&E outfit from White House Black Market." And it sure had felt good buying clothes she didn't mind leaving the tag in. Gone were the days when she clipped the XXL out of her jackets so no one would know. Like they couldn't tell by looking at her.

"What about Lillian?" Sera asked.

Dread soared through Maggie's gut. "We'll make sure she's fast asleep before we leave."

CHAPTER 17

When they got to the high school, Maggie was so busy admiring her black bootleg jeans that she almost ran into a pile of cinderblocks behind the portable buildings. She had to get her head in the game. But darned if Lycra wasn't a miracle fabric.

She tiptoed to catch up with Sera and Abby Ruth, who were already lifting a skinny metal-framed window. Maggie's insides sank. Even in her smaller-sized pants, there was no way her backside would fit through that thing.

Abby Ruth gave Sera the once-over. "You sure dressed for the job, didn't you?"

Yeah, in her body-hugging catsuit, Sera would slip through that window like a greased-up hinge pin.

"Once I'm in, I'll unlock the front door to let the two of you inside."

They boosted Sera up in their cupped hands and she wiggled through the opening. Maggie half expected a crash to sound from Sera landing on the floor, but of course, there was barely a shuffle. Maggie and Abby Ruth scooted around to the other side of the building where Sera was already standing in the open doorway.

They climbed the concrete stairs, and once inside, Abby Ruth passed out small high-powered penlights. "Meant to put these in your Christmas stockings," she said. "But I forgot in all the hullabaloo of Jenny's visit."

Sera flicked hers on and the beam illuminated the casing on Maggie's. Oh, goodness. Abby Ruth had even had the lights engraved with their initials. The woman might act like she was hardhearted, but she had an ooey-gooey center. Maggie couldn't imagine her life without these two women.

"Maggie, why don't you check the junk pile in the corner?" Sera said. "And Abby Ruth, if you'll get a closer look at the sculptures, I'll see if I can find anything in the storage room."

They all hit their areas of the room, with Sera disappearing through a door near the teacher's desk. As quietly as possible, Maggie rummaged through a large plastic bin of metal flotsam, separating them into piles as she might with her grandkids' Legos. Part of an old fireplace set. Nuts and bolts. A motorcycle fender. *Hmm.* There was the metal beater Sera had mentioned. And a stack of license plates. Colton had used license plates on the Virgin Mary's cloak. But parts alone weren't really enough to condemn the teacher as a forger.

Abby Ruth was busy turning over sculptures on the worktables and checking their buns of steel…literally.

"Find anything?" Maggie called out softly.

"With some of these things, I can't tell the ears from the ass," she grumbled. "Regardless, I haven't seen the fake-o Colton signature anywhere."

A scraping sound came from the front of the building. One that sounded a lot like shoes against concrete steps.

Maggie grabbed Abby Ruth's shirt sleeve and strong-armed her toward the door where Sera had disappeared.

"What the hel—"

Maggie yanked hard enough to rip the seam of Abby Ruth's favorite western shirt. "Need to hide. Now."

They hustled inside the storage area, and Sera whirled around. “You scared me to death—”

“Someone’s here,” Maggie whispered, her voice hoarse and shaking. This scenario was all too familiar. The last time her underarms had produced this much moisture, she, Sera and Abby Ruth had been trapped inside a bad guy’s house and Teague had been about to catch them at it.

“Well, shit,” Abby Ruth muttered. “What now?”

“The tarps.” Sera grabbed a couple of beige mounds.

“We can’t just throw them over our heads and pretend to be tan ghosts.” Still Abby Ruth snatched one and draped it over her shoulders.

“We can squeeze behind here.” Sera headed around a shelving unit filled with a collection of dustpans, metal birdhouses, and some other unidentifiable projects. Without any trouble, she shimmied between it and the wall.

Abby Ruth followed her lead, creating a tarp-colored faux wall back there.

Maggie eyed the gap and sucked in her stomach. The sound of the building’s door closing spurred her into action, and she shouldered her way behind the first support. The whole thing shook, rattling the students’ projects against the metal wiring beneath them.

Maggie froze, a metal support pole pressed against her sternum. Oh. So not good. Her right boob was behind the shelf, but the left one poked out as though it was peeking around during a game of hide-and-seek.

"Get back here," Abby Ruth whispered.

"I'm trying. Some of us are more mammarily gifted than others." Maggie tilted in her pelvis, even did one of those Kegel exercises for good measure. Then she squished her left breast almost as flat as those mammogram machines did. With that combo, she was able to wiggle her way behind the shelf.

Probably wouldn't matter. Whoever was inside was sure to spot the puddle of her nervous sweat.

Abby Ruth helped her yank up the tarp and hold it level with hers and Sera's.

Just in time too because the storage door opened and someone clomped in. A man, by the sounds of his mutters to himself. "Clamps, soapstone and solder."

While Maggie stood behind the shelf with her shaking thighs pressed together, the man wandered around the space, apparently gathering items. At one heart-stopping point, he pulled something off the shelf right in front of her tarp-covered face. Then he shoved it back into place so hard, the hunk of metal popped her in the nose. When she felt a trickle on her upper lip, it was all she could do not to sniff.

By the time the guy had done what he came to do and clicked the storage door shut behind him, the trickle was dripping onto Maggie's brand spanking new shirt. When the outer door closed as well, they all dropped their tarps. But Maggie was too frozen to squeeze her way out of their hiding spot.

Sera came around to Maggie's side and tugged her from behind the shelf. "Are you okay?"

"Imb nob sure." She tilted her head back, cracking it against the wall.

Abby Ruth shined her penlight directly into Maggie's face, half blinding her.

"Oh, no. Your nose is bleeding." Sera snatched up one of the abandoned tarps and pressed it against Maggie's face. "Keep your head back and apply pressure."

A stream of blood trickled down the back of Maggie's throat. "Ugh."

"Sera," Abby Ruth said, "did you get a look at the guy?"

"Definitely Murphy Blackwood, the shop teacher."

"Any idea what he took?"

She glanced around. "All the items he was reciting to himself, plus a canister of gas."

"Mighty suspicious, if you ask me," Abby Ruth said. "We need to follow him."

"Maggie, are you up to it?"

Heck if she'd let a little bloody nose stop her. "Yeb."

THE THREE OF THEM RACED OUT OF THE PORTABLE building toward the parking lot, but whatever the shop teacher had been driving was nowhere in sight. Sera leapt into the back of the truck and Abby Ruth fired it up. Maggie slid the back window open and called to Sera, "You okay back there?"

"Yeah." Sera pulled out her phone and started tapping buttons. "Got to love the internet. You can find everything on here." She flashed her phone in their direction. "Got it."

Murphy Blackwood lived just a few blocks away.

"Let's go," Maggie said. "I know where that is."

A few minutes later, they were cruising past the address at a slow rate of speed. Sure enough, a truck was parked in the driveway. Sera jumped out of the back of Abby Ruth's truck and peeked into the bed of the other truck. She gave the girls a thumbs-up, indicating the welding supplies were in the vehicle.

They parked a block down, waited for a looong three hours, but it looked like whatever he was doing with all those welding supplies, he wasn't up to it at his house. And they couldn't stay here until morning.

"We'll have to set up another stakeout later," Maggie said. "If we're not home when Lil wakes up, we'll have to explain ourselves."

"Things were easier before we had a keeper," Abby Ruth commented.

True, but it would be so disloyal for Maggie to admit it aloud. "I'm tired down to the marrow of my bones," she said instead. "Sera might be young enough to stay out until dawn and get up with the chickens, but I'm not."

"Sugar, that doesn't even make sense seeing as roosters crow at sunup." But Abby Ruth started up the dually and pulled away from the curb.

When they entered Summer Haven's drive, Abby Ruth cut the lights and crept up the driveway, being mindful not to rev the gas. Maybe she had learned some discretion over the past few months.

Turned out, it didn't matter how discreet Abby Ruth was. When they tiptoed in the front door, Lil was sitting on the velvet divan in the parlor. She was dressed in her favorite cotton waffle weave robe, with her arms clamped across her chest as though she was trying to keep her anger from leaping out. "And where, pray tell, have the three of you been?"

Maggie forced herself not to wince or hunch. "We went out for a little…"

"Fresh air," Sera improvised.

"Drink," Abby Ruth said at the same time.

Maggie could feel the strain of her small smile. "A little al fresco cocktail."

"Until midnight?"

"Champagne is best sipped in the dark of night," Sera said.

Her shoulders back like a queen, Lil stood and stalked over to Maggie. Then she stuck her face close and sniffed. "Only thing Maggie smells like is sour perspiration."

And blood, Maggie thought. But she wasn't about to add that tidbit to the mix.

"So why don't you tell me where you really were?"

"We're just trying to wrap up this thing with Colton Ellerbee," Maggie told her.

"I thought we agreed you would drop that silliness."

It wasn't silliness, but apparently Lil didn't

want them digging into any situations that weren't directly related to her wellbeing. That hardly seemed fair. Or neighborly. "No, Lil," Maggie said as evenly as she could. "You may have expressed your opinion, but that doesn't mean we agreed. Colton gifted us with a beautiful nativity scene—"

Abby Ruth coughed and patted her chest.

"—and hired Abby Ruth's daughter as his agent. He's been good to this family."

Lil's face drooped, little jowl pockets quivering. "This family? I thought *I* was your family, Mags."

Oh. Oh, no. Surely Lil wouldn't be so petty or cruel to pull the pout card. "You are my family. A part of my family. But, honey, whether you like it or not, life had to go on while you were away. Abby Ruth and Sera are very important to me. The Summer Shoals community is too. And if I'm called to help someone I care about, I'm sure as shooting going to step forward." Sure as shooting? That was straight from Abby Ruth's dictionary. Maggie had changed, and for the better, since she'd made new friends. For the first time since George had died, she felt alive again.

"So where were you out investigating tonight?" Lil said *investigating* as if she was spitting out sour milk.

"Just the high school," Sera offered up.

Lil made a show of checking her wrist even though she wasn't wearing a watch. "I didn't realize they were offering night classes. Not just night, but midnight classes."

The evening of excitement and fear finally caught up with Maggie, and she staggered over to the piano bench and sank down on it. "Let's not snipe at one another, Lil. Get whatever you have to say off your chest."

"You cannot tell me that whatever you were doing at the high school was on the up and up. If you were on the property, it would be a minimum of a trespassing charge."

Goodness, Lil really had learned some things in prison, hadn't she? Next Maggie knew, Lil would be quoting the penal code to her. "We were very careful." And no way in heck was she breathing a word about their close call with the shop teacher or how they'd staked out his house. Lil would scream *stalking*.

"We were just looking around," Sera said.

Lil leveled her gaze back on Maggie. "You do realize everything you do reflects back on Summer Haven. Back on me. Have you considered that if I'm associated with any illegal activity whatsoever, they could decide to toss me back in prison?"

Lord, Lil was as paranoid as a cat in a roomful

of hunting dogs. Prison had done a number on her, but Maggie could not, would not, give up this investigation. Not only because they needed the money, but because it was exhilarating.

A little trespassing isn't half as bad as being put away for fraud, Lil. Besides, you wouldn't have a secret if it hadn't been for us. Why are you so worried about my allegiance to you when I've done nothing but protect your secret?

Maggie didn't rightly like this side of Lil, but she simply said, "We'll surely keep that in mind."

CHAPTER 18

After her little chat with the girls last night, Lillian felt much more at peace. The next day dawned with beautiful streaks of pink over the Georgia sky. A perfect morning for her to take the Tucker Torpedo out for a spin. Probably best to do it by herself since her driving skills were no doubt rusty.

Before heading out to the garage, Lil glanced at the newly relocated coffeemaker. She sure could use a cup of coffee, but decided not to risk it. That chicory stuff would have to go before she would trust anything brewed in that machine. Maybe the Piggly Wiggly should be her first stop.

She reached for the car keys on the hook by the door only to find they weren't there. Why couldn't all her things be where she'd left them? When Maggie woke, they needed to have a talk about all the disarray in the house.

For now, Lil checked the long skinny drawer she used to keep stocked with postage stamps, a notepad, and a matching pen and pencil set. Now it was filled with Maggie's neatly arranged rubber bands, stapler and pen. Lil's favorite Mont Blanc pen was missing.

She took a settling breath. Later. She'd deal with all that later.

When she couldn't find the Tucker's key ring, she checked the file drawer and withdrew the spare she kept stashed under *T.* Everything in its place. Just the way she liked it.

As she headed for the garage, Lil hummed a happy tune to herself. This was a new day, and she would find a way to get through to Maggie. She twisted the garage handle and pulled to raise the manual door.

But the garage was absolutely empty.

Where is Daddy's car?

Her chest tight, Lil hurried back into the house, moving faster than she had since before Martha told her about the whole compassionate release thing. She stomped her way upstairs and banged on Maggie's door with enough force to bruise her knuckles. “Margaret Evelyn Stuart Rawls, where in the name of Pete is my car?” She didn’t wait for Maggie to respond but turned the knob and walked directly inside.

Maggie pulled herself to a sitting position on the side of the bed. She was blinking like a medicated owl and the entire right side of her hair stuck out at wild angles. “Huh?”

This was what happened when someone Maggie’s age stayed out half the night. More than half the night. “The Tucker. It’s not in the garage.”

Abby Ruth must’ve been woken by the ruckus because she was suddenly hovering in Maggie’s doorway dressed in her nightclothes and wiping sleep from her eyes. If this was their normal schedule, rising after nine in the morning, it was no wonder Summer Haven looked worse for the wear.

Maggie shot a look at the woman standing behind Lil. Lil didn’t know exactly what the silent exchange meant, but it felt horrible to be excluded. She was on the outside in her own home. How was that fair after spending all these months away? “Well?”

“Sugar,” Abby Ruth drawled. “You caught us.”

Fear missiled through Lil’s heart. What had they done?

“Maggie’s such a horrible friend that she made

the extra special effort to send your daddy's precious car to be detailed from tire to roof."

"But…but…" But she needed it back now. "I missed it so much and wanted to tootle around in it today. Mags, if you'll get dressed, you can drive me into town to pick it up—"

"No can do," Abby Ruth interrupted. "We took it to a real special place near Atlanta and paid an arm and a leg because these folks specialize in these old, valuable cars. You wouldn't want just anybody to gussy up your daddy's car, now would you?"

"No, but—"

"Good, that's settled then." Abby Ruth turned to walk down the hallway.

"Nothing is settled." Angelina expected Lil to hand over the car by High on the Hog, only a week away. But Lil wanted time to drive it again. Lord, what had she gotten herself into this time? The way things were going around here, Daddy would be haunting her in no time flat. "I didn't ask you to do this. I need you to go pick it up. Clean or not. I need it back today."

When Abby Ruth turned back, there was something in her gray eyes—a little cold and a lot stormy—that made Lil feel as if she'd just shoveled down the prison cafeteria's meatloaf. Bloated and uncomfortable. "I may not be a guest at Summer Haven on your invitation, Ms. Fairview, but I know every one of us has done things for you that you never asked us to do. I didn't know you from Adam, but I lied to Teague Castro for you. And I've known that boy since he was knee-high to a flea. Maggie has busted her behind not only to watch over a house and car you apparently care more about than you do your friend, but she's also protected your secret so you could protect your reputation. I think what you need is to be grateful."

"Abby Ruth, please don't—" Maggie started.

But the tall Texan kept rolling. "So next time you decide to pitch a hissy fit and demand people undo all the nice things they've done for you, you might want to think about how that would all play out."

With Angelina's threat looming, that was pretty much *all* Lil could think about.

MELTDOWN CITY. THAT WAS WHAT MAGGIE WAS thinking of renaming Summer Haven after the past few days. Between Lil's anger and angsty mood swings, and trying to keep Abby Ruth in check, she'd had her hands full. Maybe Colton would make her a nice sign for the estate from Slinkys, yo-yos and possibly an old merry-go-round. Because that was what life around here felt like these days.

The only two things keeping Maggie going were the art forgery case and the thought of her date with Bruce this afternoon.

"Don't frown like that. Retinol can only do so much," Sera said, pulling Maggie's hair into a tight French braid. "You look so pretty, and you don't want to ruin it."

"Thank you for doing my hair."

"Are you nervous?"

Maggie surveyed the emotion she was feeling. Nerves? Not exactly. "Maybe a little. Bruce seems so nice, and he couldn't have come up with a better first date. I love doing stuff like building birdhouses. The only way it would be better is if it was with my own grandchildren."

"He likes you. I could tell when he came up asking about you at the High on the Hog meeting."

"He did?"

"Sure did. Cornered me as soon as I walked in like he'd been lying in wait."

"Why didn't you tell me?"

"He's kind of shy. I had no idea how long it might take him to make a move. Didn't want to ruin the surprise if it took him forever, but he didn't waste any time. That means he's into you." Sera reached forward and tugged a couple small pieces of hair out of the braid and twirled them toward the front. "Don't want to look too perfect. Nice." She placed her hand on Maggie's cheek and smiled. "You are beautiful. Inside and out. Now, what are you going to wear?"

Maggie glanced down at her ratty terrycloth robe. "Not this." She got up and crossed the floral carpet of the Azalea room. She pushed hangers to the left and right, assessing her options. Pants were easy. The ones she'd worn to break into the high school would work for any occasion. She pulled a bright blue blouse with shimmering pearls from the rod. Then a red top, plain except for a drawstring at the waist giving it a faux layered look. She'd slowly been adding new items to her wardrobe since she'd begun toning up. She held them both up. "Which do you think?"

"Definitely the red. You wear it so well."

Maggie put the blue one back in the closet. Then hung the outfit from the knob on her dresser. She quickly dropped her robe and began to pull on the pants.

Sera gasped. "You're *not* wearing those panties."

"What?"

"Those are granny panties."

Maggie looked down at the high-waisted beige undies she'd bought at the discount store. Frou-frou they weren't, but they served their purpose. "Well, I *am* a granny. Give me a break. I'm sure not wearing one of those skimpy thong numbers again. You're obsessed with underwear that crawls in places it shouldn't."

"Mags, those are cotton. Cotton is for when you're at home watching Lifetime movies and chowing down on popcorn. Now, silk and satin, those are for dates. Surely you have some sexier underwear than those. Something with some high cut legs or at least a little lace."

"No one will see them. If we're in a wreck, I won't be embarrassed."

"I'm not worried about the EMTs seeing you in granny panties. I'm worried about poor Bruce. Doesn't he deserve something pretty?"

"He's not going to see my panties. Not today and maybe not ever. Stop it."

"Don't say that. You don't know what the future will hold. If you shut down the possibilities now, you and Bruce will never have a chance to flourish. Promise me you won't do that."

Maggie let out a breath. "Fine. I'll leave open the possibilities. But I'll be honest, my heart still belongs to George, and Bruce's wife has been gone about the same amount of time. I think George probably will want to move as slowly as I do."

"You mean Bruce."

"What?"

"You said George."

"Oh."

"It's okay, Maggie. That means Bruce has touched, if not pried open, a teensy part of you that was closed off to anyone but George until now. We totally need to get your star chart done. Trust me, you're moving into a new phase in your life. A good one. I just know it."

"Then why am I sweating?"

"Because you're human. Arms up."

Maggie raised her arms on command and Sera took a powder puff from Maggie's dresser and pushed her hand right up the front of Maggie's blouse to sweep a perfumed dusting of powder under each of her pits. "Good as new."

Maggie laughed. "Not sure I was ever that good."

"Pu-lease."

A soft knock came from the door, and Maggie and Sera both spun around to see Lil standing there.

"Mind if I come in?"

Maggie hesitated for a moment. "Of course not."

"You look pretty," Lil said. "Where are you two going?"

Maggie reached for her hair. She wished she knew how to braid one of these herself. It made her feel extra feminine. Sera made it fun to girly up.

Sera gave Maggie a hug. "You'll have a wonderful time. I can't wait to hear every single detail." She skipped out of the room and Maggie felt her mood dip at the sad look in Lil's eyes.

"I have a date, Lil."

"A date?"

Maggie couldn't help but run a hand down her hip. She'd never be skinny, but she was healthy. And darned if that didn't make her feel sexy. "Bruce and I have a date."

"I don't even know who this Bruce is."

Tension crawled up Maggie's throat, but she choked it back. "He works over at Dogwood Ridge Assisted Living. He's a computer guy."

Lil's lips trembled. "I can't imagine you with anyone but George."

"Me either, but he's nice. And I liked going out on those dates when we were checking out that scam of a matchmaking site, even if it was just for research."

"I'd have helped you get ready," she said.

She could tell her new friendship with Sera annoyed Lil, but their friendship was so different from hers and Lil's. Only she didn't know what quite to say to smooth it over.

"I'm getting ready to head out. Wish me luck," she said.

Lil nodded. "You don't need it. And Mags…"

Maggie paused just as the doorbell rang.

"I'm so sorry I've been so hard to get along with. I do appreciate everything you girls have done for me. Really."

Maggie gave Lil a hug. "We're all going to be fine." She stepped back with her hands on Lil's shoulders. "I've got to run, but I love you, and Sera and Abby Ruth will too once they get to know the real you."

She checked herself one more time in the bedroom mirror, then said a little prayer to George. *Honey, I hope you know that no one will ever fill the space in my heart, my soul, my life that you did. And if anyone can ever come a close second to the happiness you gave me, it will be a miracle. I love you.*

Maggie swept at the tears that nearly always fell when she talked to George in heaven, then headed downstairs. She could have glided down the stairs on butterfly power for all the flapping occurring in her stomach right now.

Before she could make it to the foyer, Sera was already there opening the door.

"Hi, Sera. I'm here to pick up—" Bruce glanced toward where Maggie stood on the stairs and simply stared, his gaze full of appreciation, "—Maggie."

Maggie's heart zinged. He had a way of making her feel special.

"You must be Bruce," Lillian said.

Maggie turned, not realizing Lil was right on her heels. "Bruce, this is my very best friend in the world, Lillian."

He held out his hand. "I've heard a lot about you, Miss Lillian. Glad to see you're home from your trip."

Lillian looked at Bruce's outstretched hand as though it were a three-day old fish, but she finally put hers in his. "Thank you." Then Lil's expression softened. "You better treat my dear friend right. Or else you'll have us girls to deal with."

"No worries about that," he said.

Maggie glanced at her watch. Quarter till noon. If she and Bruce didn't get a move on, they'd be late to pick up his grandson and miss the start of class. And Maggie was itching to get started on that birdhouse. "We should probably head out."

"Why don't you invite Bruce in for some tea and we can all get to know—"

"Sorry, Lil, but we have to be somewhere in fifteen minutes. No time to chat now."

Lil's expression closed up like chickweed just before the rain.

Patience, Maggie. She needs you, and doesn't quite know how to fit back into regular life.

Maggie squeezed Lil's hand. "Maybe another time."

"Maybe."

CHAPTER 19

When Maggie, Bruce and his grandson arrived at Curl Up and Read, the whole bottom floor of what used to be the old five-and-dime had been renovated and split into multiple stores. When the local hair salon had been bursting from its trailer seams, it had moved here and added a bookstore. The only one in Summer Shoals.

The salon side was hopping, with the cackle of gossip and the whir of blow-dryers, but the bookstore was packing them in today too. Little squeaks and whoops peppered the normal shoppers' chatter. It felt familiar in a nice way, just like back home in her and George's hardware store. Boy, she missed that place some days.

Bruce led his towheaded grandson, Austin, over

to a table already set up with pre-cut boards and a bottle of glue. *A proud grandpa.* She knew the feeling. Next time she was on the phone with Pam, she would ask her to bring Chloe and Clint to Summer Shoals when school released in the summer.

She hung back, watching Bruce and his grandson for a minute and giving her wobbly knees time to steady themselves. Before she could make her way through the crowd, the salon receptionist sang out her name, "Maggie. Are you here to get your roots done?"

Maggie felt herself go as red as her shirt. She hoped Bruce hadn't heard. "No. I'm actually here for the bookstore project."

"Oh, sorry. Well, we'll see you soon."

Lord, did she look like she needed the salon? Doubting the braid now, she felt a sweat break across her forehead. But Bruce was waving at her from across the room, and he'd saved a stool for her.

When she walked over, he looked up and smiled. "Your hair looks really pretty like that."

She lifted a hand to Sera's handiwork. "Thank you. So—" she aimed what she hoped was a confident smile in Austin's direction, "—are you excited to build a birdhouse today?"

"Yes, ma'am. Pawpaw says you're real good at stuff like this and you're gonna help us make the bestest birdhouse ever."

Nothing like a little pressure to get a gal motivated, but flattery would win both Austin and Bruce a few extra points today. Especially delivered with a *yes, ma'am* and all. "You better believe it," she assured her new best friend.

Maggie grabbed a copy of the step-by-step instructions and glanced over them as the librarian gathered the children at the front of the room and read *Even Birds Need Homes* to them.

"Excuse me," Bruce said to her. "I'll be right back."

When he returned, he had a cup of sweet tea for each of them. "Thought you might be thirsty."

"Thanks, Bruce." She pointed to the two long tables set up at the back of the room. "Looks like they want us to work back there."

She and Bruce found their reserved spot at the table, and Maggie was impressed with Darrell Holloway's clever marketing. "Look, the license plates for the roof of the birdhouse have the hardware store logo on them. Genius!"

"Thanks for coming today." Bruce took out his phone and snapped a picture of Maggie standing in front of the project.

"I'm glad you asked, and look, here come the kids."

The kids rounded up their parents, and the team projects began in a joyful ruckus of giggles and banging and clanging. Bruce was right, he wasn't very handy but he was playing photographer, and Maggie was having fun feeling like his favorite subject.

An hour later, Austin was beaming from ear to ear. "We have the best birdhouse in the whole place!" He held the length of twine from his fingers, the birdhouse swaying left and right.

"You're a natural craftsman, Austin," Maggie said, and she meant it. She couldn't wait until Pam and the kids came this summer. Now she would have someone local for them to meet and play with. And Abby Ruth's grandson would be here too. What a fun summer it would be.

"Can you come over to Pawpaw's house in two weeks and help paint the birdhouse?"

Maggie could see the likeness across the generations. Little Austin had his pawpaw's kind eyes. "How could I ever say no? If it's okay with your pawpaw, I'd love to come and help." She glanced over at Bruce, hoping she hadn't just overstepped his boundaries.

"Are you kidding? We'd love to have you over," he said.

Not exactly a date, but one didn't turn away the love of a child and the opportunity to be a part of something that might make a memory of a lifetime for him.

"And since we're on the subject," Bruce said. "There's somewhere else I'd like to take you. I have an invitation to the big charity auction over at the new Gypsy Cotton Gallery. Would you like to join me?"

And she thought she'd been nervous when he'd asked her out to build a birdhouse? The auction was even higher stakes—a public date. Maggie didn't even try to calm her ba-booming heart. "I'd love to. When is it?"

He rolled his lips in. "It's kinda short notice, so if you can't, I understand—"

"Bruce, just tell me."

"This Tuesday."

Goodness gracious, he was cutting it close. "Is it black tie?"

"The invitation said cocktail attire. I'll be honest, I'm not totally sure what that means."

Maggie reached up and straightened Bruce's collar. If he wasn't the cutest darned thing in the world, she didn't know what was. "It means if you have a tie and jacket, you'll be just fine." She, on the other hand, would have to find an outfit.

"Hey, Dad. Over here." A tall, younger version of Bruce waved from an aisle over.

"There's my son now."

Austin ran and jumped into his dad's arms, nearly bopping him in the head with the birdhouse.

Bruce and Maggie caught up to them.

"Sorry I'm late, Pops," Bruce's son said, his handsome face so similar to Bruce's. "I lost track of time."

"No worries. We had a great time. Didn't we, Austin?"

"Yes, sir. Dad, this is Maggie. She's a girl but she knows everything about tools. She's really cool."

Bruce's son reached to shake her hand. "You've made quite an impression on my boy. Nice to meet you."

Bruce beamed, and the approving glance Bruce's son flashed toward his dad didn't go unnoticed by Maggie. A million bucks? No, she felt like all the cash in banks all across the South.

She and Bruce left the store. As they walked toward the diner, he took her hand in his. "You were great back there."

His palm was a little damp, or maybe it was

hers, but holding hands was nice. "Thanks. I love that kind of stuff."

"I could tell. You're good with kids too." He held the door for her at the Atlanta Highway Diner and led her to a corner booth.

After a meal of fried catfish and macaroni and cheese, Bruce left the payment on the table, along with a very generous tip. He was so easy to talk to that time had flown by and Maggie was sorry the date was over.

He opened her car door for her. "I'm looking forward to doing this again."

"Me too." Maggie couldn't hide her delight, her grin spreading across her face. For the first time in her life, she felt like the parade queen.

WHEN LIL HAD IMAGINED HER FIRST FEW DAYS OUT of prison, she'd pictured home-cooked meals, working in her gardens, and rolling through town in Daddy's Tucker. Spending hours sitting on the front porch with Maggie, sipping her special tea even if the air was still chilly, anything that would make her feel alive and free again. But with Angelina's deadline looming, Lil felt more like hiding in the root cellar.

And now Maggie was out on a date.

Somehow that almost made Lil feel worse than her friend being the ringleader of a pseudo-detective group.

Regardless, there was no way she was about to get on board with their little investigative sideline. It was potentially dangerous, both to them and her. And prison wasn't a predicament she ever wanted to find herself in again. She'd survived it once. But twice? Well, that probably would send her into a deep, dark depression. Or kill her altogether.

Although she dreaded it, she needed to get her rear off this front porch rocker and let Angelina know she couldn't deliver the Tucker by next Friday like they'd agreed. In fact, Maggie had put in a call to the detailer and received the news it might take even longer than they'd originally promised. What were those people doing—scrubbing it down with a toothbrush? If so, Lil sure hoped it was a soft-bristled one.

Since Maggie had gone with Bruce, Lil grabbed Maggie's keys and headed toward Broussard Bed and Breakfast. In the few miles between Summer Haven and Angelina's, Lil gave herself whiplash fifty times. Amazing how easy it was to forget how to properly use a brake pedal.

Relief waved over her when she finally parked in front of the pair of candy-colored matching

Victorians, one the Broussards' home, the other their B&B. She pulled the parking brake and took a moment to roll the tension out of her shoulders. But the ache in her heart, that wasn't so easy to release.

Finally, she pushed out of the truck and made what felt like a gangplank walk up the path to the front door.

She pressed the doorbell and waited. As heavy footsteps came closer to the door, her heart seemed to inch into her airway.

The door swung open, and there stood Dr. Broussard. Lil was always struck by how handsome he was—dark hair with a little silver over his left ear, a perfect smile, and the hands of a pianist. "Mrs. Fairview. So nice to see you after you've been gone so long. How was your trip?"

"Oh, it was…fine," she said lamely. She needed to practice a response to that question. No doubt, she'd be hearing it frequently. "But I'm surprised to catch you home in the middle of the day."

"No office hours on Saturday anymore. Didn't you get the postcard my clinic sent out?"

"Um…yes, but it totally slipped my mind." Phooey. So many things had happened while she was away. "I…you…is Angelina at home?"

"Matter of fact, she is. Let me get her for you. Won't you come in?"

She'd rather not. She'd rather turn and run than talk to Angelina while her husband was there. Did he know about Angelina's blackmail? Doubtful. He was such a kind man. Summer Shoals had been so fortunate to get a big city doctor like him to take over old Doc Wilson's practice after he died.

"In fact, would you like to join us for lunch?" He smiled, his white teeth almost twinkling, and Lil could see why Angelina would want to give him such a special gift. If only that gift weren't Lil's car. "Angelina made my mother's meatloaf recipe. It makes the best sandwiches around."

"No," she blurted, too quick and too loud. After the junk they passed off as meatloaf in prison, she couldn't eat it again if it were the last food available. There couldn't have been a speck of real meat in the prison loaf. "I've already eaten. You know, perhaps another time would be better."

Angelina stepped into the hall. "Who's at the… oh, Lillian, what a nice surprise." The honey dripping from Angelina's mouth didn't sound like the woman Lil knew, but the sparkles on her shirt were a dead giveaway.

"I was just asking Ms. Fairview to stay for lunch." Dr. Broussard turned his smile on his wife, and Angelina snuggled up to his side.

"What a lovely idea," Angelina said, her voice all soft and sweet. "You will join us, won't you?"

Who was this woman and what had she done with the Angelina who'd given Lil so much grief since the Broussards moved to town a few years ago?

"Thank you, but I really can't stay."

"I totally understand," Angelina said, then batted her eyelashes at her husband. "Honey, go on and get your lunch while it's still hot. I'll be right there."

"If you're sure."

"Only the best for you." She squeezed his arm as a high school cheerleader might hang on to the star quarterback. Angelina was either head over heels for her husband or she was worried about something.

Could Angelina be insecure in her marriage?

Dr. Broussard gave her a peck on the cheek and said to Lil, "Don't be a stranger."

When he was gone, Angelina turned back to Lil with a sharp gaze and an even sharper whisper. "The car is supposed to be a surprise for him. Please tell me you didn't blow it."

"About that…"

Angelina's sharp eyes gave way to a darting

gaze that held an edge of panic. "I don't have time for a sob story."

"Angelina, is everything okay?"

"It will be fine once you hand over the car. Like I said, only the best for my husband." There was a certain desperation to her words that pinched Lil's heart.

"I'm sorry." And the crazy thing was, she *was* halfway sorry to be the bearer of bad news when Angelina seemed so stressed about this whole exchange. "But the Tucker isn't available right now. Maggie and the others sent it to be detailed and it won't be back in Summer Shoals for a few days."

"You did this on purpose. If you think procrastinating will somehow make me change my mind, you're wrong."

"I'm not trying to change your mind. I'm just asking for a grace period. What's a few days between friends?"

"Friends, Lil? You've always believed you were better than everyone else in this town, especially me. Do you have any idea what it feels like to always be looked down on?"

As a matter of fact, she did now that she'd been in prison. But Angelina's question hit uncomfortably close to home. Had she really come across that way before she left for Walter Stiles?

Her heart sank. Maybe that was why Angelina had taken such an immediate dislike to her when she and her family arrived in Summer Shoals. "I never meant to make you feel like you're not worthy. You're a lovely woman, but perhaps sometimes you come on a little too strong."

"Not all of us are born with the Summer family sterling silver in our mouths. Some of us have to scrap for what we want. And by goodness, I want that Tucker." Angelina popped her fist against the side of her thigh hard enough to leave a bruise.

Lil winced in sympathy. This was a woman on the edge. And whether it was greed or insecurity, Lil wasn't sure.

"Do you really know what your friends have been up to while you've been away, Lillian?"

Something about Angelina's tone chilled Lil's skin. "What do you mean?"

"You're so worried about your secrets, you've turned a blind eye, and they've been running amuck all over this county like some kind of geriatric caped crusaders."

Now, wait a darned minute. *Geriatric* made them sound as if they each had a foot in the grave.

"Come with me," Angelina demanded and waved Lil into a formal living area featuring a beautiful bay window overlooking her expansive backyard. Pointing to an area near the fence, Angelina said, "Do you have any idea what used to be there?"

"A flowerbed?"

"Not just a flowerbed, but a collection of very rare Hooligan hybrid roses. Each bush costs over $250 to import from a tiny village in Turkey. Tell me, do you see any bushes out there?"

"No?" Lil said tentatively, but who needed Turkish roses in her garden? "It looks quite nice wide open."

"Precisely. Wide open and bare. Which it wasn't before your friends created havoc here. It's a barren wasteland because the women you left in charge of Summer Haven drove a golf cart like they were a NASCAR team and killed every last one of my roses. Because they felt it was their responsibility to capture an alleged criminal. At the end of the Halloween event, my yard looked like a band of wild bears had thrown a frat party in it. I promptly sent Maggie a bill for reparations."

The word *reparations* made Lil even colder. She was already in debt to her eyeballs to the federal government for the money she'd borrowed from Social Security. "How…how much?"

"Five thousand."

Holy hotdogs.

"So if you've been thinking of backing out on our deal, you might want to reconsider. Because not only will I let your sordid secret leak, but I'll also tell people how you don't pay your debts. And I'll slap you with a judgment for that amount. I'm tired of playing nice guy."

If this was playing nice, Lil had better work fast.

CHAPTER 20

Sera contemplated the status of Colton's case as she sat on Summer Haven's wooden front porch. She inhaled and lifted through the top of the sternum, then exhaled with a twist to her right. "I think we need to move in on Murphy Blackwood."

"Shh." Maggie glanced over her shoulder at the front door. "We don't need Lil overhearing this conversation."

"Ridiculous to have to tiptoe around her," Abby Ruth snapped.

Sera took in another deep breath and let it out slowly.

Maggie pointed toward the driveway. "Looks like we've got company."

Colton Ellerbee pulled right up near the front porch. Did the guy have no regard for landscaping at all?

When he got out of his car, the look on his face—thin-lipped and tight—made Sera's butt-muscles cramp. Not good when she was in the *bharadvaja* twist pose. He walked closer, and the deep flush on his face more than said he wasn't happy. Good thing the man wasn't overweight because carrying extra pounds might push him right over the edge into a coronary. That was all they needed. A dead artist composting in the garden.

Sera put on a reassuring smile and rose. "Hi, there. We were just discussing the sculpture, and you'll be glad to know we have an excellent lead." They would solve this forgery case just like they had the ones before it. She was sure they had the right suspect. Now all they needed was to figure out where the teacher was making the forgeries so they could prove it.

"Don't bother," he said. "I know exactly who's forging my work."

"Oh." Disappointment threaded through Sera. Would that mean the chase was over?

"And the sheriff will be here any minute."

That had an ominous sound to it.

"That's great news." Maggie got up and headed

for the door. "I think this calls for some special iced tea. I'll be back in a jiffy." The panic in her eyes told Sera she was more worried about Lil overhearing this conversation than she was about being hospitable.

"Why don't you sit?" Sera invited Colton.

"I'll stand."

Oookay.

Colton shoved a sheet of printer paper into Sera's hands. "What do you have to say about this?"

Sera reached into her pocket for her cheaters. Close-up reading had become more of a challenge lately. She popped them on her face and studied the page. It was an email to Colton. Someone was explaining they'd purchased one of his sculptures and planned to dedicate it. They were inviting him to take part in the ceremony in California. "This is near where I used to live. It's beautiful. And this seems like a nice gesture, so why are you upset?"

He stabbed a finger at the paper, denting the middle and almost pushing it from Sera's grasp. "It would be a nice gesture if that…that…thing in the picture was something I made."

Abby Ruth ambled over. "Looks about like every other pile of sh—I mean, piece of your art I've seen."

"What's that supposed to mean?"

Abby Ruth began to backpedal. "I know you're good at what you do, else my daughter wouldn't be representing you. But I don't understand the thrift-store conglomeration you call a sculpture, or why someone would want one, original or fake. But no offense."

"Oh, you would say that," he snapped. "Because you're the one most invested in this cover-up."

"Excuse me?"

He pointed at the picture embedded in the email printout. "Do you see this? I sent a piece almost exactly like it to your daughter a few weeks ago. It was never out on general display. I'd say it's becoming crystal clear who's benefitting from the forgery of my art."

Abby Ruth stepped into Colton's space. "So what's your point?"

He didn't back down. Nope, he just stretched his spine, reminding Sera of a grizzly poked with a stick. "You approached me about finding the forger because you're trying to cover for your own daughter."

Maggie was already worried Lil might overhear them whispering and this conversation was getting louder by the minute, so if Sera didn't calm down these two, no telling what would happen.

"Wait a damned minute," Abby Ruth spit out. "Are you accusing Jenny of having something to do with this?"

"Not something. Everything," he huffed. "In fact, she's probably not only making inferior copies of my work, but she's probably already sold the original and pocketed all the money."

Abby Ruth advanced on him, getting a good handful of his sweater vest. Sera scooted between them before Abby Ruth could draw a weapon on him. Colton bleeding out on the steps would be tough to explain when Teague showed up.

"Whoa, whoa, whoa," Sera said. "Let's all calm down here and go to our separate corners."

One good shove from Abby Ruth and Colton stumbled, bumping right into Maggie as she stepped out on to the porch, sending one of the tea glasses arcing off the tray and into the flower bed.

Maggie put down the tray and ran for the garden. "Now y'all just calm right down. All we need is for Lil to be upset over one more thing."

"If you can tell us what's going on without getting combative, you can stay." Sera pointed Colton to one of the rocking chairs. "If not, we'll have to ask you to leave."

"She started it." He jabbed a finger in Abby Ruth's direction.

The man had a point, but still Sera waited until he was settled in the chair and said, "Now, why in the world would you think Jenny had anything to do with forging your work? We have an excellent suspect right here in Summer Shoals."

"It's no secret Jenny wanted to win the holiday art show more for the money than for the residency. That was one reason I took pity on her and hired her as my agent."

By this time, Abby Ruth had wandered around behind Colton's chair and not so accidentally elbowed him in the head. "You hired her because she's good at her job."

"That's true. She was an excellent agent up until the point she decided she could make more money by imitating me than supporting my career."

"Hogwash," Maggie said. "That girl is as honest as her momma. And I can attest to the fact that Abby Ruth's honesty is sometimes downright painful."

Sera added, "You say Jenny is the only other person to see this sculpture?"

"Yes, it was supposed to be a cornerstone piece for a new series of sculptures. It's all been very hush-hush, and we haven't unveiled the series title.

I'm creating sculptures representing the Chinese New Year calendar. 2014 was the year of the horse. Then, we have the sheep, the monkey and the rooster." His words sped up in his excitement. "It's quite genius, actually."

"Very innovative," Sera agreed.

"Jenny planned to pitch an exclusive showing to a big time Boston gallery. I was very careful, only worked on it at night. No early reviews or pictures on Facebook or the online gallery. This was going to be my big break."

"Would you be willing to send this email to me?" Sera asked.

"I guess," Colton said grudgingly. "And now that I'm thinking more clearly, I do need to take this to the authorities."

Sera addressed Maggie and Abby Ruth, "There's Teague now." The blue lights bounced across the front of the house until Teague shut down the motor and approached the porch.

"On second thought, I don't think he's the one to handle this situation. That man is so crazy over Jenny there's no way he could be objective. In fact, maybe he's covering for her too."

This time, Abby Ruth didn't bother to make her whack at Colton's head look like an accident. She jack-slapped him so hard his temple bounced against the chair's finial. "Only a complete idiot would make an accusation like that against Teague Castro."

The sheriff strode up the steps and said, "Who's an idiot and what's he accusing me of?"

IN RESPONSE TO TEAGUE'S QUESTION, THEY ALL started yammering at once. Heaven help him. When dispatch had given him the message from Colton Ellerbee, they'd said he was in a state. Teague shifted his gaze around the porch. First Abby Ruth, then Sera. Maggie, then Ellerbee. The grannies all looked worried, but Ellerbee was drawn up tighter than a dehydrated prune.

Teague stuck his fingers between his teeth and let out a whistle.

The porch went silent and all eyes swept toward him.

"Whoa! Now what's going on here?"

They all began to speak at the same time and Colton looked as if he was darned near ready to blow a gasket.

"Stop. One at a time." He stepped toward Colton. "You. Tell me what's going on here."

Colton sneered at Abby Ruth, never a good

move. "No offense, Sheriff, but I'm not sure you're the right guy for this."

"Spill it."

"Fine. You're not going to like it, but if you insist." Colton glared at Abby Ruth, then stabbed a finger in her direction. "She and her daughter are in cahoots. Forging my art."

"Abby Ruth Cady is a lot of things, but artistic isn't one of them."

"I believe she had a major hand in trying to pass off a barbaric-looking replica of my nativity scene's Jesus at one point. Am I right?"

Abby Ruth shrugged.

"Well," Colton said, "I think she took a liking to the whole creative process and here we are."

Colton had a point. Abby Ruth's choices hadn't been artistic, but the way she'd pieced that sculpture together had been pretty impressive. That being said, her talent ran more toward assembling guns. If Colton was accusing her of building AR15s, Teague could see it as a possibility. But animal sculptures? Not likely.

"She's a forger, and her daughter is moving the goods. These women have supposedly been looking into the whole mess, but now it's clear they've been trying to keep me off their tracks while they forge and move more pieces. Cashing in on my fame."

Fame was stretching it, but no one deserved to have their art forged. Regardless Teague knew darned well Abby Ruth and Jenny weren't in on it.

Sera sidled up next to Teague. "We have not been duping Colton. We've been trying to help. Even have good leads, which we were trying to tell him about. Abby Ruth would never do anything like that."

"You know that's horse hockey, Teague. If I was going to steal or forge something, it damn sure wouldn't be that junk."

"Not helping, Aunt Bibi," Teague said.

"And I want you to arrest these frauds and then get on the horn to have Jenny Cady taken in up in Boston. She claims to be an agent, but she's a thief. And my art is worth big money. We're not talking a misdemeanor. This is a felony."

Teague's stomach knotted. If he weren't the sheriff, he'd probably have knocked the over-dramatic artist halfway across the porch for talking about the woman he loved like that. "Why would she do that? Colton, it doesn't make sense. She gets paid a percentage of your sales. It's in her best interest to keep your sales moving, and your reputation growing."

"Not if she's double-dipping. Getting a

percentage of my work, and then taking the whole cash value of those forgeries she's making."

Teague knew Jenny was a woman of many talents, but dumpster diving and welding were not among them. "There's bound to be a better explanation."

"Right. Her momma's been keeping me off her trail while she packs away some more cash."

"Or—" Abby Ruth stepped forward, "—you're such a jerk that plenty of people want to take advantage of you and wouldn't feel bad for it. I told you we are getting close to solving the case. Tadpole, we have a suspect. Most of the proof is circumstantial to this point, but give us a few more days. I promise we can put this puppy to rest."

Teague glanced at Colton.

Colton sputtered. "Not on your life. The forger has to be Jenny because she's the only other person who's seen it. I shipped it to her myself. If she isn't the actual forger, then I bet she sent my work to the forger she hired, all the while thinking I'm working down here in Georgia completely unaware of her scam."

Teague raised a brow. "When did you ship it?"

"In March. Dropped it off at the Shipper Shack on my way to pick up more Rhode Island license plates for my current sculpture. A rooster representing the Chinese New Year coming up. There's a subliminal message there with the Rhode Island and the rooster. Get it? Rhode Island Red." He paused for agreement. When he got none, he blundered forward. "Lots of people don't ever get to the depths of why I choose the things I do. Whatever. Those who matter do."

"Hold that thought." Teague spun around, his back to the group, and dialed Jenny. When she picked up, he brought her up-to-date on the nonsense down here in Summer Shoals.

He kept his voice low, but Jenny wasn't so restrained. When she responded, he had to hold the phone away from his ear. "You tell that pompous—"

Teague quickly shoved the phone to his head again to keep her insults and threats between the two of them. He was in love with a passionate woman, but sometimes that passion went wild. And not in a good way.

"Give me a second, Jenny. We're gonna get this all straightened out. Take a deep breath, okay?"

Jenny's words petered out and he heard her doing one of Sera's yoga breaths on the other end. Finally, she said, "I have his damned sculpture right here."

"Ellerbee," Teague said, "she still has your monkey."

"I don't believe it."

"FaceTime me," Jenny snarled.

"Hang on." He pressed the FaceTime button and connected with Jenny. Then he motioned for Colton to move closer. The grannies moved in too, as if they were all connected by one big fishing net.

"Colton. Why didn't you just call me?" Jenny demanded. "I'm your agent. I'm here for you. I'd never do something like forge your work."

Colton's mouth took on a sulky pout. "The evidence points to you."

"You're wrong. Look."

Teague held the phone so they could all see Jenny standing in front of a four foot sculpture of a monkey with wings made from Kansas license plates, a garden hose tail, and wacky conglomeration of seemingly random parts.

"See," Jenny said. "It's right here."

Colton waved a piece of paper in front of Teague's phone. "Show her this."

Teague positioned the phone so Jenny could see the invitation and the sculpture in the picture.

"It's kind of hard to see," she said, "but if you look closely, you can tell the two sculptures aren't the same. The hat on the one here in Boston is made from pillboxes. But the hat on the one in the picture looks like it's made from Copenhagen cans. And what are those feet—spatulas? That doesn't even make sense. If I wanted to rip off your art, Colton, don't you think I'd be smart enough to make it look the same as yours?"

Hopefully Teague was the only one to hear her mutter, "Or better?"

Colton's frown deepened. "Yeah, it's a crummy forgery at best. My reputation will be shot."

Teague wasn't sure what Jenny saw in Colton's art, but then he was no artist.

Jenny's voice steadied. "Colton, I'll straighten this out for you. I'll go to the wire with the information. The people who matter in the art world will be on your side."

Abby Ruth shouldered in between Teague and Colton. "Maggie, Sera and I think we know who the forger is and have been tracking him down."

Jenny caught Teague's gaze, a plea clear in her eyes. "Teague?"

"Don't turn away from me, young lady," her mom snapped. "We've been working hard on this case and we're only steps away from resolving it."

"Momma, please don't make a mess of this."

"We've got this. And I'll keep Teague in the loop," Abby Ruth said to Jenny. Then she turned to

Colton and, in the most sincere tone Teague had ever heard from her mouth, said, "Colton, will you please let us try to solve this? I promise you I won't let you down."

Colton stepped away and turned his back.

"Please, Colton. She's sincere, and Maggie and I will help her," Sera said softly.

He grumbled and then nodded. "What are my choices? Fine. But if you don't get some answers soon, I'm calling…the…the…FBI. I'll have you all arrested, Jenny too, for conspiracy." He spun toward Teague. "And I don't know what good you'll be in all this, but if I'm right, you'll be thrown out of office when the county hears about your favoritism."

Colton stomped off the porch and slammed his car door before peeling out. New spring grass floated in his wake as he punched it out of Summer Haven's driveway.

When the front door whipped open behind Teague, he went for his gun.

Lil's chin cocked at a stubborn angle. She walked outside and pinned them all with a glare. "What in blazes is going on here?"

Teague motioned for Maggie to fill Lil in, then moved into the yard. "Hey, babe," he said to Jenny, "I'm sorry all this is going down. I know you're under a lot of pressure up there as it is. I miss you like crazy. But don't worry about a thing. I'll handle this, and I won't let your mom make a move without telling me about it. While they're looking around here, I'm heading to Palm Beach to check out the first forgery."

CHAPTER 21

After all the hullaballoo Lillian had overheard on her front porch, one way or another, she would stop Maggie and the others from poking around any more. She felt responsible for letting them get involved in that first case, and darned if they weren't apparently addicted to the adrenaline rush. That wasn't smart or safe. After being on the inside, she was much more aware of things that could go wrong when dealing with criminal types.

As if she would believe Maggie and the others were just helping Teague through a lover's quarrel with his girlfriend. Although if Abby Ruth's daughter was anything like her mother, Lil had trouble believing that girl was Teague Castro's Miss Right.

Lil had decided to sleep on it before taking action, figuring she'd have a better perspective this morning. But when she got out of bed, she was more determined than ever to make sure those girls didn't get into more trouble. If they did, it could land her fanny right back in prison and she sure wasn't up for another go at that.

It was her obligation as a real friend to protect Maggie, and she had every intention of doing so. Today.

Even though her lavender Etienne Aigner clutch didn't exactly match the mauve lounge pants and tunic she'd found at the back of her closet, she tucked it under her arm and marched right down Main Street and up the steps to the sheriff's office. She was Lillian Summer Fairview. She could make things happen in this town.

The sergeant at the front desk recognized her immediately. "Miss Lillian, how've you been? Heard you were traveling the world or something. Good to have you back."

"Thank you. You know I couldn't stay away for too long. There's no place like home and Summer Shoals will always be mine."

"So true. What can I do for you?"

"I need to speak with the sheriff."

The sergeant gave her a nod and picked up the phone. "Yes, sir. Mrs. Lillian Fairview is up here. She'd like to see you. Yes, sir."

"He said to send you on back."

"I know the way," she said with a quick double-tap on the counter as she walked by. The utilitarian color of the cinderblock walls gave her an eerie sense of déjà vu. Since that darn Angelina hadn't wasted any time snatching almost every position Lil used to have in this town, maybe she'd start up a new event to raise money for a sheriff's office facelift. Plus, a new cause might keep the girls busy enough to keep them out of trouble too.

"Hellooo," she sang out as she stepped inside Teague's office and took one of the leather chairs in front of his desk. "Brought you a little something." She dug a small mason jar out of her purse and set it on his desk. "Sugared peanuts."

"Why thank you, Miss Lillian. It can be hard readjusting after being gone for so long."

If he only knew. She gave him a polite chuckle. "Well, couldn't be happier to be back home. Although, I do have one teensy-weensy problem I think you'd be better suited to help me with."

"Don't tell me, you need some tree trimming done again?"

"Not this time." This time the laugh was for real. He'd fallen right into her trap that day. Bless his heart. "You know I have a few guests staying over at Summer Haven with me."

"That's seemed to have worked out for everyone."

For them maybe. Me? Not so much. Now that she was back, she wanted things the way they were when she left. But with Maggie off escapading with Sera and Abby Ruth all the time, things wouldn't be the same. Not unless Lil took action. "Yes, well, I'm worried."

"What's wrong?"

"It seems Maggie and her new friends consider themselves some sort of modern-day *Charlie's Angels* or something. Slipping away in the middle of the night snooping around the goings-on in this town. I think they're going to get themselves in trouble they can't handle."

"Really?"

She leaned forward, lowered her voice. "Let's not pretend, Teague. You were at the house when Colton Ellerbee came by."

"So?"

"So that man is a volcano waiting to blow. You can't tell me you think women Maggie's age should not only put up with his baloney, but also traipse all over creation trying to solve his so-called case. Art, my hind foot."

Teague's chair squeaked as he leaned back in it, tapping his fingers against each other.

"I told them to stop this silly investigation, but they won't listen to me." She scooted forward in her chair. "But if you tell them to stop, they'd have to listen."

"I'm not sure I can do that, Miss Lillian."

"Of course you can. You're the sheriff. You can do anything you like."

"I'm not sure I want to. I have to tell you, I saw those girls in action over Halloween. They did a better job than my own deputy could have. I was impressed."

Lil nearly collapsed back in her chair. She hadn't expected this kind of response from him. "But…but…I go away on a little vacation and come back to find these ladies have set up an impromptu business in my home. That's plain wrong. Was it too much to ask they just watch over things for a few months? You'd think they'd appreciate the roof over their heads and do me this one favor."

She was frustrated and her words were coming

out choppy and rough. For a moment there, she sounded more like Big Martha than herself. Probably not flattering.

"Where exactly were you?" He leveled a stare at her, and she wasn't sure if it was her imagination or he was taunting her.

"A-A-Alaska and a few other places." Hell's bells, Maggie and Sera had promised a full briefing on the charade, but she'd be darned if she could remember anything except for the picture from Alaska right now.

"Alaska, huh?"

"I'm just glad to be home. Vacations are nice, but home is all that matters to me. And my friends, of course, and I'm worried for their safety."

"A ten-month vacation?"

She swallowed and opened her mouth, but she couldn't lie to him. Not a word came forth.

"Miss Lillian. I know where you were."

Even though her heart was zinging around, she had to bluff. He couldn't know. Could he? "Well, you know after you're hopping from place to place and time changes and all that, the destinations seem the same."

"Salisbury, Georgia, is not that far away. And last time I looked, it was in the eastern time zone, same as Summer Shoals."

Her zinging heart dropped like a cinderblock. And there it was. He knew. "How did you know? How long?"

"I got a little suspicious at the Fourth of July parade when I saw a woman with a belly button ring and bare feet sitting in your spot of honor in the back of your daddy's car. Somehow that didn't seem like you."

"And you've kept my secret all of this time? Do the girls know that you know?"

"No. It wasn't my place to share it. That information didn't change the safety of this town. I didn't feel obliged to pass it along."

"Thank you, Teague."

"You're welcome. But about your request to have Maggie, Sera and Abby Ruth back off the Colton Ellerbee case? Well, I promised Jenny I'd head down to Palm Beach to check things out. I'm short-staffed and strangely enough, those ladies are helping me. They're not in danger. I wouldn't let that happen."

"But—"

"Miss Lillian, they've kept up one helluva charade for you for nearly a year, and it hasn't been easy for them. That house has been a handful. Not only that, but I'm pretty damn convinced they helped you solve your Social Security problem. I can't prove it, but I have a hunch."

His disappointment in her was worse than the guilt she'd harbored all those months ago when she'd been forced to pawn Daddy's pocket watches. If she'd learned to be more grateful and less selfish, she wouldn't be feeling this way right now. What happened to the no more Miss High & Mighty she'd promised herself?

Teague was right. They'd gotten involved in both of those cases for her. If she kept raising a ruckus over every little thing, she might just end up all alone in that big house.

Feeling deflated and ashamed, she forced herself to stand. "I promise I'll make you proud of me and happy you kept my secret."

LILLIAN WENT STRAIGHT HOME, BUT HER HEART WAS heavy. She didn't even bother going inside, instead collapsing into one of the rockers on the front porch. She'd made so many mistakes.

The familiar rumble of the Tucker Torpedo pulled her from her silent pity party.

Maggie walked outside, glanced at the car coming up the drive and then at Lil.

"Did you know they were bringing the car back today?"

"No," Maggie said. "I'm as surprised as you are."

Lil jumped to her feet, sending her rocker thudding against the white clapboard of the house to catch up with Maggie, who was making a beeline for the Tucker.

Lil's breath caught in her chest. Letting Angelina have this, even for a nice sum of money, would be the hardest thing she'd ever had to do.

A bright orange Dodge pickup pulled up behind the Tucker. A puff of smoke came from the driver's side window as the man got out of the Tucker and gave the guy in the truck a nod.

Maggie practically hip-checked Lil as she raced toward the nose of the Tucker.

Lil watched her run a tentative hand over the metal and hood ornament. She overheard the man say, "We finished up and know how eager you've been to get the car back before your friend comes home. That hood was a real booger bear to fix."

Hood fixed? Lil's jaw tensed, her teeth clenching as tightly as if they'd been wired together like the grid of the Tucker Torpedo's grill. She saw the gulp Maggie had just taken.

"Figured I could drop it off since my buddy and I had to cruise straight past here on the way to the North Georgia Car Rally. I have to tell you I impressed myself on the paint match. I enjoyed the heck out of this project. Sure glad you tracked me down."

"Thank you so much," Maggie said.

Since when had Margaret Rawls become devious and kept secrets from her? Probably since those other two women started hanging around. Lil tried to hold back the jealousy nagging at her about Maggie and her new friends.

"It looks perfect," Maggie said, and boy, did she look relieved.

I'll be the judge of that. Lil raised her chin and cast a critical eye on the car. As she quite honestly couldn't tell it had ever left her care, her misgivings and anger fell away. It looked to be in tiptop shape, and detailed to boot.

Tears of relief welled in her eyes. Lil blinked them back and slid behind the wheel of the beloved car. Her last connection to Daddy.

The man ran his hand along the shiny hood ornament.

"Where did you find one?" Maggie asked.

"I didn't," he said. "Your friend Serendipity didn't tell you?"

Maggie glanced over at Lil, nerves clear in her expression. “Tell me what?”

“She showed up begging me to get the car done early. She’d superglued the pieces together and filled the pits with something organic. I don’t know what it was, but my guy did some sanding on it and sent it to be chromed. I swear it’s nicer than the original Tucker hood ornaments.” He handed her the invoice. “No charge on the ornament.”

Maggie looked down at the paper in her hand. And although she leaned close to the man and lowered her voice, Lil still heard her say, “I know I told you I’d have the money, but would you be open to a payment plan?”

He rubbed his bristly face. “Sure was hoping for the whole amount today.”

“I’m good for it. I promise. It would really help me if we could spread it out.”

He nodded once, and Maggie continued to thank him profusely.

Lil got out of the car and tried to be patient and polite as the man closed his deal with Maggie.

They watched him hop into the Dodge and pull a tight circle to leave Summer Haven, Lil turned and tried to keep her cool. “What exactly is going on here?”

“It was an accident, Lil. The tree in front of the

garage got struck by lightning and one of the limbs fell."

"Right through the roof of the garage?" Lil walked over to the side of the house eyeing the garage, but the roof looked just as rough as it had last summer. Probably should have been replaced long ago.

"No. We'd pulled the car out of the garage. It's a long story and most of it doesn't matter. The bottom line is the car was outside just long enough to end up with a bonk on the nose."

"I can't believe you didn't tell me."

"I didn't want you to worry."

"Why didn't you call Daddy's mechanic? I left you all the details."

"He croaked. I had to go on a wild search to find someone else."

"That couldn't have been easy. I'm surprised you found someone so close, and young. Daddy said he had the only guy on the whole coast who could work on that car. I guess I should be grateful you took the time to find the right person to fix Daddy's car."

"Don't thank me, Lil. It just makes me feel worse for letting it happen in the first place. You trusted me. I didn't mean to let you down. I know how much that car means to you, and I have to tell you—"

"Look, Daddy loved that car to the point of treating it like a family member, but if there's one thing I learned the hard way in my little home away from home, it's that things aren't what are important." How could she ever tell Maggie she was about to hand the car over to Angelina?

Maggie's mouth went slack.

"I know." Lil raised a hand. "Surprised the heck out of me too, to hear myself say that out loud. I hope you'll understand when I tell you I'm selling the car."

"What?"

Lil wasn't sure if it was just an awkward surprise or if Maggie was mad, but she'd never seen her look like this. Her lips twitched like an out-of-sync left blinker and she sputtered, "Y-y-you're selling the Torpedo? I've worried myself skinny trying to be sure I didn't let you down and you're selling the thing?" Her voice rose in volume with each word. "We've scraped and scrambled. When we all thought that car was worth the better part of a million dollars, you were dead set against ever selling it."

"What—"

"Don't you think you've been a bit unfair?" Maggie pushed at her hair, and her hand shook.

"Now that it's worth next to nothing, you'll sell. Geez, Lil, forgive me, but this is a bit hard to swallow."

Next to nothing? That couldn't be right. "Perhaps I heard you wrong. Did you say the Tucker is worthless?"

"It's not a Tucker."

Lil laughed. Her homecoming had been one big loop of ups and downs. Obviously, Maggie was pulling her leg to get back at her for being so moody and snappish lately. "Don't be ridiculous. I know you're just trying to get a rise from me."

"Dennis, the guy who just left, is not a Tucker mechanic."

"And yet you let him work on Daddy's car?"

"When the accident first happened, I called a Tucker Torpedo expert out here. Smart guy and he had some very interesting things to say about this car."

Maggie's matter-of-fact tone had worry curling tight in Lil's insides. "Like what?"

Maggie took a deep breath. "That car is not a Tucker Torpedo. I'm not kidding, Lil."

"How can you say that? Look at that big wonky Cyclops eye headlight in the middle. Have you ever seen another car like that?"

"Oh, it's an amazing replica, but it's not a

limited edition anything, and most definitely not a Tucker Torpedo."

The tight wad of worry inside Lil inflated into a beach ball of anger. "Of course it is. Says so right on the emblem."

"No, Lil. I don't know what the circumstances were, but that car was one heck of an impressive project. The Tucker Torpedo expert thought it was real at first glance too, but it's just a replica. Isn't even all metal. Half of the thing is car filler. But here's the real kicker. The Tucker Torpedo was a rear engine car."

"Like a VW bug?"

"Yep."

No, Daddy'd treated the Tucker as though it was as precious as Lil and her mother because it was special. Not because it was a replica.

Then again, he'd never claimed it was terribly valuable. Abby Ruth had been the one to say it was worth tons of money.

But he'd taken so much pride in driving that car around the county. What if honest William Summer wasn't nearly as upstanding as she'd always believed? Maybe the reason he'd asked her not to sell it was because he didn't want to be exposed as a liar even after his death.

He didn't want people to know the car was a big fat fake.

And how could she sell a fake Tucker to Angelina? It was bad enough she knew Lil had committed fraud, but now she'd think the whole Summer family tree was nothing more than a bunch of lawbreakers.

CHAPTER 22

Maggie, Abby Ruth and Sera finally got back to the business that would help clear Jenny and keep Colton from firing her. They were all exhausted after the brouhaha with Lil and the Tucker not-a-Torpedo. Still, relief at having 'fessed up further loosened Maggie's muscles.

Over the past ten months, too many secrets and lies had swirled around Maggie and Summer Haven. It felt good to finally have one less weighing her down.

"Let's take a closer look at the picture Colton sent me," Sera said.

They'd gathered under the awning of Serendipity's van rather than take a chance on bumping into Lil or having her overhear.

Maggie had made a thermos of her tea and poured them each a medicinal—if a quart jar could be considered medical—portion of her special brew. Then they settled in.

The photo the sculpture owners had emailed to Colton was slightly blurry, making it even harder to see the individual pieces of, as Abby Ruth would say, crapola. But Jenny had emailed a clear picture of the original, so side by side they could see the subtle—and some not so subtle—differences. Hopefully, there'd be a clue in all this squinting and find-the-difference game they were playing.

Still, the larger-than-life-sized winged monkey itself made Maggie giggle.

She nudged Abby Ruth with her shoulder. "You must've inspired Colton when you dressed up as the Wicked Witch of the West for Halloween. He made you some friends."

Abby Ruth gave her the stink eye, but then she grinned. "He wouldn't be the first artist I've inspired. When I was in college, I modeled for an all-male art class."

"Why doesn't that surprise me?" Maggie said.

"Let's just say I never wanted for dates after those boys got a peek at my…assets."

Sera clicked on a little magnifying glass icon encircling a plus sign. The photo zoomed in and in. Then she manipulated the mouse until they could inspect one small area of the sculpture at a time.

"Gotta give the guy credit," Abby Ruth said. "Not many people would think to make those wings out of license plates. And the letters on those plates are lined up to actually spell words. Even I have to admit it's pretty genius. The faker didn't go to nearly that much trouble."

Sera continued to shift the picture from area to area.

"Wait a minute." Maggie pointed at the computer screen. "Scroll back." Something familiar dangled from the monkey's arms—paws, claws? What were monkey hands called, anyway? "Can you make that any clearer?"

"Best I can do," Sera said.

Maggie's eyesight wasn't what it used to be, but she was pretty darned sure of what she was seeing. "Take a look at his paw-claws. That stir up a memory with either of you?"

Sera's face brightened as though she'd been offered free tofu for life. "*Stir* being the operative word there, Mags. I knew there was something to Hollis' case."

"Well, I'll be a monkey's uncle," Abby Ruth said quietly.

"Looks like we may have swept his concerns under the rug a little too soon," Maggie agreed.

"Our two cases are connected!" Sera slapped her thigh. "How lucky could we be?"

"Why didn't we notice until now? I mean junk is junk, right? Y'all load up," Abby Ruth said. "It's time for another field trip to the dump."

"We should call Teague," Maggie said.

"Won't do any good. He headed down to Palm Beach," Abby Ruth said.

Maggie shrugged. "Well then, I guess we've got a job to do."

Sure enough, when they arrived at the county landfill, Hollis Dooley and his dog were in the security booth, snoozing away in the early April sunshine streaming through the open door.

"Hollis, wake up," Maggie said in a low volume.

Nothing. His jaw was slack and his dentures hung loose, making him look long in the tooth.

"Hollis," Sera sang.

Still nothing.

"Hollis Dooley," Abby Ruth yelled, "wake your ass up or I'm gonna make off with your walker and your dog."

The old guy sat up, his sparse hair and eyes wild. His arms flailed around. "I gotta gun. You take my Ritter and I'll pump you full of lead quicker than you can say Jiminy Cricket."

Maggie patted him on the shoulder. "It's just us. No one's stealing Ritter."

Hollis' eyes cleared, and he raised his forearm to his mouth to wipe away a spot of drool. "Maggie, Sera, you're both a sight for sore eyes." Then he narrowed his gaze at Abby Ruth. "You, on the other hand, just make me sore."

Abby Ruth laughed and patted him on the shoulder. More of a whack, but friendly nonetheless.

"We have a few questions for you about the missing trash." Maggie took out a small spiral notebook where she'd jotted down some questions on the way over. "By chance, has Mr. Blackwood been out here lately?"

"The shop teacher? What's *he* got to do with missing trash?"

Maggie didn't want to unduly accuse a man of criminal behavior before they were sure he was the baddie. "We thought he might've struck a deal with you to drum up some supplies for his classes' auction projects. They were inspired by the winning Art Fest work Colton Ellerbee did, and they're making their own sculptures out of old stuff."

Hollis drew himself up on his stool, which still

only brought his head to around Abby Ruth's shoulder. "What kinda man do you think I am? You think I'm out here takin' bribes? Just because I work for the county don't mean I'm—"

Sera cut in, "Of course we don't think that. There's no one more upstanding in Summer Shoals. We know how diligent you are about keeping an eye on things around here."

Abby Ruth snorted. If she didn't stop that, she'd have sinus troubles soon.

"We wondered if you've noticed anything else missing lately," Maggie said.

"Well, once you gals told me there was nothing to worry about, I didn't much pay attention. After all, I paid y'all a pretty penny to figure it out."

He called five hundred bucks a pretty penny? After paying for Sera's impromptu muffler repair, there wasn't enough left to even put a dent in the Tucker-that-wasn't-really-a-Tucker's repairs.

"What kind of things do you think might be missing?" he asked.

Maggie pulled out the printed picture of the forged sculpture and held it out.

"What in hell is that mess?"

"I knew I liked you, Hollis," Abby Ruth said.

"It's a winged monkey," Sera offered.

Hollis shuddered. "When I was a kid, those things used to scare the bejesus outta me."

"We were hoping you could tell us if you noticed any of these items missing from the dumpsters."

Hollis glared at the photo, squinting and moving it close to his face. Then he hefted himself up with the help of his walker and toed his dog. "C'mon, Ritter. We got work to do."

The old hound rose to his feet so slowly, Maggie wondered if they should get him a walker too. But he shook himself and lumbered out of the small building.

She, Sera and Abby Ruth followed Hollis as he slowly stumped his way around the landfill. He stopped at one container and stretched his neck. "Could one of you gals climb on up there and see if there's a big old blue lobster pot full of stuff still in the bin?"

Abby Ruth rocked back on one boot, but Sera just hitched up her skirt, threaded it through her legs, and tucked it into her shirt. Then she climbed up the metal structure. "Was it on top?"

"Doubt it," he said. "Quite a few people have been in since then. Probably under Mr. Barton's old mattress."

Sera dived in.

"Oh, and you might not wanna touch that mattress. Mr. Barton said it came from one of his rentals. Had bedbugs."

A little squeak came from inside the bin. When Sera surfaced a few minutes later, she was brushing at her arms. "No lobster pot."

Maggie consulted the picture. "What about pipes like those? Looks like some kind of water lines or something."

Hollis waved them over to another location. "Last time I saw something like that, it was in here."

"How long ago?"

He scratched his chin, then scratched his dog's ears. Then his chin again. "Few weeks ago, I think?"

Maggie cast a hopeful look at Abby Ruth, but she was shaking her head. "Paid near on five-hundred big ones for these boots."

Pretty much what Maggie figured. "You really should buy some rubber boots."

"Those ugly things?"

If Maggie had to scrounge pennies from the parlor sofa, she was buying Abby Ruth some muck-around boots. But for now, she allowed her friends to boost her up. Without Sera's grace, Maggie hung like a dead fish on the bin's lip, the metal pushing into her midsection, almost cutting off her breath. She teetered forward and backward, finally building enough momentum on the front side. Unfortunately, she wasn't as lucky as Sera going through the shop classroom window. She went head and hands down into the trash, and by the squishy-lumpy feel of it, her right hand had landed in a heap of banana pudding.

Maggie's stomach revolted. Dang it, and she'd loved banana pudding up till now. She tried to shake it off, but that only sent her further into the pile. *This is for a good cause, Maggie. Money and Jenny's reputation. Hold your breath and keep going.*

She finally made her way upright, balancing one foot on a sturdy liquor box and the other on a cracked Frisbee. The odor around her was a miasma of days-past-manager's-special meat and greens gone bad. Would she be able to rid herself of it before Bruce picked her up for the auction tomorrow evening?

She scanned the gunk around her and called out, "What were we looking for?"

"Did you hit your head in there?" Abby Ruth yelled.

"You climb in here and tell me if your brain keeps working."

That shut her up right quick.

Sera said, "White corrugated pipe. Plastic-like stuff."

That's right.

Maggie gingerly picked up a moldy-headed doll, then a plastic trash bag that made a noise like a nest of rattlesnakes. She slowly worked her way through the shoulder-high stacks. But no sight of the white, bendy pipe. "Nothing here either," she called.

It took four attempts to scramble up the bin's interior wall before Maggie could throw a leg over the side and she clung there, one arm and leg in and one set out, heaving in a semi-relieved breath and trying not to smell herself.

When she dropped to the ground, her legs wobbled and she sank into a crouch.

Abby Ruth waved a hand in front of her nose. "Odiferous."

But Sera reached out and gave Maggie a helping hand to her feet. "Do you think two missing things is enough to prove this is where the forger is getting his supplies?"

"It occurred to me while I was in that stinky mess that when we came out to the landfill the first time, we found a pile of things on the back fence line. Do you remember seeing a one-armed mixer?"

"I do. One beater was missing, and the other was a beater just like the one in Colton's real sculpture. Do you think we thwarted their attempt at a better forgery so they had to resort to the spatulas?" Sera asked.

"It's a possibility," Maggie said.

Sera turned to Hollis. "Are you sure about seeing the pipe and the spatulas?"

"I may be old, but I ain't feeble. If I said I saw 'em, I saw 'em."

"I'm convinced," Abby Ruth said.

"What in the tarnation is going on here?" Hollis demanded.

"Long story, but someone is forging Colton Ellerbee's artwork."

"Them junk things?"

"Finally," Abby Ruth said, "someone who appreciates art the way I do."

"If you could keep this quiet for the time being, we'd appreciate it." Maggie reached out to touch Hollis' arm, but for a man using a walker, he sure did scoot out of the way in a flash. "We think we know who the forger is, but the last thing we want to do is spook him."

"So Mr. Blackwood is ripping off trash to make more trash. I always knew that boy wasn't right in the head."

Maybe Maggie and the others needed lessons on questioning witnesses because stealthy they weren't. "Let's keep that between the four of us for now," she told Hollis.

"Guess I'll know when it's okay to say something when the gossip starts humming down at the Atlanta Highway Diner," Hollis said.

Sera patted Ritter and gave Hollis a goodbye wave. "Thanks for all your help, but we need to head back to Summer Haven now."

When they made it out to Abby Ruth's truck, she looked Maggie up and down, lingering in the vicinity of her hip. Maggie glanced down to find a big snotty wad of something plastered to her like an octopus. Lord have mercy.

"Sugar," Abby Ruth drawled, "you know I love you like a sister, but on the way back, you *will* be riding in the truck bed."

THE EVENING OF THE AUCTION AT THE GYPSY Cotton Gallery, Bruce opened the passenger door for Maggie, and she stepped out in a flowing black skirt Sera had loaned her. It felt incredibly sexy to have the wispy fabric move around her bare legs, and being able to fit into anything of Sera's was a boost. Maggie wouldn't have believed she'd ever fit into Sera's headband, much less a piece of the younger woman's clothing.

Lil slid out of the backseat, looking a little uncomfortable. Being out and about in Summer Shoals was probably a big change from prison life. Maggie was trying desperately to keep that in mind and be patient with Lil as she transitioned back home.

Bruce hooked his arm and Maggie wove hers through his.

She leaned in. "Thanks so much for letting Lil join us this evening."

"That's fine."

He seemed okay with it, but it was kind of a damper on a date. She'd have to make it up to him. They walked up the sidewalk past the original cotton scales and through the massive wooden doors that had replaced the trailer-height sliders once allowing big cotton trailers through.

"Tassy has worked some magic in here," Lil said. "I can't believe she transformed this place in such a short time. It was only an idea when I left… on my trip last summer."

The high-ceilinged warehouse gave the gallery a New York loft feel. Tassy and Sherman Harrison had done as they'd promised the town planning committee in keeping the legacy of the old cotton gin. They'd even used a couple modules of cotton at the far end of the building to partition off an office, and hung art along the tufts of natural cotton. Round bales of cotton served as super-sized pedestals for two huge sculptures, giving them an out-of-this-world look as they rose close to the rafters of the two-story open space.

Bruce led Maggie along the velvet-roped path to the podium where he handed over his invitation, and a young man in a black suit and tie checked them off the visitors' list. Then Lil handed hers over, and the invitation-taker gave her a double-take. "I haven't seen you in ages. Heard you were back from your trip. I can't wait to hear all about it."

A tinge of pink rose in Lil's cheeks. No one else would probably notice, but Maggie knew it meant Lil felt guilty as sin.

Maggie and Bruce walked in and meandered through the exhibit of at least forty sculptures up for auction. Each was a unique and personal interpretation of a dog, or what was supposed to be a dog. Seeing these gave her a little more respect for Colton Ellerbee's work. At least she could tell what his were.

Maybe turning junk into art really was a special talent. But what some of these kids had done was nothing short of disturbing. Spanish moss covered one sculpture, which by the looks of the shape was probably supposed to give the appearance of the fur on a Bichon Frise. But Lord have mercy, who wanted a hunk of fungus moss hanging in their living room? And that one with the skinny bedspring legs looked as if it might leap from the shelf and attack her with its handsaw jaw.

One sculpture in particular had a suspiciously familiar look to it. Probably because of the bobber eyes, just like the ones they'd had to repair on the sweet baby Jesus from Colton Ellerbee's nativity scene. Suspicion tickled Maggie's senses. She tried to push the feeling away. She was here on a date with Bruce, and she would not worry about the investigation tonight.

"What do you think?" Bruce said.

"I…well…hmm…" She wasn't sure how impressed he was, but she sure couldn't say what she was thinking with Sherman standing just feet away from her, bragging about the gallery. He was busy talking it up to some out-of-towner city types.

Bruce gestured to some seats. "Would you like to sit down or keep looking? I could get you a drink? A glass of wine?"

"That would be wonderful. I'll take some sweet

tea if they've got it." Something told her she needed to keep a clear head.

"I'll be right back."

But Maggie couldn't help herself. As soon as Bruce walked away, she edged closer to Sherman and listened in on his conversation.

"The gallery has really made a name for itself in some of the bigger cities lately. I'm so proud of Tassy. And we do love supporting the youth in the arts. After all, they are our future. And what better test of their skills than to turn trash into treasure?"

The people he was talking to nodded and rubbed their chins as though they were very impressed. Then one mentioned something about a friend of Sherman's in Palm Beach.

Bells and whistles went off in Maggie's head. *Bong! Whoo-whoo!*

What if there was a connection between Sherman and Colton's work? After all, most farmers could weld. Sherman might not be much of a farmer, but he could be a heckuva welder.

Maggie glanced toward the bar. Bruce stood talking to some people, but he hadn't yet made it to the front of the line.

As she turned to study the kids' sculptures more closely, Maggie spotted Murphy Blackwood entering the room. Could he and Sherman be working together? She snagged an auction program off a chair and ran a finger down the items on the page. Next to each item was a description of the art and the student who'd created it. She counted the items, and then counted the ones on display. They matched.

Darn it. She'd had a hunch maybe there'd be a lead here. So much for that.

Maggie casually strolled over to Mr. Blackwood's side and smiled up at him. "Hi, there. I was hoping I would get the chance to meet the man responsible for opening these children's minds tonight."

"Thank you. It's such an honor to work with the kids." He motioned to the work. "Their creativity amazes me."

"Yes. They certainly have fertile imaginations," she said. "Tell me, have you ever created sculptures like this?"

"No. All my welding was done in a steel factory back home. That's why I went back to school to get my teaching degree. Welding all the time was hard work. Not nearly as rewarding as teaching either."

"I'm sure. Well, Summer Shoals is lucky to have you. Of the art here tonight, is there any one student's work you think stands out from the bunch?"

He scanned the room but held his tongue. The silence went on and on, but Maggie wasn't about to break it. Finally, Blackwood said, "They're all special in their own way."

"I'm sure," Maggie took one more quick look at the sculptures on display. It was unlikely any of these could be mistaken for Colton Ellerbee's work. Maybe she was seeing connections where none existed.

CHAPTER 23

Lil picked up her bidder's paddle and took a seat in the third row. Two of the pieces displayed would look so cute in the gardens around the gazebo, and people would be suspicious if she didn't at least bid on a few things. After all, the Summer family had long been supporters of the arts and charity events in town. She'd bid a couple of times just to keep up appearances, then drop out and fake a deeply disappointed expression.

Or could she? What if people began to question her financial straits? That could lead them too close to the truth of her whereabouts these past few months.

You promised to curb your high and mighty

ways when you left prison camp, Lil. Why is being humble so darned hard for you?

If anyone asked, she could claim she wasn't buying anything this evening because she was planning to redecorate Summer Haven and didn't yet know which art would be best for the estate. Then again, had anyone ever questioned her on something like this? Maybe she was the only one who really cared about keeping up appearances.

She watched as Bruce carried two glasses of tea toward Maggie. His date. It was so odd to think of Maggie dating. She and Lil had both married the loves of their lives. How did a woman move on after that? Especially at her and Maggie's age.

But Maggie's slimmer face lit up when Bruce approached her. And the way she looked up at him while they talked, she was clearly enchanted by the man. Bruce reached for Maggie's hand and gently tucked it inside his.

Something inside Lil's chest moved. It was good to see someone care for her best friend that way.

At the sound of her name, Lil turned. She'd swear it had come from a group of people engaged in a hushed conversation over by an oil painting. Why in the world would they be talking about her? She didn't even know those people.

And when had that happened? She used to know every single soul in Summer Shoals.

Determined to be stoic about the possibility people were talking about her, she turned her attention back to the students' sculptures. From the corner of her eye, she caught Winnie, the owner of Love 'Em or Leave 'Em Florist, staring at her. Lillian wandered over and pretended to look at a painting in the back corner of the gallery. She could feel people's gazes following her as she moved, and a warm flush crept up the neckline of her dress. She dabbed at the sweat on her lip with a tissue from her pocketbook.

Winnie wiggled her bulk in next to Lil and threw her arms around her. "I can't believe you're finally back. Do you know how much we've missed you? This town is not the same without you. Angelina Broussard has been trying to fill your shoes, but she'll never take your place."

Lil scanned Winnie's face for signs of distrust or disgust. None, but that darned Angelina had to have let the cat out of the bag. People were talking, and their hushed whispers sounded like the Mormon Tabernacle Choir singing "Lillian Summer Fairview is a criminal" in an explosion of altos and sopranos. Her heart picked up pace, and suddenly breathing was an effort. It took all she had to pant out a response to Winnie. "Almost time for the bidding. Let's chat after."

She made a mad dash for her seat, and almost immediately, Bruce sat down next to her holding two glasses. "Are you okay?"

Lil fanned her bidder number across her face. The air felt soothing against the heat of her skin.

"Here." He pressed a glass into her hands. "Sweet tea. Take a sip, and it'll fix you right up."

"Thank you, Bruce." But her hands shook as she lifted the tea to her lips. Her sip was more of a slurp, and a rivulet of liquid escaped her mouth and ran down her chin.

Maggie's beau immediately pulled out a snowy handkerchief and passed it to her. If there was such a thing as death by humiliation, Lil was done for. She had to do something to divert Bruce's attention from her nerves.

"Where's Maggie?" She craned her neck, searching the crowd.

"Maybe the ladies' room? I'm sure she'll be back before the bidding starts." He pointed toward a dog sculpture that looked like the love child of Hollis Dooley's bloodhound and something from a science fiction movie. "I'd like to buy her a little gift. Do you think she'd like that one?"

Just then, Lil spotted Maggie across the room.

She looked right and left, then slipped behind a cotton module. Lil knew the restrooms weren't back there. Oh, no. That wasn't good. It meant Maggie hadn't listened to a darned thing Lil had told her about dropping these so-called "cases."

"Bruce—" she placed a hand on his arm and stood, "—if you'll excuse me, I'd like to freshen up before the bidding starts as well."

"What about the sculpture?"

Maggie had wanted a pet for as long as Lil had known her, but George had been highly allergic. "I'm sure she would love it."

Whether or not she deserved it was another question altogether.

MAGGIE SLIPPED BEHIND A TALL COTTON MODULE. The space was partitioned off as an office with a beautiful wooden desk in the center sitting atop what looked to be a very expensive rug. The desk lamps, with their multicolored glass shades, were too ornamental for her taste, but they were obviously expensive. The wall on the far side was filled with artwork and a bookcase with lighted shelves. Next to the bookcase was a door standing slightly ajar.

Somewhere behind her in the main gallery area,

the auctioneer was starting things up with his fast-talking explanation of how the bidding would work tonight. Maybe she should just go back and take her seat next to Bruce. If the Harrisons found her back here, they'd be upset.

Although the sign said "Employees Only," Maggie pressed on the wood, and the door swung open easily.

The large space was a shipping area connecting to a loading dock. She took a quick glance over her shoulder to be sure no one had followed her. Then she tucked in behind the door and scanned the room. Packing material dotted the floor. Several crates were stacked against the wall. To get a better look at those, she pulled at their wooden corners, inching them out to reveal the shipping labels.

The crates contained framed art pieces. Huge oils that would never sell around Summer Shoals. No one had a wall that darned big, and besides, who wanted to hang what looked like melted brown crayon in their living room?

But next to the back door sat a crate too square to contain a painting. Maggie walked over and took a closer look at the box. The barcoded label had already been prepared, and the return address label listed Colton Ellerbee as the shipper.

Probably wasn't unusual for an artist to ship

from the local gallery, but Colton had said he shipped from the Shipper Shack. Plus, Tassy didn't even handle his artwork. Why was this box here? Did he no longer trust the Shipper Shack to handle his work, or could this be another forgery?

Maggie's breathing hitched with excitement. She pulled out her phone and snapped a picture of the label and the crate, like Sera had taught her. Maggie squatted next to the box and pulled away one of the copies from the packing slip. She tugged at the crate's edge, but it had been nailed tight. Spotting a claw hammer hanging on a pegboard over a long table, she jumped to her feet. Hammer in hand, she went to work on the top of the wooden framed crate.

"What do you think you're doing?"

The hammer slipped from Maggie's hand, and gravity introduced it to her toe. The pain shot clear up to her shin, and she let out a thin scream. "Lil, what are you doing? You scared the living daylights out of me."

Lil strode to Maggie's side and grabbed her arm, her small hands squeezing with surprising strength. "I could ask you the same thing, since you have absolutely no business being back here."

"I was just taking a look, and I found this crate.

Look at the return address label. Says this is being shipped from Colton. It might be another forgery."

"Or it might be Colton's shipping out art. It's none of your business." She yanked on Maggie's arm, forcing her to stumble a couple of steps. "I told you to leave this alone. You'll get us all in trouble."

Maggie pulled away from Lil's grip, wincing at the pain shooting from her big toe. She pitched her voice to a whisper. "If anyone is going to get us in trouble, it'll be you. You need to lower your voice."

"If I saw you come back here, there's no telling who else saw you. Come on." Lil headed for the door.

"No. This is a solid lead, and I need to check it out."

Lil spun back around to face Maggie. "Excuse me?"

"Look, Lil, you're used to being the queen of Summer Shoals, and that every little thing you say goes." Maggie tossed her hands in the air. She'd about had it with all Lil's high-handed ways. "But since you went to prison…"

"Why are your eyes suddenly the size of salad plates?" Lil whispered.

"Probably," Bruce drawled, "because I caught

you two back here snooping. So why don't one of you tell me about Lillian going to prison?"

SITTING IN ABBY RUTH'S DUALLY WITH A CLEAR view of the alley behind the Gypsy Cotton Gallery, Sera smoothed a hand down her black catsuit. She was becoming quite attached to it. If they were going to make this crime-fighting stuff a regular pastime, she might have to invest in a second one. Too bad organic cotton didn't stretch the way spandex did.

Then again, she had to consider more than just what she wanted at this moment. She had loose ends to tie up before she could make a decision about staying here in Summer Shoals or returning to California for good. The clock was ticking, so loud she could hear it in her dreams at night.

The thought that she might not be in on these adventures with Maggie and Abby Ruth for much longer made her insides ache.

Her hand lingered on the black fabric. Technically, she didn't need to be wearing the catsuit now since it was nearly daylight. But once Maggie told her and Abby Ruth what she'd found last night, they'd known they needed to track that package from the gallery. It was still dark when they'd left Summer Haven this morning.

"So," Sera said to Maggie, "was Bruce really upset when he found you and Lil snooping around the gallery?"

"He was polite enough to drive us home," she said. "But the silence in his car was so loud it almost busted my eardrums. Pretty sure I blew it with him. Something about me lying to the whole town didn't settle well with him."

Sera reached for her hand. "Sweetie, I'm so sorry."

And by the mopey look on Maggie's face, she was too.

Abby Ruth popped her steering wheel with the flat of her palm. "Am I the only one thinking if the box hasn't moved in the past four hours that it's probably not gonna grow legs and walk outta there on its own?"

"We can't give up now," Sera said. Especially if this was her last hurrah with the two women. Solving crimes with them would be hard to leave behind.

"Maybe we need to regroup," Maggie said with a yawn. "Besides, Teague may get the clue needed to break this thing wide open."

Abby Ruth cranked the dually and they rode

back to Summer Haven with the windows down, allowing the chilly spring air to slap their cheeks and keep them awake. From the back seat, Sera gazed out at the rolling Georgia landscape.

They trudged into the house only to once again find Lil sitting in the parlor. When she spotted them, her furrowed forehead and tight mouth relaxed. "I've been worried about you."

"Lil," Maggie said, exhaustion filling the word, "we're too tired for you to give us a hard time. If you could save that until morning over a cup of coffee, I sure would appreciate it."

"I said I was worried, not mad." For the first time since Lil had arrived home from prison, she looked relaxed rather than uptight. "Besides, I have some information I think might help you."

"You made it terribly clear last night how you felt about all this," Maggie said. "I don't have the energy for another of your lec—"

Sera grabbed Maggie's hand. "Let's hear her out."

Lil reached into her robe pocket and pulled out a notepad-sized piece of paper. Held it out to Maggie. "Think this might help you track down whoever's been forging Colton's sculptures? You dropped it last night."

Maggie's mouth fell open and she reached out

to take the page from Lil. "You stole the box's packing slip. Why in the world?"

Lil pressed her lips together and took a deep breath, obviously wary of how to respond. "Ever since I returned home to Summer Haven, I've felt I don't belong anymore. Not only that, but it's strangely difficult to function on the outside after months in a place where I wasn't free to go where I wanted. But I walk back into what I believe is my home to discover you've built an entirely new life, a new family without me. And I had no part in it."

"I never meant to make you feel—"

"I'm not blaming you." Lil took a shaky breath, almost breaking Sera's heart with the pitiful sound. "I came in with an attitude, and believed for some crazy reason the world should've remained suspended while I was away. That's not only naïve, but it's downright self-centered. And you were right, I wanted everything to be about me. How childish I've been."

When Lil buried her face in her hands, Maggie broke away from Sera to embrace her. "You just wanted to be home."

Lil's face was slightly tear-streaked but determined. "The three of you have done so much for me. Not only for me but other people who've been wronged. How horrible I've been to demand you stop helping others."

"I hate to interrupt this touching scene," Abby Ruth said, pulling the packing sheet from Maggie's grasp. "But this package is due to leave the Shipper Shack this morning. If we're going to catch this guy, we need to get going."

"What about Teague?" Maggie asked.

"Far as I know, he's still on a plane from Palm Beach to Atlanta. By the time he gets back to Summer Shoals, that crate could be long gone." Abby Ruth pulled out her phone. Sera looked over Abby Ruth's shoulder as her fingers tapped the screen.

ABBY RUTH: T- ON OUR WAY 2 SHIPPER SHACK. goods r being shipped out this a.m.

TEAGUE: sit tight. on my way frm aport.

ABBY RUTH SHOVED HER PHONE BACK INTO HER pocket.

"Oh. Oh, no." Sera swiped her finger across her phone screen. "I put the tracking number from the shipping slip Lil gave us into the shipping company's website. The package isn't long gone, but it has already left the Shipper Shack. And that handwriting on the form? It's the same as on the forged art. I'd know those Mickey Mouse ear *L*'s anywhere."

"Girls, we've got to move."

"I want to come too." Lil stuck out her chin. "It'll only take me a minute to change."

Both Sera and Abby Ruth turned to Maggie. This was her call.

"Lil, this could be dangerous," Maggie said. "We don't know who this guy is or how he might react."

"Yet you're willing to put yourself at risk for a friend. Well, I'm willing to put myself at risk for *my* friends. Besides—" she elbowed Maggie, "—you can bet your sweet patootie that of anyone in this foursome, I have the most experience with criminals."

CHAPTER 24

When he drove back into Summer Shoals, Teague spotted Lil's blue Tucker Torpedo at the corner of Main and Merchant Streets across from the Shipper Shack. *Dammit, I told them to keep me in the loop.*

He pulled the sheriff's car right behind the Tucker. When he tapped on the car's driver's side window, Lil flinched, dropping a huge pair of binoculars in the lap of her bright yellow outfit. Her head spun around so fast she resembled a half-crazed Linda Blair in *The Exorcist*, and looked more than a little guilty.

Lil cranked and cranked to lower the window. "Hi there, Teague. Beautiful day to be in town, isn't it?"

Beautiful, my ass. The weather doesn't have a thing to do with why you're casing the Shipper Shack. "What are you doing here? Because it sure isn't sightseeing or shopping."

"Well, you see, I was keeping an eye on things until you got here. Watching to see who was coming and going. Abby Ruth said to not get involved at all. To sit tight just like you said. That's what I'm doing. Promise."

"Where are Abby Ruth, Sera and Maggie? They aren't inside the Shipper Shack, are they?" He tried not to yell, but his words came out as if he'd bitten them off in tiny chunks.

"Of course not."

Relief eased his tight lungs. He still wasn't a hundred percent sure what they were dealing with here, and he'd be damned if any of these old gals would get hurt on his watch. Maybe for once they'd half listened to him. "Then where are they?"

Lil waved a casual hand. "Oh, you know, running some sort of errand."

Lord, this woman needed to take lying lessons from Abby Ruth if she ever planned to be halfway decent at subterfuge. "Like a trip to the Piggly Wiggly or the post office?"

"They didn't say exactly."

"And they left you here alone to watch the place?"

She drew herself up, but still she was only a hair taller than the top of the steering wheel. "I am quite capable, you know." She lowered her voice and leaned out the window. "I learned things while I was inside."

Yeah, he'd just bet she had. But she wouldn't put any of it in practice today. Last thing he needed was for this mess to somehow land her in trouble again.

"Well, thanks for keeping an eye on things," he said, putting on his confident law enforcement officer smile. "But you can move along now. I've got this."

Lil nodded and started the Tucker's engine. With her tiny hands at eleven and one on the steering wheel, she barely peered over the top of it. She edged away from the curb and motored down Main Street.

Teague walked across Main to the Shipper Shack. When he strolled inside, the owner wasn't there, but Tassy Harrison was sitting behind the counter. "Hey there," he said. "You filling in here again? Thought you'd be busy with all the goings-on down at the gallery."

"Oh, I am, but in a small town, you have to help

your neighbors out. I really don't mind. Besides it gives me time to catch up on some good reading." She lifted a book, flashing him the red-and-white cover of the latest Pick Your Passion novel.

And cover for your husband, no doubt. He'd been a little suspicious of the Porsche-driving farmer when he and his wife moved to town, but they'd seemed interested enough in the community and were beginning to fit in. Maybe his first gut reaction about Sherman had been right all along.

"Know when the owner will be back?"

Tassy gave him a flirty smile. "Not sure. He's gone to get supplies today, but I can help you with anything you need."

"I wanted to follow up on a shipment." If his suspicions were true and this whole forgery thing landed directly in her husband's lap, he doubted Tassy would be forthcoming with the information. But her clamming up would be just as telling.

She set aside her novel and tilted a computer screen toward her. "I can help you with that. Do you have the shipping number?"

"I do."

"Excellent."

Teague passed her the sticky note with the Palm Beach shipment's details, then his phone beeped.

"Excuse me a moment." He turned his back on Tassy and took the call.

"Hey, boss," his one remaining deputy said. "The information from Palm Beach just came in. Fingerprint came back as a Veronica Karlov. White female. 35. I can send the details to your phone."

"Do that."

Teague lifted his head and nodded politely at Tassy. Then when his phone sounded with the *buh-doop* of an incoming text, he bent over the screen again. He thumbed open his deputy's message and enlarged the picture of one Veronica Karlov.

Well, I'll be damned.

MAGGIE WAS STILL A LITTLE WORRIED ABOUT leaving Lil all by her lonesome at the Shipper Shack. Then again, riding with the gas-pedal-loving Abby Ruth was probably way more dangerous than sitting across the street from a building. There was something to be said for staying on stationary ground.

But as she and her partners in crime fighting sped down Georgia Highway 26, Maggie wouldn't trade this exhilaration for anything in the world.

"Are you sure we're headed in the right direction?" Abby Ruth asked Sera.

Sera checked her phone. “The next distribution center is fifty miles ahead. It’s a straight shot. Wouldn’t make sense for the driver to take any other route.”

Not ten minutes later, they topped a rise and Maggie spotted the recognizable brown-colored van. “There!”

“Got you in my sights,” Abby Ruth said between her teeth, and the already flying dually bucked like a frisky horse.

Sera grabbed Maggie’s headrest while Maggie clung to the chicken stick above the window. Didn’t take them long to pull abreast of the van. Unfortunately, they were the ones barreling down the wrong side of the two-lane road.

Her heart going ninety-to-nothing, Maggie jabbed the down button for the window, and the van driver glanced over at her, his eyes wide and eyebrows like carat marks above them. She waved frantically and hollered, “Pull over.”

All the silly man did was hunker over the steering wheel as if he were some kind of rally racer. Sometimes men’s egos did get in the way of their good sense.

She tried again. “We need to talk to you.”

“I’m calling the cops,” he yelled back.

“Idiot,” Abby Ruth grunted from her side of the

truck. "Wonder if he's ever heard of *Hey y'all, watch this.*"

"If he hasn't," Sera said, "bet he's about to."

Abby Ruth jerked the wheel to the right, sending Maggie into an intimate relationship with the door handle. Might be a good time for a quick prayer.

Please God, let us get out of this alive. I'd really like one more date with Bruce before I see you on a permanent basis.

The delivery driver goggled at them, as if he couldn't believe a truck full of over-fifty women would be so bold as to make a move on him.

Maggie shouted again, "Pull over. If you don't, she'll just keep at it until you're upside down in a ditch."

He gave her a narrow-eyed stare, but the van began to slow. He veered onto the grassy shoulder, but rather than pull in behind him, Abby Ruth parked at an angle that would make it impossible for the driver to get back on the road without plowing through her truck.

Maggie would place her bet on the dually any day of the week.

Behind her, Sera was bouncing in her seat. "I can't wait to see if this sculpture is the year of the rooster."

The driver stood in the truck's open doorway with his arms spread as though he could protect his cargo with his body alone. "You're not taking my truck."

Abby Ruth climbed out, and Maggie opened her own door to make the long jump to the ground as did Sera. Abby Ruth's long-legged stride brought her around the hood in a snap. She gestured back at her dually. "You think I want your claptrap van when I drive that?"

"Stay back. I'm armed," the driver said.

"Oh, please," Abby Ruth sighed and reached into her boot holster to pull out her handgun. "I'll bet you all the peaches in Georgia that mine's bigger than yours. And it's not like we're pirates. We don't want your truck."

Why, oh, why couldn't Maggie ever convince her that carrying a gun wasn't a fashion statement or in everyone's best interest?

"Who are you and what do you want?" he asked.

With a flick of her hand, Abby Ruth reached into the back pocket of her jeans and produced a leather wallet. She flipped it open to reveal what looked like an authentic deputy's badge.

"Where did you—" Maggie started.

"Abby Ruth Cady. Chief Deputy of the Bartell

County Sheriff's Department. I'm authorized to confiscate a crate from your cargo under suspicion of art fraud. Maybe mail fraud too."

Maggie closed her eyes to gather her bearings. Over the course of this case, they'd broken about as many laws as they'd tried to uphold. Teague would either kiss them or kill them.

"Fraud," he said. "I don't know anything about—"

"Just get out of our way." Abby Ruth grabbed the driver by the uniform and *persuaded* him to step down from the truck and stand in the grass. "We'll get what we need and then you can go on your way."

By this time, the driver's face was the color of pea soup.

Abby Ruth called from inside the van, "Found it!"

Maggie and Sera made their way to the cargo hold to find Abby Ruth standing over the very crate Maggie had tried to pry open at the gallery last night.

"Hey, driver boy," Abby Ruth bellowed. "Open up the back and help us with this thing. After all, we're just three frail old ladies."

. . .

TEAGUE LOVED IT WHEN THE PIECES OF A CASE finally fit together like a kid's puzzle. Perfect. No gaps. And he'd just been handed the one completing this whole thing.

He turned back to Tassy. She must've seen some small warning in his face, because her lips parted kinda like a sexy Victoria's Secret model posing on the runway. But in a blink, her eyes flashed wild, like a deer that had spotted a hunter carrying a thirty-aught-six.

She whirled around and bolted.

As she kicked it into high gear and made for the back door, all he saw were the soles of her shoes and her hair flying like a banshee.

Teague shoved his phone into his pocket, took two strides, then vaulted over the shipping service counter without disturbing a single sheet of paper. He landed on the other side and caught the back door before it slammed shut.

Outside, Tassy was still in plain sight, running toward the end of the alley.

Teague radioed in his status and picked up speed. This wasn't his first rodeo. He'd catch her, but when would word get out to criminals that it didn't do a helluva lot of good to run? Rarely worked out for them. Mainly pissed off the pursuing officer.

Teague closed in on Tassy, and she glanced over her shoulder. She started picking up speed again, but a swoosh of yellow came sailing from behind the dumpster and hit Tassy broadside. Tassy went down in a tangle of blond hair, arms and legs and remained on the ground. Lord, he hadn't seen a tackle like that since he was a kid and Texas A&M's Wrecking Crew football defense was still at the top of their game.

Tassy thrashed around under a tiny body dressed in yellow. Lil used Tassy's shoulders as leverage and climbed to her feet. She dusted her hands together as if she'd singlehandedly taken down an organized crime boss. Which in a way she had.

Teague stepped forward and pulled Tassy off the ground. "Well, I thought your husband was the one behind all this, but your little sprint has confirmed what the evidence already proves, Ms. Karlov."

Without fanfare, he spun her around and handcuffed her. "You have the right to remain silent."

"Yeah, yeah, yeah."

He finished reciting her Miranda rights, then turned to Lil.

She was bouncing on her toes and clapping. “I took her down, didn’t I?”

“Yup, but you’re not off the hook, Miss Lillian. I told you to go home.”

“Well, technically, you just told me to move along. Which I did. Behind the building, and I’d say it was lucky I did.” She ran a hand down her skirt, brushing away a spot of dirt.

“Did you hurt yourself?”

She winked at him. “I’m tougher than I look.”

Those old ladies would be the death of him. Then again, he shouldn’t be surprised by Lil’s daredevil actions. This was the same woman who’d been on top of her house last summer wielding a chainsaw.

“Is she the one that—” Lil stopped mid-sentence when Teague’s glare shot daggers in her direction.

Someone like this Karlov would love to know exactly what Teague knew before he questioned her. *Not happening.*

“I’ll explain it all later. You go directly back to Summer Haven. Do not pass Go or anything else. Clear?”

“Yes.” Lillian turned and headed for her car.

Relieved she hadn’t given him an argument, he

turned his attention back to the real issue at hand. His deputy pulled up, and Teague led Tassy over to the car and put her in the backseat. Once the door was securely closed, he called in the status to Dispatch.

Once his deputy pulled away, Teague headed around the building and back to his own cruiser.

He tapped one button on his phone, and Jenny answered on the second ring. "Please tell me you have good news for me."

"Only if you do the same."

"Teague…"

"Fine. I just arrested the person behind the Ellerbee forgeries."

"Thank goodness. I was afraid I would lose my client, and that sure would've put a snag into my move to Summer Shoals. But who? What?"

"I'll give you all the details later. I need to get to the station now."

Before he could say goodbye, Jenny's whiskey-smooth voice lowered. "Thank you for always being there for me."

"Never doubt it. Or the way I feel about you."

"Does that mean we're even?"

"Oh, not hardly. But handling your mom? Now *that* you owe me for. You owe me big."

"Bet you already have some ideas of how I can repay you."

More than he could shake a stick at. “You better believe it.”

“You know I love you, right?”

After all the years he and Jenny had been apart, hearing those three words from her over the past few months had been heaven. “Love you too. But I’m still wondering what I did to deserve you.”

She laughed. “I’ll be sure to help you understand the next time we’re together. Tell Mom I’ll call her later.”

“Will do.” He smiled as he hung up the phone. Abby Ruth was a handful, but without her there’d be no Jenny. And without Jenny, there’d be no happiness.

CHAPTER 25

The next afternoon Lillian picked her way across the pitted field of the fairground parking lot where the Ruritan Club had pulled off another transformation. The Annual High on the Hog event was already in full swing. Colorful flags marked the path to the entrance and giant tents had been set up for the festivities.

She stood at the entrance, waiting for the man she'd agreed to meet here before Sera's dress-a-pig competition began. Strange, Lil used to run this entire event, but when Sera had asked her to judge the competition in Tassy's stead, the rush of gratitude and pleasure Lil felt was as grand as anything she'd ever experienced as High on the Hog chairperson.

The smell of pork cooking low and slow on the smokers filled the air. Every once in a while she'd get a whiff of tangy, peppery vinegar or a smooth, fruity apple. There were as many ways to sauce a whole hog as there were to laugh, and they served up all kinds at this big shindig.

Within minutes, Bruce Shellenberger walked up. Lil did like a man who was punctual.

"Hi, Lillian." He ducked his head, then looked back up and squared his shoulders. "Thank you for meeting me here today. I want to apologize for judging you at the auction the other night. I was out of line. I had no right to—"

"No need to apologize, Bruce. Come with me." She patted his arm and wrapped her hand around it to lead him toward the barn, and then pulled him aside. "I was the one who strained things between you and Maggie. She was only doing what I'd asked of her by keeping quiet about my true whereabouts."

"That's a mighty big burden, even for a best friend."

Yes, she'd asked too much of Maggie. And she certainly didn't want to stand in the way of her future happiness. Although it tore a corner of her heart to think of sharing Maggie, it was wonderful to have someone else recognize how beautiful and special she was. "You like her."

He patted his chest. "So much that sometimes I'm not sure this old ticker can handle it." Then his happy expression melted. "But I was a complete jerk the night of the auction. I wouldn't blame her if she never talked to me again."

"What does your family think of her?"

"Austin, that's my grandson, he hasn't stopped talking about her since the day she helped him build the birdhouse. And my son thinks I should—as he put it—just go for it."

"But now you think you've blown your chance?"

"Haven't I?"

Lil smiled up at him. "Bruce, if I haven't ruined my friendship with Maggie after all the shenanigans I've pulled lately, I seriously doubt your little fit of pique the other night will put her off."

"I have no idea how to get back in her good graces."

"I think I can help you out there. Let's go in here." Lil led him inside the big barn. Laughter and animal snorts and squeals bounced off the metal roof. She nodded toward the judging box where Maggie was helping Sera get two of the costume competition judges—Teague and Abby Ruth—settled.

Lil waved to them and said to Bruce from the corner of her mouth, "Here's your chance."

Bruce followed along with Lil.

"Look who I found in the crowd," she said.

Maggie wore a clear look of panic on her face.

"Oh gosh, Bruce, would you and Maggie go get us some of the yummy strawberry lemonade?" Lil asked. "I saw the band is trying to raise money to get down to Florida again."

"But…but I'm helping Sera," Maggie sputtered.

Lil looked from Maggie to where Teague and Abby Ruth were already perched in their judges' chairs. "I think everything will be under control once I take my place."

Bruce looked shell-shocked at the sight of Maggie, so Lil bumped his arm, and he spurred into action. "Yes, Maggie, would you help me?" He was pale and Lil was half afraid the poor guy would hyperventilate. "Please?"

"Great," Lil said. "After the judging, why don't we all go over to the food tent and Teague can give us the scoop about the mess with Tassy."

Maggie smiled, but there was a little quiver in her lip. Lil squeezed her hand and gave her a bolstering wink as she walked by.

Once Maggie and Bruce were off in pursuit of lemonade, Lil hung her pocketbook on the back of her chair and took her seat.

"What are you up to now, Miss Lillian?" Teague asked.

She smiled at him. "Love's not just for you younger folks."

"Ladies and gentlemen." Angelina Broussard's voice came over the loudspeaker, and Lil spotted her standing in the middle of the ring. "This year, the High on the Hog committee is proud to present a new and creative competition for the kids. In a moment, you'll be treated to a parade of the finest animals and the best costumes you've seen since my Halloween party last fall." Her face took on a tightness and she waved a hand toward the judges' box. "And I'd like to thank our judges. Sheriff Teague Castro. Ms. Abby Ruth Cady. And certainly not least, Lillian Summer Fairview."

The crowd around them clapped up a storm after Lil's name was announced. And if that didn't warm her heart, nothing in the world could.

"So without further ado, I give you the Soooo-weeeeetest parade around." Angelina swept an arm toward the ring entrance.

Abby Ruth leaned over the rail separating them

from Sera. "She didn't even give you credit for the idea."

As the kids began to file out, Sera's sunny smile increased by a thousand watts. "Doesn't matter. This isn't about me." She clapped with excitement.

That Sera, she was so much smarter than Lil had ever imagined. A lesson in this-isn't-about-me was just what Lil had needed for a long time now.

But for the moment, she concentrated on the adorable children leading their pigs into the ring. One little boy urged along a pig dressed all in black and wearing some kind of pointy-eared hat. A girl had hold of two pigs—both dressed in red and blue, one with silver cuffs around its front legs and the other with a flowing red cape. What in the world?

Teague pointed to a pig swathed in all green with a bow and quiver strapped to its back. "Is that…the Green Arrow?"

Sera clapped and bounced on her toes. "Aren't they fabulous? I mean, it's much harder to consider eating one of those adorable little piggies when you think of them as superheroes, right? In fact, they might just fight back."

Abby Ruth muttered, "Wouldn't bother me a bit to take down Batman and Superman."

Lillian choked on a laugh. The woman was

outrageous, and she had a feeling nothing in the world could change that.

At least thirty children coaxed their pigs around the ring, showing off outfits for everything from Aquaman to the Hulk. One girl was especially enterprising and was holding a stiff leash with nothing attached.

Teague leaned over and said, "The Invisible Woman."

"Definite points for creativity."

By the time they'd each cast their ballots and Angelina was announcing the winners, Lil spotted Maggie and Bruce heading their way with a box of drinks. At the sight of their smiles—wide as the Mississippi River—her heart picked up an extra hurry in the beat department.

Lil couldn't stand it another minute. She'd been dying to hear the whole story about Tassy Harrison for two days. "All right, everyone, let's head to lunch so Teague can tell us everything."

But before they could make their way out of the barn, a middle-aged fellow wearing very expensive-looking shoes walked up to their group. It was clear from the expressions on everyone's faces that no one knew him, but he looked dead straight at Sera.

"Serena Johanneson?"

"It's Johnson," Maggie corrected him. "Serendipity Johnson."

Sera sucked in a breath. "No, he's right." She lifted her chin. "Yes. That's me."

Teague cocked his head, his eyes narrowing.

The stranger flipped an envelope in Sera's direction. "You've been served."

SERA WATCHED THE MAN TURN AND STRIDE TOWARD the barn's exit. Around her, her friends' silence was heavy and pressed on her heart.

So she'd waited too long and her time had run out. She shouldn't be surprised. She'd been gone from home for well over a year now. Marcus couldn't be expected to wait forever.

Then again, maybe this was something else.

She gently pushed a finger under the envelope flap, folded it back and slid out the papers. *Petition for divorce. Petitioner - Marcus Johanneson. Respondent - Serena Johanneson.* And it seemed as if everything stood still. The squealing kids, the rides, the microphones, it all fell silent under the static in her mind.

She folded the papers in half, then stuffed them back into the envelope.

"Sera," Maggie said softly, "what's going on here?"

"And why the hell did that man call you Johanneson?" Abby Ruth demanded.

"Could we walk?" Sera asked. She couldn't stand inside for another second. She needed air and space. But she owed her friends the truth. She felt like a very sad Pied Piper leaving the barn with five other people trailing her. Their worry and confusion was so thick she could've reached out and touched it.

Once they were out in the April sunshine, she turned to them and took a deep breath. "I've been served with divorce papers."

"You're married?" Maggie's face crumpled, which was a punch right to Sera's heart. "But…but…"

Bruce wrapped his arm around Maggie's shoulders and she turned her face into his body.

"I'm sorry, Maggie." But Sera's words were completely inadequate. She'd hurt the woman who'd become the best friend she'd ever had.

"Johanneson?" Teague said. "Isn't there some bigwig director-producer type guy named Marcus Johanneson?"

Sera patted her skirt pocket, but she'd neglected to drop a box of Mike and Ike's in there this morning. Of all the days to be without her small sugar stash. "Yes."

"And you're married to *him*?" Abby Ruth's voice was flat, indicating she was just as hurt as Maggie.

"Apparently not for much longer." The words almost choked Sera.

Unbelievably, Lil was the one to slip an arm around Sera. "Why don't we all go sit down and get some food? There's no news in the world that's good news on an empty stomach."

Inside the food tent, the women settled at a table while Teague and Bruce went off in search of lunch. Sera swept her hand across the blue-checked plastic tablecloth to smooth away the wrinkles. She couldn't look her friends in the face.

Lil grabbed her hand. "Dear, if there's one thing I've learned in the past few months, it's that hiding from the truth doesn't make it go away."

Running from it had given her a small reprieve, but she'd known it wouldn't last. She'd just thought she had a little more time. "I'm married to Marcus Johanneson."

"And you never told us. Why?"

"Because I desperately needed a break from that life."

Abby Ruth tapped a finger on the table. "I saw a

spread in *People* magazine, the one with your house. That damn thing's ten thousand square feet if it's an inch. Why in would you need a break from that? And why are you driving that shabby piece of sh—steel? What do you drive back home?"

Home. Serendipity flinched at the word. Was that her home…back in California? Or was it here? Or had she ruined the most true and precious friendships she'd ever made in her life? "My birth name was Serendipity Meadow Blu. My parents were what most people would call hippies."

"Well, at least that's not a lie," Abby Ruth muttered.

"About a year and a half ago, my dad passed away and left me his van. I can't tell you how many miles my family put on that thing."

"Oh," Abby Ruth said. "Sorry I called it a piece of sh—steel."

"Death has a certain way of making life incredibly clear," Maggie said.

Sera looked at her friend, pleading with her to understand. "Yes. And after my dad died, it was like I was looking at my life through a painfully clean window. I had a big house, a famous husband, but I felt like a black hole."

"And so you ran away."

"I didn't run. I told Marcus I needed some time

to get my head on straight. To figure out what I wanted from life. My life, not his."

"But now it's time to fish or cut bait."

"He's been so patient, but yes, it's time. The decision might've been so much easier if I hadn't made such wonderful friends. I honestly feel like I belong here." She swept away the tears as she choked out the words.

The men returned to the table with two trays full of food. And although Sera wasn't hungry in the least, that piece of chocolate cream pie Teague was passing her might soothe her wounded soul.

Everyone dove into the goodies.

Sera was thankful for the break from the prying questions and also the chocolate because no sugar-free gluten-free tofu chicory natural stuff would make a girl feel better after being served like that.

She took an oversized bite of pie and closed her eyes, praying the sugar would somehow soften the day's blows.

A hand rested on her shoulder. "We love you, Sera. You're family to us," Maggie said.

And like her dad had always told her, the world's problems rebalanced themselves. *We must shift and stay in tune.* Lil was back and her problems were finally righting themselves. Now Sera's past had to be dealt with. She prayed she hadn't waited too long to do the right thing, because frankly she still wasn't sure what the right thing was.

GOODNESS GRACIOUS, LIL THOUGHT. SERA HAD certainly just dropped a bomb on them. And by the way the gal was stuffing chocolate pie into her mouth, she didn't want to talk about it anymore.

Time to change the subject. "Okay, Teague," Lil said. "We need to know everything."

"Well," he said, "it was a little more complicated than any of us realized. And Tassy Harrison aka Veronica Karlov was right in the big middle of it."

Abby Ruth stomped her foot, sending the whole table wiggling in a shimmy. "I knew it. That Tassy was too pretty to be true."

"Not just pretty," Teague said, "but pretty darned smart too."

"Spill it, Tadpole."

"This whole thing was way bigger than just Ellerbee. In fact, his piddly few sculptures were a fraction of the whole operation."

"Operation?" Sera said around a mouthful of pie. "That sounds serious."

Teague rubbed a palm across his forehead. "If

I'd known how dangerous this might've been, there's no way I would've let the three of you investigate the forgeries."

Lil piped up, "Four."

"Excuse me?"

"The four of us," Lil said, tapping a finger in the air counting off Maggie, Sera, Abby Ruth and herself. "Or did you forget I was the one who stopped Tassy?" Lil suddenly knew exactly why the girls were so keen on continuing the investigations. She wouldn't soon forget the thrill of taking down that woman.

Teague cleared his throat. "I stand corrected. Anyway, Veronica Karlov is the daughter of Dimitri Karlov."

Abby Ruth snapped her fingers. "Wait a minute, something about that name sounds familiar."

"Probably because law enforcement agencies here and abroad have been trying to track down Dimitri Karlov for years. Lots of people knew he was moving fakes through the art world, but no one could seem to catch him. Up until recently, he dealt mainly in oil paintings."

"What in the world made him turn to junk art?"

"Apparently, his daughter took a real liking to Ellerbee's work and convinced her dad they could make millions off the stuff," Teague said. "She expected Colton's reputation to explode and her family would profit when it did."

"Well," Abby Ruth drawled, "in a backwards sort of way, I think that was a compliment to Jenny's skill as an artists' agent."

Maggie leaned forward on the table. "But Colton was so adamant that no one had seen the sculpture he shipped to Jenny."

Sera raised her hand and waggled it as if she had the right answer to a teacher's question. "I've got this one. During the High on the Hog committee meeting, Tassy mentioned she'd asked Colton about fixing the smokers and he kicked her out of his workshop. What do you want to bet that's when she saw it?"

Teague pushed away his now empty plate. "And you'll be glad to know we located your wayward nativity scene sheep. It was hidden under a draped packing table at the gallery. I'm not sure when or how she took it from your garage. She hasn't 'fessed up to that yet."

"I think I can fill that one in," Maggie said. "She brought us banana nut bread. Oh, I guess it must've been the end of January. We all thought it was such a nice gesture. Should've known she was up to something."

"Good news is Veronica was willing to give up

her dear old dad and her brother in order to get immunity. The dad and brother will be facing federal charges."

Maggie pushed back her bangs. "You mean to tell me we busted up an international art fraud ring?"

With a sigh, Teague looked up at the tent's ceiling. "I don't even know how to answer that."

Abby Ruth whacked him on the back. "Just say yes. Then you can say thank you and ask if we're available for consulting jobs."

Her heart full of satisfaction and hope, Lil smiled. Somehow, she knew this was only the beginning of what she and these women could accomplish together.

She looked up from her pulled pork sandwich to find Angelina striding through the crowd directly toward the table. She stopped across from Lil, one hand on her hip and her toe tapping. "We have a little business to take care of."

Lord, this wouldn't be easy. Lil had debated with herself for days about how to handle Angelina. Pride, nostalgia and responsibility had been duking it out inside her. But now it was time to make a decision and stand by it.

She bumped Maggie with her hip, asking for her to scoot her chair over so Lil could get up from the table. Maggie wouldn't budge. "You don't have to do—"

"I do, Mags. It's time to deal with this."

Bruce pulled Maggie's chair closer to his own, so Lil could get up. Standing next to Angelina, Lil barely came to the woman's shoulder. Apparently, she'd lord over Lil one way or another.

Lil walked outside with Angelina. "I must be honest with you," she said. "My daddy's car has ten times more sentimental value than anything else. I don't understand why you'd want it. I mean you and your husband have fancy cars. New ones with sexy features. Have you ever driven a car this old? No power steering or brakes, and believe me, it's not the easiest thing to park."

Angelina swung around and glared. "A deal is a deal, Lillian. Don't you go trying to manipulate me. I want that car and you already promised it to me for fifty thousand dollars. I've got the cash right here." She patted her garish animal-print purse.

Still, Lil felt as though she needed to dissuade her. After all, the car wasn't really a Tucker. "I don't feel right about this."

"Don't you back out on me now, or I'll make quick business of spreading the word about your little time share location." Angelina leaned in so close that Lil nearly choked on her perfume and glitter. "Do. Not. Try. Me."

Lil didn't like to be threatened, but then Angelina wasn't holding anything over her head anymore. If people had been talking about her the other night at the auction, the gossip about her being in prison had spread all over town by now.

Maybe selling Angelina Daddy's car was like all the karma stuff Sera always talked about. A way for the universe to even out the ebb and flow of energy. Of negativity and positivity.

Lil's momma would call it Angelina getting her just desserts.

Lil pasted a sweet smile on her face. "You're right. A Summer never goes back on her word." Lil dangled the keys in front of Angelina.

Her eyes turned sharp with greed. "Oh, the keychain matches the pretty blue paint!" She lunged for the keys and Lillian snatched them out of her reach.

"But first, I must insist on the money."

Angelina's mouth drooped, but she looked over one shoulder, then the other. Finally, she slipped a hand into her purse and pulled out a quart-sized baggie with two stacks of bills inside it. "All in hundreds."

Lil took the bag and unzipped it.

"It's all there. I wouldn't cheat you."

Maybe not, but Lil had learned in prison that you couldn't always take a person at her word. She flipped through the corners of each stack like one of those books that made it look as if a cartoon character were running. Excellent. Lots of zeroes running through both stacks. "It all looks in order. You can come by Summer Haven later, and I'll sign over the title."

Lil slipped the baggie into her own pocketbook, then pressed the keychain into Angelina's hand. "I hope this car brings you everything you deserve. It's been a wonderful part of my family. The memories. They're the most special thing about this car."

Then Lil simply turned away, walking back to join her friends in the celebratory meal. Even though Angelina was getting exactly what she deserved, Lil couldn't bear to watch her drive off in a car that had been a part of the Summer family all these years.

When she strolled back inside the tent, she paused for a moment to gaze at the table full of people—Maggie and Bruce, Sera, Teague. Even Abby Ruth. Full of her family. Blood or no blood, they were hers.

And losing a car wasn't going to change that.

Before Lil could take her seat again, Darrell Holloway rushed over to the table and said in a voice that probably carried clear across the fairgrounds. "Lordy be, you will not believe what I just overheard. Some people are talking about you, Miss Lillian. Is it true, you being in Walter Stiles Prison Camp? That's too much to believe."

Only the look on Darrell's face wasn't horrified. More like surprise and interest.

Lil glanced around at the surrounding tables. It was true people were looking her way, but no one seemed to mind one bit that she'd gone to jail. There were no snarls or gasps. People were smiling and nodding, looking right darned impressed.

She'd paid her dues after all and been released early. Now it didn't seem like such a scandal anymore. Good manners never went out of style. And lying was far worse than the truth.

Regardless of whether or not Angelina had spilled the beans, Lillian's time in prison was public record. And it was time to not only be honest with others but with herself as well. "A Summer always pays their debts. I did wrong, and I paid for it."

Darrell dragged a chair over and sat right down. "Have you seen that show *Orange is the New Black?* Did *you* have to wear orange? I can't imagine it was a good color on you. And have mercy, I bet prison was so dangerous and scary. You probably saw some fights." Darrell's mouth and eyes rounded. "Maybe you were in some. I'm sorry, but it's just so darned exciting. I mean, someone I know. A lady like you, a member of the Summer family, in a place like that!"

Lil's first instinct was to lift her chin or deflect the conversation, but she wasn't that woman anymore. "I wouldn't say it was exciting—" although it had been at times, "—but I will say it was educational."

"You should write a book."

Her, write a book? Such a thing had never crossed Lil's mind.

"He's right, Lil," Maggie said. "I can only imagine the stories."

Darrell rocked back and nodded. "If Miss Lillian wrote a book like that, she'd totally be sitting in high cotton."

A slow grin spread across Lil's face. "In high cotton? Now that sounds like a pretty good place to be."

Thanks bunches for reading *Deviled Eggs and Deception*!

Want more of Lil and the gals?

Discover what happens when they try to nab a gun thief in **FRIED PICKLES AND A FUNERAL.**

When Hollywood A-listers swarm the small town of Summer Shoals, Georgia, for a celebrity funeral, Lillian takes in a temporary houseguest. She's put him up in Abby Ruth's empty bedroom, but after the charming visitor leaves, her adored arsenal has also disappeared.

Lil, Maggie, and Sera are in a tizzy trying to find the guns before Abby Ruth returns home. Then, when Abby Ruth divulges a heartbreaking secret, her friends are more determined than ever to solve this crime. Only this time the gals have crossed the line into deeper, more dangerous territory than ever before.

Will these female sleuths recover Abby Ruth's guns, or will they find themselves buried under a heap of lies?

Read the first chapter of FRIED PICKLES AND A FUNERAL at the end of this book.

RECIPES

ABBY RUTH'S TEXAS DEVILED EGGS

INGREDIENTS

- 6 hard boiled eggs, peeled
- 1 tablespoon chopped green onions
- 1 tablespoon chopped fresh cilantro
- 1 small serrano or jalapeño pepper, seeded and finely chopped
- ¼ cup mayonnaise
- 1 teaspoon yellow mustard
- ½ teaspoon salt
- ¼ cup shredded sharp cheddar cheese

- Chili powder or Seasoned Salt

DIRECTIONS

1. Cut eggs in half lengthwise; carefully remove yolks, and place them in a small bowl.
2. Mash egg yolks and stir in the mayo until smooth.
3. Add green onions, cilantro, finely chopped and seeded (or leave 'em in if you like it hot. Abby Ruth does!) pepper, yellow mustard and salt.
4. Spoon yolk mixture into egg white halves.
5. Sprinkle with cheddar cheese and desired amount of chili powder or seasoned salt for a colorful dash.
6. Cover and chill until ready to serve.

TRULY SOUTHERN DABBA DEVILED EGGS

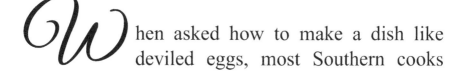

When asked how to make a dish like deviled eggs, most Southern cooks will tell you a dabba this and a dabba that. If you have to measure things too closely, it takes all the fun out!

INGREDIENTS

- Boiled eggs, peeled. Doesn't matter how many because you'll be eye-balling all the rest of the ingredients.
- Pickle relish, either sweet or dill, but probably not both
- Mayonnaise, Duke's preferred
- Mustard, plain ol' yellow or you can fancy it up with Dijon or whatnot
- Salt and pepper, to taste
- Cayenne pepper, to taste
- Paprika
- Any other mixin's you've got a hankering for

DIRECTIONS

1. Boil, peel and halve your eggs. (Want perfect boiled eggs? Put them in a pan of water and bring to a roiling boil. Once

the water boils, turn off the burner. That's right--OFF. If you're cooking on electric, move the pan off the burner. If you're cooking with gas or induction, just leave the pan right where it is. Let the eggs sit in the hot water 13-14 minutes before draining and cooling with cold water.)

2. Pop the yolks into a bowl and smush 'em up with a fork.
3. Dump in several tablespoons of relish, depending on your fondness for pickles. (If you want super smooth filling, you can stir in the condiments first.)
4. Do the same with the mayo and then toss in a teaspoon or so of mustard.
5. Add about a teaspoon of salt and somewhere in the neighborhood of ¼ to ½ teaspoon of pepper.
6. Dump in some cayenne. Unless you're a weenie, then you can leave it out all together.
7. Stir everything up and give it a taste. It'll probably need a tad more salt. It always does.
8. Once you've got your filling the way you like it, spoon it back into the egg

halves and sprinkle on a little paprika (or more cayenne) to make 'em pretty.
9. Elbow everyone else outta the way and enjoy!

TASSY'S BANANA NUT BREAD

Lil and the gals have to give credit where credit is due, and Tassy does cook up a mighty fine Banana Nut Bread.

INGREDIENTS

- ¼ cup canola oil
- ¼ cup salted butter, softened
- 1 cup granulated sugar
- 2 whole ripe bananas, mashed
- 2 large eggs, room temperature
- 1 teaspoon vanilla
- 1½ cups all-purpose flour
- 1 teaspoon baking powder
- ½ teaspoon salt
- ¼ cup buttermilk
- ¾ cup walnuts, chopped

DIRECTIONS

1. Preheat oven to 325 degrees. Grease light colored loaf pan with non-stick cooking spray and set aside.
2. In a large bowl, mix oil, butter, and sugar until well combined. Stir in eggs, vanilla, and banana until smooth.
3. Gently stir in dry ingredients and buttermilk until a uniform batter has formed, scraping sides to remove any lumps.
4. Stir in ½ cup walnuts. Pour into prepared pan and top with remaining ¼ cup chopped nuts.
5. Bake for 50 to 60 minutes in the lower half of the oven or until completely baked.
6. Remove from the oven and cool at least 15 minutes before removing from pan (if you can wait that long!). Slice and serve.

MAGGIE'S SPECIAL ICED TEA

When Maggie and the gals have a hard day (or a celebration), they turn to Maggie's special iced tea recipe. Its sweet taste with a kick tends to soothe any troubles or make a good day just that much better. Oh, and if you're tempted to leave the "special" outta this tea, then please note that it'll still taste pretty darn good, but it won't be Maggie's tea!

Maggie recommends a glass jug for this recipe, but heck, use what'cha got, people!

INGREDIENTS

- 3 family-sized tea bags (or 10 regular-sized tea bags)
- Water
- 1½ cups sugar
- A bit of "special" - either bourbon or Irish whiskey. Maggie's been known to enjoy some Crown Royal, but Abby Ruth is solidly in the Jameson camp.

DIRECTIONS

1. Place the tea bags into a gallon-size glass jug (or whatever you have on hand).

2. Boil up your water (a tad less than a gallon because you'll be adding in some sugar and some "special").
3. Once the water has come to a full rolling boil, gently pour it over the tea bags in your jug.
4. Let the whole shebang steep for about 3-5 minutes, depending on how strong you like your tea. Maggie prefers it strong, so she goes the whole 5 minutes.
5. Stir it up a bit and then remove the tea bags. Use a slotted spoon, or a wooden spoon if you want to wrap the tea bag strings around it and squeeze all the liquid out.
6. Toss in about a cup and a half of sugar and stir until dissolved.
7. Chill the tea in the fridge for as long as you can stand it. Once the tea is cool, add the "special" one jigger at a time until you're satisfied with the taste and strength.
8. Pour that deliciousness over a tall glass of ice, take it to the front porch, and sip your worries away!

BOOKS IN THE SERIES

IN FOR A PENNY

COLLARD GREENS AND CATFISHING

DEVILED EGGS AND DECEPTION

FRIED PICKLES AND A FUNERAL

WEDDING MINTS AND WITNESSES

Jenny & Teague Stories

CHRISTMAS COOKIES AND A CONFESSION

SWEET TEA AND SECOND CHANCES

ACKNOWLEDGMENTS

We are so grateful to the fabulous team of people who help us bring these books to you.

Heartfelt appreciation to our amazing editing team: Deb Nemeth, who has been with us every step of the way. We've decided she gets to be an honorary granny with the two of us. Thanks for always making us look smart and the grannies look good! And to Kimberly Cannon, thanks so much for being the clean sweep before we go to press.

A toss of colorful confetti to celebrate our artistic team: Michelle Preast, who originally brought our vision of the grannies to life, then put both of us in character format so we could all play together. We're having a ball with the cartoons, especially as we hit the road on our Spring 2015

2600-mile road trip to celebrate book three in this series.

A big 21-gun salute to our law-abiding technical advisors: Wilson, you swooped in at just the right time to help us work through the bad-guy scenarios and reined us in when we went a little loco. Not an easy job. And thanks again to Adam Firestone, who outfitted Abby Ruth with her gun collection and taught us about antique Spanish firearms. That research has been so much fun to pull back out every time Abby Ruth gets wild. And that's pretty often.

Most importantly, we both have the best support system in the world. Our families—especially Miss Bettie, Tech Guy, and Smarty Boy—and closest friends make every moment we spend creating this series that much more special because you're all a part of it.

AND TO ALL OF YOU READING THIS ~ THANK YOU!

ABOUT KELSEY BROWNING

USA Today bestselling author **Kelsey Browning** writes contemporary romance, romantic suspense, and cozy mystery. Her Georgia-set, co-authored Seasoned Southern Sleuths mystery series is described by readers as "The Golden Girls meet Dirty Harry." Her single title romances garner reviews that call her writing funny, sassy, and full of sizzling chemistry. Originally from a Texas town smaller than the ones she writes about, Kelsey has also lived in the Middle East and Los Angeles, proving she's either adventurous or downright nuts. These days, she makes her home in northeast Georgia with her tech-savvy husband, her smart-talking son, and a (fingers crossed) future therapy pup. Find Kelsey online at KelseyBrowning.com.

For info on her upcoming releases, subscribe to her Sass Kickin' News.

ABOUT NANCY NAIGLE

USA Today bestselling author **Nancy Naigle** whips up small-town love stories with a dash of suspense and a whole lot of heart. She began her popular contemporary romance series, Adams Grove, while juggling a successful career in finance and life on a seventy-six-acre farm. Two of Nancy's novels, Christmas Joy and Hope at Christmas, premiered on Hallmark Countdown to Christmas in 2018. Now happily retired, she devotes her time to writing, antiquing, and the occasional spa day with friends. A native of Virginia Beach, she currently calls North Carolina home. Join Nancy on Facebook and sign up for her newsletter at www.NancyNaigle.com.

ALSO BY KELSEY BROWNING

PROPHECY OF LOVE SERIES

Sexy contemporary romance

Stay With Me

Hard to Love

TEXAS NIGHTS SERIES

Sexy contemporary romance

Personal Assets

Running the Red Light

Problems in Paradise

Designed for Love

SEASONED SOUTHERN SLEUTHS MYSTERY SERIES w/NANCY NAIGLE

Southern cozy mysteries

In For a Penny

Collard Greens and Catfishing

Deviled Eggs and Deception

Fried Pickles and a Funeral

Wedding Mints and Witnesses

JENNY & TEAGUE STORIES

Contemporary romance with a dab of mystery

Christmas Cookies and a Confession

Sweet Tea and Second Chances

STEELE RIDGE SERIES

Romantic suspense collaboration with Tracey Devlyn & Adrienne Giordano

The BEGINNING

Going HARD

Living FAST

Loving DEEP

Breaking FREE

Roaming WILD

Stripping BARE

Enduring LOVE

Vowing LOVE

STEELE RIDGE: THE KINGSTONS

Romantic suspense collaboration with Tracey Devlyn & Adrienne Giordano

Craving HEAT

Tasting FIRE

Searing NEED

Striking EDGE

Burning ACHE

STEELE RIDGE CHRISTMAS CAPERS

Romantic suspense collaboration with Tracey Devlyn & Adrienne Giordano

The Most Wonderful Gift of All

A Sign of the Season

His Holiday Miracle

A Holly Jolly Homecoming

Hope for the Holidays

All She Wants for Christmas

Jingle Bell Rock Tonight

Not So Silent Night

A Rogue Santa

The Puppy Present

For the Love of Santa

Beneath the Mistletoe

NOVELLAS

Sexy contemporary romance

Amazed by You

Love So Sweet

ALSO BY NANCY NAIGLE

The Adams Grove Series

Book 1:: Sweet Tea and Secrets

Book 2:: Wedding Cake and Big Mistakes

Book 3:: Out of Focus

Book 4:: Pecan Pie and Deadly Lies

Book 5:: Mint Juleps and Justice

Book 6:: Barbecue and Bad News

Boot Creek Series

Book 1:: Life After Perfect

Book 2:: Every Yesterday

Book 3:: Until Tomorrow

Single Titles

Sand Dollar Cove

Christmas Joy

Hope at Christmas

Christmas in Evergreen

Dear Santa

The Secret Ingredient

Christmas in Evergreen: Letters to Santa

Recipe For Romance

Christmas Angels

inkBLOT – co-written with Phyllis Johnson

Read on for a fun excerpt from book four, FRIED PICKLES AND A FUNERAL.

Chapter One

The six-shooter was pointed right at Sera, momentarily jolting her out of her sorrow.

Thank goodness it wasn't a real gun, but a float-size wreath in the shape of a revolver, which might've looked right at home had she been back in California for the Rose Parade, rather than in Georgia with Lil and Maggie.

As Sera and her friends walked closer to the massive building looming in front of them, Holy Innocence Mausoleum looked anything but innocent today. A crowd was growing in the area surrounding the cannon-size handgun wreath. So lowbrow. Besides, hadn't these people been taught never to point a gun? Even one made of flowers.

Sera lifted a handkerchief graced with tiny, hand-stitched hummingbirds on one corner to dab at a tear beneath her Miu Miu sunglasses. "I still can't believe she's gone."

"I hate that these terrible circumstances brought you back to us." Maggie grabbed Sera's hand. "But it's good to see you."

Lil tugged at the peplum of her yellow suit jacket. "Look at all these people. I've never seen so many Western hats in one place. She was obviously loved by many. Bless her heart."

"My goodness. Would you look at that wreath over there?" Maggie pointed toward a spray of all-white carnations with a fringed cowboy boot in the center. "Wish Abby Ruth was here to see this. She'd have loved it."

Sera sniffed back a tear. "Only Abby Ruth would have expected that boot to be blazing red."

Lil and Maggie both nodded, the tender thought lightening the heavy mood.

"It's odd not to have her here," Sera said. Standing tall and strong, Abby Ruth was always the one anchoring their foursome. Instead, Sera's husband, Marcus, made up the fourth today. Well, he would be once he parked the car and caught up to them.

More floral arrangements stood nearly eight-feet deep along each side of the mausoleum's entrance, giving the otherwise cold, harsh facade an inappropriately festive look.

"I know folks are trying to show their love and appreciation." The words caught in Sera's throat. "But she'd have hated the waste of all of these flowers. The money could've been spent on something that would help others."

"Even if they were cheap sunflowers and alstroemeria, with so many, the money adds up quickly," Maggie agreed.

"More than Summer Shoals raised at the last High on the Hog event," Lil said with a quick *tsk*.

"Easily, and they'll all be wilting and dying before sunrise," Sera said. One more dreary sign of death, which seemed to be the subtitle in every direction.

The tiny pillbox hat balancing atop Lil's freshly dyed blue-blond curls—a combo not too many people could pull off—gave the matriarch of Summer Shoals a look of royalty. A thin man with a bad highlight job darted out in front of them and snapped pictures, clearly focused on Lil, who looked like a Hollywood A-lister today.

"No pictures," Sera said, waving the skinny guy away, a habit she fell back into so easily. "How are we supposed to mourn with these vultures all over the place? What was her family thinking with all this fanfare?" If she had to guess, they'd probably tipped off the paparazzi themselves.

Once the photographer moved on to another victim, Maggie said, "Everyone shows their love in a different way. Can't really judge that, can we?"

Sera, Lil, and Maggie walked in lockstep. Three styles. Three sizes. But three women equally affected by today's sad affair for their own reasons.

True friends.

Sera was thankful that Lil and the other girls hadn't pitched a hissy fit and thrown her out on her fanny when they'd found out the truth about her life in California. During the time she lived with them here in Georgia, she'd omitted the tidbit that she was the wife of Marcus Johanneson, one of the most influential men in the Hollywood film industry. A triple threat, Marcus had been an actor first, then he began directing and producing his own movies. Only a few people had a résumé as impressive as his. He had the magic touch when it came to selecting blockbuster movies, and everyone who was anyone wanted to be considered for one of his projects.

"There are so many people here." Lil's head swiveled right and left. "I think I saw Michael Douglas over there. Sera, tell me you've met him. Or even better, his daddy."

"We've met." Although Sera had told herself she'd never keep anything from her friends again, elaborating on the fact that Michael and Kirk were much more than business acquaintances didn't feel appropriate.

Lil touched her heart. "I do love those men. I swear, I think they could wake up my last working hormone."

Maggie nudged her best friend. "Lil, we're not *that* old."

Lil's eyebrows danced. "That might be true, because I do believe that I'd be tempted to rise from the dead if all these folks showed up at my funeral."

Sera would've never expected anything less than a standing-room-only, Hollywood-style full house for Jessie Wyatt. Even in death. Jessie might've been one of the most famous movie stars of her time, but to Sera, she'd been a dear friend. Since the day they'd met on one of Marcus's movie sets, Jessie had been Sera's lifeline and advisor during the tumultuous tides of her marriage.

Sera wished Finn, could've made it for the funeral. She would've simply said, "Lil, Maggie,

Abby Ruth, please meet my son." Then they would've been so taken with his good looks and charm that they would've easily forgiven her. And it would've kept her from having to explain yet one more thing that she'd hidden from her friends.

She shook back her long hair, chasing away the nostalgia and past mistakes to focus on today.

Although the interment would be inside the mausoleum, the family had opted to have the service outside. Probably a good decision with this many people in attendance, and the May weather was perfect for it. The crowd of thousands mingled close to the building. The mourners' muted wardrobes were occasionally punctuated by a bright spot of white and fringe. One that couldn't be ignored, because an entire group of women were dressed up like Jessie, in all-white cowgirl costumes.

"Mrs. Johanneson, excuse me."

Sera turned to face another reporter with a cameraman hovering behind him. "Jessie starred in several of your husband's films. Someone said that you two were very close. Could you comment?"

She sucked in a breath. "Jessie Wyatt was one of the most genuine people I've ever met. She was not only a friend but also a mentor. I'll miss her terribly." She lowered her head after her statement.

Once, she and Jessie had spent three weeks together when Marcus was shooting in the wilds of Zimbabwe. If anything could bring two women from different generations close together, it was sharing toiletries in the jungle. And Jessie had been generous with not only hard-to-attain supplies but also advice and encouragement. A gift that had changed Sera's life in so many ways.

The excited reporter closed in on her again. "Wasn't Jessie from Macon? Why did they decide to bury her here in Myrtle Knolls?"

"Someone in her family can answer that. We're here to honor the woman, not the location. No more questions, please. This is a difficult day for us all." Sera raised her hand politely, and the reporter backed off. Automatically, she scanned the crowd for security. She'd learned to be sure she knew where help was in case the reporters got out of control. Happened all the time with Marcus.

Off to the far side of the funeral area, Teague Castro stood tall, wearing his Bartell County Sheriff uniform. His dark good looks and muscular build fit right in with this attractive Hollywood crowd. Myrtle Knolls wasn't his jurisdiction, but that was the cool thing about small towns. The attitude of the residents was one of community and goodwill. Teague and his men were here to help keep things under control because it was the neighborly thing to do, something that would never happen in Hollywood.

Lil's fingers dug into Sera's hand. "Is that Luke Bryan?"

The reporter who'd still been hovering around must have heard Lil because he took off in Luke's direction, waving over his shoulder for the cameraman to follow.

Whoomp-whoomp-whoomp. One look at the helicopter circling overheard told Sera the bottom-feeders who couldn't score a press pass to the funeral weren't letting that stop them. Paparazzi. Those fools would crash any event if they thought it would tantalize the public. The funeral location should've been kept under wraps, but with this many attendees and Jessie's family's propensity to blab, that had probably been unrealistic.

Sera and her little group finally made it close enough to get a glimpse of Jessie's casket through the throng of family, fans, and A-listers, where a young preacher stood holding a leather folio.

"The deceased has often been described as a force of nature," he said, his gentle but strong voice calming the crowd to an eerie silence. "She will be sorely missed by many, including the NRA, which she supported generously throughout her lifetime."

A smile touched the corner of Sera's lips. She should've thought to introduce Abby Ruth and Jessie. Those two would've gotten along like a house on fire. Then again, together they might've set the house on fire.

On her left, Lil squeezed closer to her. The older woman looked like a tiny Vienna sausage among a tall package of frankfurters.

Sera tapped the huge man in front of Lil on the shoulder. "Mr. Hogan, would you mind giving us a bit more room?"

He pulled his massive arms into his body and smiled down at Lil, his bushy blond mustache twitching to one side. "You want to climb up on my shoulders?"

"Lord have mercy," she breathed, that little hat hanging on by a bobby pin. "No, thank you."

"Let me know if you change your mind."

Lil gave him a vague, star-struck nod.

The huge tan man turned to the side and ushered all three of them in front of him. A front-row view.

"If you'll bow your heads and join me in blessing Jessie Wyatt's soul so she may pass peacefully to the other side," the preacher said. At the end of his prayer, multiple words rippled through the gathering.

"Amen."

"Blessed Be."

"Namaste."

Finally, the crowd pulled back, and Lil and Maggie worked their way closer to the casket.

Before Sera could move to join them, a warm hand brushed the small of her back. Marcus. There was a time when he'd led her into a crowded room with that gesture and she'd felt as if she was the most special woman in the world. Today, she wasn't sure what his touch made her feel.

Still, she smiled up at her husband—as handsome as ever with his lean build and million-dollar smile. He'd aged gracefully with sexy silver lacing his hairline now. Had she caused those grays? He'd have worried about her even though he'd left her alone to find her way. He was like that.

"Did you get the car parked okay?" she asked him, her nerves insisting that she make small talk with her own husband. Her mind needed the break from the overwhelming sadness if only for a moment. "I thought you'd missed the service."

"Sorry it took me so long. Ran into Sylvester Stallone on the way back from the lot and stood by him while the preacher was talking."

Of course he had, because Marcus Johanneson

was a magnet for Hollywood types, and a slew of them had shown up today.

"It was a beautiful ceremony." He wrapped his arm around her. "How are you doing?"

She rested her head against his shoulder, needing his strength today. "It was lovely, made more so by how pretty it is here in Georgia."

"But nothing can compare to you," he said, dropping a kiss into her hair.

Sera reached for his hand and gave it a squeeze. Returning to her adopted state for Jessie's funeral had been hard, but being back a few days, Sera knew this was where she belonged. Marcus seemed to want their marriage to return to the way it had been when they were newlyweds, before Finn came along, when she'd always been the one to mold to Marcus's career, his life. Yet she yearned for her days back here in Summer Shoals, where she was simply Sera. No reputation. No money. No expectations.

Only Marcus wasn't a part of that life, and she didn't know if she could live here in the place she loved without the man she loved.

"Georgia, and Summer Shoals in particular, has become one of my favorite places in the world," she said with complete honesty. Saying the words aloud seemed to give them wings but left her shaky. She needed to be away from Marcus for a moment to get her head together. "I'm going to go pay Jessie my respects."

"Then let's—"

"Alone, please."

He dropped her hand. She regretted hurting him. But she needed a little more time and space to work out how she planned to go forward with her life. And her relationship with Marcus was still a work in progress. Jessie's death made it even clearer that a person's time on this earth was limited. Each day needed to be cherished.

A crush of people had quickly separated Sera from Maggie and Lil. So Sera tried to slowly edge her way around and was captivated by the elaborate casket spray. The blanket of the tiniest perfect bluebonnets, with Indian paintbrush tickling stalks of red clover, resembled a Texas sunset. Jessie hadn't ever lived in the Lone Star state, but most people considered her the perfect Texas cowgirl. Funny how a fictional role could change the whole world's perception of a woman.

Not only had someone spent a fortune on the out-of-season Texas wildflowers, but they'd also integrated Jessie Wyatt's signature Wild West outfit of white leather into the flowers. And right on top were her famous deerskin gauntlets with fringe of gold and stones that had once been rumored to be genuine sapphires, rubies, and diamonds.

"Are they going to entomb her costume?" a woman next to Sera asked.

"Sure looks that way," someone else whispered.

"But it's a collector's item—a representation of an important Hollywood icon. Seems like it would be better served in a museum somewhere."

Sera couldn't agree more. Especially the gauntlets, because although Jessie had owned several skirts and vests, only one pair of authentic gauntlets existed. One night over sangria at an after-party, Jessie had shared a secret with Sera. Those gauntlets were insanely valuable, given to Jessie by her husband as an anniversary present. Not that anyone else knew that. Rumors had been bandied about for a few years, but with some well-executed PR by Jessie's agent, the gossip had eventually been written off as Hollywood lore.

The helicopter took another spin above, and camera lenses shimmered in the bright sunlight. Then more flashes and clicks came from beyond a private family mausoleum less than fifty feet away, just outside the funeral's security perimeter. Entertainment rag reporters were wily and persistent.

Apparently, she wasn't the only one to spot the

intruders, because several Bartell County deputies raced off toward the culprits.

One of Teague's guys hollered, "Y'all need to get on out of here. This is a private event."

"Dude, this is a free country," a so-called reporter yelled back. "Maybe I'm here visiting my grandma."

"With that camera equipment? What? Were you planning to take family portraits?"

Sera tried to suppress a smile, because truthfully, those country boys weren't prepared for the likes of ruthless paparazzi. They had no remorse and no manners. And if a story put them in the position to make a buck, they didn't care one bit who they hurt.